E. M. FOSTER, THE CORINNA OF ENGLAND, AND A HEROINE IN THE SHADE; A MODERN ROMANCE (1809)

E. M. Foster,
The Corinna of England,
and a Heroine in the Shade; a Modern Romance (1809)

<small>EDITED BY</small>

Sylvia Bordoni

LONDON AND NEW YORK

First published 2008 by Pickering & Chatto (Publishers) Limited

Published 2016 by Routledge
2 Park Square, Milton Park, Abingdon, Oxfordshire OX14 4RN
711 Third Avenue, New York, NY 10017, USA

First issued in paperback 2016

Routledge is an imprint of the Taylor & Francis Group, an informa business

BRITISH LIBRARY CATALOGUING IN PUBLICATION DATA

Foster, E. M., fl. 1795–1803
The Corinna of England, and, A heroine in the shade: a modern romance. –
(Chawton House library series. Women's novels)
1. Women – Fiction
I. Title II. Bordoni, Sylvia
823.7[F]

ISBN 13: 978-1-138-23602-8 (pbk)
ISBN 13: 978-1-8519-6924-1 (hbk)

Typeset by Pickering & Chatto (Publishers) Limited

CONTENTS

INTRODUCTION

The Corinna of England, and a Heroine in the Shade was published anonymously in two volumes in 1809 by B. Crosby & Co., based in London. This was the first and only edition of the novel. The anonymous author was well known to the reading public of the time, having previously published numerous novels, amongst which the most famous were *The Duke of Clarence; a Historical Novel* published in four volumes as early as 1795 by the London publisher William Lane, *Frederic and Caroline, or the Fitzmorris Family. A Novel*, published in two volumes by B. Crosby & Co. in 1800, *The Winter in Bath*, published in four volumes by the same publisher of *The Corinna of England* in 1807, and *The Woman of Colour*, published in London by Parry & Co. in 1808. After 1809, another novel, *The Dead Letter Office; and a Tale for the English Farmer's Fire-Side*, published in two volumes in London in 1811 by Crosby, has been attributed to the same author. On the whole, the author published fourteen novels between 1795 and 1811, most of them under the pseudonym of E. M. F.[1]

The identity of the anonymous author, however, is still being debated and has never been entirely clarified. *A Feminist Companion to Literature in English* (1990) identifies the author as E. M. Foster. The editors describe Foster as a prolific and conservative author, based in London, who was well known at the end of the eighteenth and at the beginning of the nineteenth centuries. More recently, Peter Garside, James Raven, and Rainer Schöwerling have observed how the identity of the anonymous author has been variously attributed to Mrs E. G. Bayfield, J. H. James and to Mrs E. M. Foster.[2]

---

1 The full title of the novel refers to the author's previous novels: 'The Corinna of England; and a Heroine in the Shade; a Modern Romance, by the Author of "The Winter in Bath", "The Banks of the Wye", "The Woman of Colour", "Light and Shade" &c. &c'. *The Banks of the Wye; or Two Summers at Clifton: a Novel* was published in London by C. & R. Baldwin in 1785, *The Woman of Colour: A Tale* was published in London by Parry & Co. in 1808, and *Light and Shade: A Novel* was published in Bath by R. Cruttnell in 1803.

2 James Raven, Peter Garside and Rainer Schöwerling, *The English Novel 1770–1820: A Bibliographical Survey of Prose Fiction Published in the British Isles* (Oxford: Oxford University Press, 2000), p. 210. E. G. Bayfield, however, published a collection of poems, *Fugitive Pieces*, in 1805, thus making it unlikely that she published her novels anonymously.

The difficulty of identifying the author with certainty has affected the reception of the novel, which had almost entirely been neglected until recently. However, as the unravelling of its connections to the more famous *Corinne, or Italy* (1807) by Germaine de Staël will demonstrate, the novel acquires a fundamental importance for a comprehensive understanding of the cultural and philosophical context which influenced British writers at the beginning of the nineteenth century. In particular, the detailed discussion of and direct references to some of the most topical issues of the time makes *The Corinna of England* a precious text for the interpretation of the British reception of the political, social and cultural influences coming from continental Europe.[3]

The Corinna of England was one of the first British responses to the publication of Germaine de Staël's *Corinne, or Italy*. It was prevalently directed to a conservative portion of the contemporary reading public, reiterating a defensive attitude towards British culture and society against an increasingly popular continental influence.

Soon after its publication in 1807, Staël's novel had an enormous success all over Europe. It was translated into English the same year and went through fourteen editions between 1807 and 1810. In spite of its phenomenal success, however, the novel was received as a controversial work and it was often criticized for the moral dubiousness of its eccentric heroine. Many contemporary critics stressed not simply the unconventionality of the character of Corinne, but emphasized her foreignness, or, more precisely, her un-Britishness.

The *Annual Review*, for example, in 1807 claimed that Corinne's apparent forwardness and freedom of manners 'would be deemed perfectly irreproachable in the softer climate of Italy', but they 'might be received with a frown in these drilling regions of the north'. The anonymous reviewer continued by stressing the national specificity of Corinne's character:

> In appreciating its merits, we must constantly bear in mind that the scene does not lie in England, but in Italy. Nothing can be more improbable than the conduct of Corinna, or more unnatural than her character, if, as is commonly the case, with vulgar and ordinary readers, our own country is to be considered as the epitome of general character, and as the standard of propriety for general conduct.[4]

Of a similar opinion was the anonymous reviewer of *Le Beau Monde*, who, in September 1807, commented that Corinne was a character utterly incomprehensible for Englishwomen accustomed to a different social environment and suggested

---

3   Only recently the novel has been the object of critical attention. In particular see: Angela Wright, 'Corinne in Distress: Translation as Cultural Misappropriation in the 1800's', *CW³ Journal*, 2 (Winter 2004), http://www2.shu.ac.uk/corvey/CW3journal/issue%20two/wright.html, and Silvia Bordoni, 'Parodying *Corinne*: Foster's *The Corinna of England*', *CW³ Journal*, 2 (Winter 2004), http://www2.shu.ac.uk/corvey/cw3journal/Issue%20two/bordoni.html.

4   *Annual Review*, 6 (1807), p. 673.

that Madame de Staël should 'give us one of her own accomplished and fascinating heroines, in English customs, and with English virtues, and English morality'.[5]

This general perplexity with regard to Corinne's un-Britishness and the call for a British counterpart to the popular heroine was cleverly exploited by the author of *The Corinna of England*. Perceiving a common discontent with the foreignness of Corinne's manners and talents, the author clearly saw an opportunity to recreate such character in a British provincial context and to exploit its comic potentiality. The parodical intent of the novel, however, serves not only the evident purpose of ridiculing the character of Corinne and what it represents, but also to advocate the rightness and the superiority of British society and culture. In this way, the comic surface of the novel only hides a more serious concern about the invasion of British literature by fashionable foreign heroines and, consequently, the need to re-impose the traditional morally impeccable and timid heroine.

This rejection of the eccentric and foreign woman in favour of a more nationally pure and domestic model was actually part of a widespread literary phenomenon which recently has been signalled as a British counter-tradition to the Italianate Corinne. As Eric Simpson has argued, this counter-tradition popularized the figure of the domestic-oriented and conservative British woman poet.[6] This tradition became very popular soon after the publication of Staël's novel and it was actually the first widespread response to *Corinne*, much before the novel and its heroine became popular with the works, amongst others, of Byron and Hemans.[7]

The Corinna of England is part of this counter-tradition which felt the need to re-establish the predominance of British society and British values in the contemporary literary production. The fact that the author chooses to satirize and parody one of the most successful foreign authors of the time in order to communicate the need to re-impose British secular values is not, therefore, surprising. Staël's novels and philosophical works had contributed enormously to popularize the influence of foreign cultures and literatures. In particular, Staël's philosophical works had discussed the importance of cultural and national pluralism, whereby the contamination between cultural and literary traditions of different European nations becomes the key element to social progress and

---

5   *Le Beau Monde*, 2 (September 1807), p. 91.

6   Eric Simpson, '"The Ministrels of Modern Italy": Improvisation Comes to Britain', *European Romantic Review*, 14 (September 2003), pp. 345–67.

7   For a detailed discussion of the influence of *Corinne* on Byron, see Joanne Wilkes, *Lord Byron and Madame de Staël: Born for Opposition* (Aldershot: Ashgate, 1999); Silvia Bordoni, 'From Madame de Staël to Lord Byron: The Dialectics of European Romanticism', *Literature Compass*, 3 (2006), pp. 1–16. For the influence of *Corinne* on Hemans, see Nanora Sweet and Julie Melnyk (eds), *Felicia Hemans: Reimagining Poetry in the Nineteenth Century* (Basingstoke: Palgrave, 2001).

political emancipation.[8] *Corinne*, furthermore, had introduced the figure of the eccentric, independent and talented woman artist, who, by definition, defies early nineteenth-century traditional ideas of womanhood and questions the well-rooted notions of national purity and feminine propriety. As it will become progressively evident, therefore, *The Corinna of England* parodies not simply Staël's novel, particularly the character of Corinne, but, more broadly, what the novel represented in the emerging Romantic and sentimental tradition.

The Corinna of England recreates the dynamic of Staël's novel. The opposition between Corinne and the angelic Lucile, Corinne's half-sister, is replicated in a reversed way. Clarissa, the Corinna of England, is an eccentric, untalented and morally ambiguous anti-heroine, while the young, timid and chaste Mary Cuthbert, Clarissa's orphaned cousin, becomes the real heroine of the story, or, as the novel's subtitle suggests, 'a heroine in the shade'. The triangular love plot which dominates *Corinne* is similarly replicated, with both Clarissa and Mary aspiring to conquer the reserved and conservative hero, Montgomery, the Lord Nelvil of the story.

As it soon becomes clear, the character of Clarissa takes inspiration from Staël's Corinne and it is represented as a travesty to the famous *improvisatrice*:

> But the superiority of Miss Moreton's talents [...] were calculated only for display; there was nothing solid or substantial in her abilities or acquirements, no depth of argument in her declamatory harangues, in which she had practised, from the early age of fifteen, to the attentive auditors round her father's table. (p. 13)

To some extent, Clarissa is the victim of her father's romanticized imagination, which had seen in her the British equivalent of the talented Italian *improvisatrice*. He encourages her to cultivate and express talents she does not possess with the devastating effect of creating a totally awkward creature, alienated and isolated from her surroundings.

The English provincial setting which constitutes the background to the novel is also an important element of the parody. The story of *Corinne* is for the most part set in Rome, one of the most cosmopolitan and artistically stimulating cities in eighteenth-century Europe. By contrast, *The Corinna of England* is set in a small village near Coventry, the manufacturing and commercial core of the emerging English bourgeoisie, anchored to the traditional moral and domestic values. The conversion of the Italian setting into an English provincial setting accentuates the absurdity and therefore the comicality of the character of Clarissa.

Corinne, or Italy became such a literary success during the first decade of the nineteenth century that few could ignore or remain indifferent to it. The parodical construction of the novel and its comic effect, therefore, must have been striking

---

8   See in particular, *De La Litérature* (1800), *De L' Allemagne* (1810) and *De L'Esprit des Traduction* (1817). Germaine de Staël, *Oeuvres Complètes*, 17 vols (Paris: Treuttel et Wurtz, 1816).

to contemporary British readers who were experiencing the *Corinne* effect. Even those who had actually resisted reading the novel, knew about this literary phenomenon and were familiar with the character of Corinne, her artistic talents and her unhappy love story. By using the story of Corinne and transposing it into a parodical novel, therefore, the anonymous author of *The Corinna of England* was aware that she could appeal to a vast portion of the contemporary reading public, entertaining both those who liked and those who did not like Staël's novel.

More importantly, *Corinne* influenced more or less directly much of the literature produced in Britain in the first few decades of the century, thus coming to symbolize and being identified with the new emerging sensibility and philosophy. Parodying *Corinne*, therefore, had implications far beyond the mere comical reproduction of the novel. It implied satirizing on a whole set of emerging notions, sentiments, philosophical and political ideas.

The fact that the parodical intent of the anonymous author was in fact directed not simply to the character of Corinne but, more generally, to the new literary fashion that Staël's heroine had come to represent is clear. Describing the faults in the character of Clarissa, for example, the narrator easily extends the critique to a more generalized state of mind:

> Superficial in every acquirement and every accomplishment, she attempted every thing; fond of the new school of manners, and of philosophy, 'philanthropy' and 'benevolence' were words which were constantly jingling in her ears; and, the inflated victim of vanity and self-conceit, was easily persuaded, that she was the succouring angel that was sent to patronise genius and virtue on earth. She had a great tincture of romantic fervour and enthusiasm in her manners, which was called '*energy*,' a word well understood in the new vocabulary of the moderns, and which has been too frequently made use of to require any explanation here [...]. (pp. 13–14)

In this passage, the author is questioning the very essence of the new emerging Romantic sensibility. Through the ridiculousness and artificiality of the character of Clarissa, the novel is dominated by the critique of what the narrator defines as the 'new school of manners' and his devotees.

Staël's novels and philosophical works are taken as emblematic of the romantic fervour and enthusiasm to which Clarissa has ridiculously devoted herself. Staël had firstly introduced her idea of enthusiasm in her travel journeys and in *Corinne*, before developing it into a philosophical concept in *On Germany*. In Chapter IV of *On Germany*, in particular, Staël defines enthusiasm as 'the nature of all [...] disinterested and exalted sentiments', representing the attempt to fuse moral, aesthetic, religious and metaphysical ideals into a single attitude: 'enthusiasm rallies itself to the harmony of the Universe, it is love of the beautiful, elevation of the soul, the delight in unselfishness all united into one and the same feeling'.[9] What the author of *The Corinna of England* sarcastically describes as the 'new school of philosophy', therefore, represents, the artistic and philosophical ideal which the emerging Romantic authors in general, and Staël in particular, had expressed in the forms of sentiments, feelings, emotions and a philanthropic and benevolent attitude towards human nature.

By the time *The Corinna of England* was composed and published, however, this Romantic ideology had progressively been associated with a tendency to over-sentimentalism both in literature and society.[10] The author exemplifies this over sentimentalized attitude in the character of Clarissa and in her ridiculous actions. The exaggeration of her feelings and the artificiality of the language she uses serve the purpose of ridiculing a whole set of attitudes which had become extremely fashionable in sentimental literature and amongst its reading public, especially young women.

The character of Clarissa and her international circle of friends, for example, serve the purpose of ridiculing the emerging cosmopolitan and multicultural fashion in British culture and society. Staël's works are particularly ridiculed for proposing and perpetrating such anti-British ideology. In *Corinne* Staël created a cosmopolitan heroine whose character and talents are the result of her being the hybrid product of Italy and Britain, and of her wide knowledge of European literatures and cultures. Corinne hosts an international salon in Rome where she discusses the differences and similarities between literatures of different countries and where she preaches the need of integrating European cultures. In *The Corinna of England,* the author sarcastically reproduces a similar context. Clarissa patronizes an international group of artists which reminds the readers of Corinne's cosmopolitan salon, with the important difference that Clarissa's protégés are actually people with no talents. Rather than promising artists in search of success, the group consists of an extravagant Italian singer who spends her days reclining on a sofa, a French musician with ridiculous manners, a painter who can only paint copies of copies and an old biologist whose only field of research is Clarissa's garden. Clarissa's closest friend, Chevalier d' Aubert, is a married French emigrant, who enchants her patroness by praising her talents and stressing her similarity to Staël's *improvisatrice*. All, the author clearly suggests, live in promiscuity with no respect for moral boundaries. By reconstructing Corinne's international circle of friends in

9   Germaine Staël, *De l'Allemagne*, ed. Jean de Pange and Simone Balayé, 4 vols (Paris: Librairie Hachette, 1960), vol. 4, p. 187 (my translation).

10 See Markman Ellis, *The Politics of Sensibility: Race, Gender and Commerce in the Sentimental Novel* (Cambridge: Cambridge University Press, 1996) and Syndy McMillen (ed.), *Sensibility in Transformation: Creative Resistance to Sentiment from the Augustans to the Romantics* (London: Associated University Press, 1990).

a comical way, the author clearly criticizes Staël's philosophical considerations on nationalism and cosmopolitanism.

In *On Literature* (1800), in particular, Staël had articulated the importance of national distinctiveness and cosmopolitanism at the same time. While she still promoted national identity and cultural specificity, Staël also suggested the need to overcome the limits of national belonging in the effort to integrate and amalgamate aspects from different cultures and societies. By celebrating the possibility of choosing 'une patrie de la pensée' (an intellectual homeland) over any imposed ideal of national identity, Staël promotes forms of interaction and cooperation between different national and cultural entities. This idea emerges also in *Corinne*, where by creating an Anglo-Italian heroine, Staël celebrates nationalism in terms of confrontation and interaction, instead of promulgating the idea of nationalism constructed in terms of opposition. Corinne's multicultural salon, where different cultures and societies are discussed and compared, is exemplary of Staël's promotion of national interaction.

The comical reproduction of Corinne's international circle of friends in *The Corinna of England* suggests a critique of Staël's ideas. The anonymous author exaggerates national stereotypes in such a way to present them as irreconcilable. More specifically, she depicts Clarissa's international friends in contrast to English values and customs. The laziness, promiscuity and superficiality of Clarissa's multicultural salon is clearly in opposition to the integrity and morality of the conservative English characters who embody English values in the novel, especially Mary Cuthbert, Clarissa's innocent cousin, and Montgomery, the Lord Nelvil of the story, who aspires to become a clergyman. By ridiculing Staël's philosophy of multiculturalism, the author promotes national and cultural purity. More importantly, she depicts conservative English values and customs as superior to those of the other nations represented in the novel, such as Italy and France. In the novel, national purity clearly triumphs over any form of cultural contamination.

References to Staël's works become explicit in the course of *The Corinna of England*. In particular, Clarissa and her French friend are enchanted by the reading of *Delphine* and *Corinne*.

In Chapter XI of the first volume, Clarissa and her entourage of friends are reading *Delphine*, Staël's first widely-read novel, published in 1802. Delphine is a beautiful and young widow of independent means and independent views, who likes brilliant conversation. She preaches enthusiasm and displays a romantic and passionate nature. She dislikes constraints and loves liberty, promotes women's independence and advocates divorce. She falls in love with Léonce, a charismatic nobleman who respects honour and social conventions and who will eventually marry Delphine's chaste and religious cousin.

Clarissa admires both Staël and Delphine for their common pathos and passionate feelings. Even the conservative and cynical Montgomery has read the novel and seems to appreciate at least some of its parts, as he comments that the novel is 'an interesting production' and the author 'certainly very great' (p. 50). The discussion, however, is soon orientated towards two opposite poles, that of the libertine and over-sentimental Clarissa and that of the conservative and morally strict Montgomery. Both positions centre around extreme opinions: Clarissa admires Delphine for her sentiments, feelings and passions and she describes her behaviour as 'enchanting'; Montgomery, on the contrary, sees Delphine's sentiments and passions as dangerous, if not despicable. He defines 'pernicious' and 'immoral' her principles, with particular reference to the disrespect of marriage vows, and criticizes Staël for delivering her thoughts on the subject of divorce 'very freely for a woman writer' (p. 51). His admiration is undoubtedly directed towards Mathilda de Vernon, the chaste and reserved cousin of Delphine, who will become the wife of the contended Léonce, and refers to her as an 'exemplary character', while Clarissa considers her as a 'cold-hearted prude', a 'rigid devotee as ever professed Catholicism', and 'as chilling, and forbidding in her manners', as her own aunt Deborah Moreton (p. 51).

Although the discussion of *Delphine* is mainly structured quite simplistically on the two different moral views of Clarissa and Montgomery, the issues at stake appear, in fact, to be more complicated. The Chevalier D'Aubert, Clarissa's French protégé, assuming that Montgomery had read the English translation of Staël's novel, suggests that this divergence of opinions is actually due to the differences between the two languages. This initiates an important dialogue between Montgomery and D'Aubert, which is not simply based on moral differences, but on national and cultural confrontations. The two seem to agree on the fact that Delphine is 'no common character'. However, while D'Aubert seems to perceive some similarities between Delphine and her patroness, Montgomery clearly states that 'it is a character not to be found with *us*' since, he continues, 'our atmosphere is too foggy for such volatile spirits; it is not composed of such inflammable materials; the imagination of *our* ladies (bating a few exceptions) is not so vivid; and the genius of the nation yet makes the prudent conduct of our women its peculiar care!' (p. 52). This is a clear reference to Staël's philosophical discussion of the differences between northern and southern countries, societies and cultures, which she first introduced in *On Literature*. In it, Staël developed the idea that the cultural habits which differentiate the north from the south are mainly originated by the difference in climate and society. This idea is even further developed in *Corinne*, where the eponymous heroine is a half-English and half-Italian woman poet who finds success and freedom in Italy but is rejected and misunderstood in Britain.11

11 For a discussion of Staël's works and ideas see: Madelyn Gutwirth, Avriel Goldberger and Karyna Szmurlo (eds), *Germaine de Staël: Crossing the Borders* (New Brunswick: Rutgers University Press, 1991).

To some extents, Montgomery's discussion of *Delphine* seems to reiterate Staël's ideology. Women such as Delphine, Montgomery argues, cannot exist in Britain, since British women are generally educated following the principles of propriety and good moral conduct. A libertine and passionate woman such as Delphine would be at odd in Britain, exactly in the same way that the eccentric and sentimental Clarissa is alienated in the provincial English setting of the novel. The idea that Clarissa is seen not simply as an eccentric and unconventional woman, but also as being 'foreign' to British customs, and therefore unaccepted by the surrounding conservative society, becomes even more explicit when she tries to imitate Staël's Corinne.

The reading of *Corinne* is introduced in Chapter XV of the second volume. The novel enraptures Clarissa. She feels that she can fully identify with the Italian woman of genius. The narrator observes that *Corinne* 'was the very work to suit the taste of Miss Moreton; for though she had neither judgment or knowledge to appreciate the beauty or the truth of the historical remarks [...] yet her imagination was enamoured of the character of Corinna' (p. 76). The reading of Staël's novel triggers in Clarissa the need to emulate Corinne with evident comic outcomes. Clarissa perceives in the heroine's energetic pursuit of Lord Nelvil, in her rejection of all common forms, her enthusiastic disposition and her extemporizing faculty an image of her own character and talents. Chevalier D'Aubert remarks that Clarissa's genius is similar to Corinne's, and he starts addressing her as 'the Corinna of England'. From here, the narrator explains, 'the sickly brain of Miss. Moreton became inflamed, and she resolved to imitate the inimitable Corinna, whenever opportunities should offer of discovering her genius to the world' (p. 77).

At this point of the novel, the anonymous author constructs an overtly comic parallelism between the story of Clarissa and that of Corinne. With the intention of imitating Corinne, for example, Clarissa decides to improvise a speech for the peasants of Coventry. Her improvisation is a mockery of Corinne's famous improvisation at the Capitol, on the occasion of her coronation as poet laureate. In it Corinne displays her physical beauty and her intellectual powers; she celebrates the poets who have preceded her in representing the poetic talents of Italy and she boldly encourages her compatriots to regain the political freedom and the cultural dignity that for so many years had characterized their country, presently enslaved by foreign tyrants.[12]

Clarissa's speech is sarcastically shaped after Corinne's improvisation: she celebrates her ancestor Lady Godiva, and she praises the glory and power of the arts. She then turns her speech into a quasi-political declamation when she instigates

12 Germaine de Staël, *Corinne, or Italy*, ed. and transl. Avriel Goldberger (New Brunswick: Rutgers University Press, 1987), pp. 26–31.

the peasants to abandon their honest and humble jobs in order to pursue artistic careers:

> Citizens of Coventry! my countrymen, attend! Accident has led me hither to be a pleased witness of your spectacle of this day, and of the patriotic enthusiasm which is excited in your bosoms! [...] – Ye Citizens of Coventry, free men of an ancient city, behold this day *another* woman speaks! *another* woman asserts the glorious preroga-tive of her sex, the bold freedom of thought and action, hitherto so exclusively, so unjustly confined to men alone! – People of Coventry, and I do I then behold you sunk to a state of effeminacy and servitude! [...] *Men*! possessed of capacious minds, of soaring genius, of depth of intellect; how do I behold you engaged? (p. 82)

At the answer that they are engaged in providing bread for themselves and their children, and in 'honest industry, Clarissa replies: 'Shame, shame on these inglorious occupations', since men have arms 'to chisel out the hero's form', and eyes that 'with Promethean fire can animate their work' (p. 82). Significantly, the result of the Corinna of England's improvisation is the instigation of a riot and public turmoil among the peasants. Instead of acclamation and glory, like Corinne, Clarissa receives only scorn and disrespect.

Clarissa tries then to imitate Staël's heroine and to act as Corinne does in the novel. She, for example, prefers walking the streets of London unprotected instead of going in a carriage, since, in strict obedience to Corinne's model, she chooses the pedestrian excursion, like Staël's heroine had done in Rome. Of course, Clarissa observes, Corinne had never chosen a female companion; but 'had she been left the guardian of an orphan cousin, Miss Moreton was confi-dent she would not have left her behind' (p. 98). In hearing of the illness of one of her friends, Clarissa rushes to visit him, since 'Corinna gone immediately to Lord Nelville on hearing of his illness!', even if this means worsening her already scandalous behaviour and compromising her cousin's reputation (p. 97).

The effects of Clarissa's actions are morally disastrous, and, at the end of the novel, she dies while trying to escape a fire in Covent Garden. This leaves the true heroine, Mary Cuthbert, the only inheritor of a large fortune. With the death of Clarissa and the marriage between Montgomery and Mary Cuthbert, the author replicates the ending of Staël's novel, where Corinne dies in solitude after Lord Nelvil's marriage with her half-sister Lucile.

The parallelism between the two novels is mainly constructed with a parodi-cal intention. However, Clarissa is often associated with Corinne and Delphine not simply for comical purposes. In particular, the narrator and the most con-servative characters in the novel, such as Deborah Moreton, Clarissa's aunt, and Montogmery, consider Clarissa together with Staël's heroines Delphine and Corinne as characters belonging to the same category of women. All are seen as unconventional, eccentric, feminist, egocentric, and exhibitionist women. More importantly, they are seen as 'foreign' to English customs and society. Delphine is seen as 'impetuous in her feeling, so hasty in her resolves, so regardless of the customs of the world!', and Corinne is described as a passionate, unconventional and enthusiastic character, while her artistic talents and poetic genius are never mentioned in the novel (p. 52). In the narrator's words, Clarissa, like Delphine and Corinne, appears as 'no common character'. From a conservative point of view, therefore, women seem to be judged not for their genuine or pretentious artistic talents, but for their ability to conform to a strict and morally impeccable idea of femininity. After all, the final message of the novel seems clear: the death of the eccentric Clarissa erases from society the unordinary woman, while the triumph of the timid and chaste Mary re-establishes the supremacy of the proper lady. The death of both Corinne and Clarissa, although tragic in Staël's novel and comical in Foster's, takes us straightforwardly to a conclusion: there is no place in society for unconventional and unordinary women, but only for chaste and angelic women, like Lucile and Mary. The triumph of the Lucile/Mary kind of woman implies that the talented Corinne and the eccentric Clarissa are both unfitted for society. Their strangeness eludes the passive end domestic ideal of womanhood that the author seems to propose as the only acceptable model.

In this way, *The Corinna of England* seems to confirm what Staël had initially suggested in *Corinne*: England, specifically provincial England, does not welcome eccentric, exuberant, artistic women who want to display their more or less genuine talents in public. This does not exclude the possibility that England would welcome a different kind of genius in women, one that could co-exist with the ideal of the proper lady. *The Corinna of England*, however, does not suggest any alternative model for female talent, since the other female characters are only concerned with domestic duties, and do not show any interest in the arts. This seems to assert the superiority of conformity over any form of eccentricity and to establish British religious and moral values as exemplary.

Furthermore, both *Delphine* and *Corinne* were politically controversial novels. Soon after the publication of *Delphine*, Napoleon banished Staël from France for the revolutionary and anti-Napoleonic content of the novel. Similarly, *Corinne*'s celebration of political and social freedom in a country tyrannized and enslaved by Napoleon had a clear political meaning. From this point of view, therefore, by parodying Staël's novels, the anonymous author of *The Corinna of England* also expresses a political opinion, dominated by an anti-revolutionary, anti-French attitude and by a reinvigoration of the idea of Britain as politically and morally superior to other European countries. In creating an anti-heroine on the example of the liberal, politically engaged and cosmopolitan Corinne, the author reiterates her own beliefs in the traditionally conservative and nationalistic heroine.

SELECT BIBLIOGRAPHY

Primary Material

Bonstetten, Charles Victor de, *Etudes de l'homme, ou Recherce sur les Facultés de sentir et de penser* (Paris, 1821).

[Foster, E. M.], *The Duke of Clarence; a Historical Novel by E.M.F* (London: William Lane, 1795).

—, *Frederic & Caroline, or the Fitzmorris Family by E.M.F* (London: William Lane, 1800).

—, *A Winter in Bath, by the Author of Two Popular Novels* (London: B. Crosby & Co., 1807).

—, *The Corinna of England, and a Heroine in the Shade; a Modern Romance by the Author of a Winter in Bath etc.* (London: B. Crosby & Co., 1809).

—, *The Dead Letter Office; and a Tale for the English Farmer's Fire-Side. By the Author of the Corinna of England* (London: B. Crosby & Co., 1811).

Montesquieu, Charles de Secondat. *The Spirit of Laws*, trans. Mr Nuget, 2 vols. (London: J. Nourse, 1758).

Staël, Germaine, *Oeuvres Complètes*, 17 vols (Paris: Treuttel et Würtz, 1821).

—, *Corinne or Italy*, ed. and trans. Avriel H. Goldberger (London: Rutgers University Press, 1987).

—, *Major Works of Germaine de Staël*, ed. Vivian Folkenflik (New York: Columbia University Press, 1987).

—, *Delphine*, ed. and trans. Avriel H. Goldberger (DeKalb: Northern Illinois University Press, 1995).

Secondary Material

Alliston, April, 'Of Haunted Highlands: Mapping a Geography of Gender in the Margins of Europe', in Gregory Maertz (ed.), *Cultural Interactions in the Romantic Age: Critical Essays in Comparative Literature* (New York: State University Press, 1998), pp. 55–78.

Blain, Virginia, Patricia Clemens and Isobel Grundy (eds), *The Feminist Companion to Literature in English* (London: Batsford, 1990).

Bordoni, Silvia, 'Parodying *Corinne*: Foster's *The Corinna of England*', *CW3 Journal*, 2 (Winter 2004), http://www2.shu.ac.uk/corvey/cw3journal/Issue%20two/bordoni.html.

—, 'From Madame de Staël to Lord Byron: The Dialectics of European Romanticism', *Literature Compass*, 3 (2006), pp. 1–16

Claeys, Gregory, *The French Revolution Debate in Britain: The Origin of Modern Politics* (Basingstoke: Palgrave, 1995).

Ellis, Markman, *The Politics of Sensibility: Race, Gender and Commerce in the Sentimental Novel* (Cambridge: Cambridge University Press, 1996).

Esterhammer, Angela, *Spontaneous Overflows and Revivifying Rays: Romanticism and the Discourse of Improvisation* (Vancouver: Ronsdale Press, 2004).

—, 'The Cosmopolitan Improvvisatore: Spontaneity and Performance in Romantic Poetics', *European Romantic Review*, 16 (2005), pp. 153–65.

—, 'Improvisational Aesthetics: Byron, the Shelley Circle and Tommaso Sgricci', *Romanticism on the Net*, 43 (August 2006), http://www.erudit.org/revue/ron/2006/v/n43/013592ar.html

Fairweather, Maria, *Madame de Staël* (London: Constable, 2005).

Felluga, Dino, *The Perversity of Poetry: Romantic Ideology and the Popular Male Poet of Genius* (New York: State University of New York Press, 2005).

Garside, Peter, James Raven and Rainer Schöwerling (eds), *The English Novel 1770–1820: A Bibliographical Survey of Prose Fiction Published in the British Isles* (Oxford: Oxford University Press, 2000).

Grenby, Matthew, *The Anti-Jacobin Novel: British Conservatism and the French Revolution* (Cambridge: Cambridge University Press, 2001).

Gutwirth, Madelyn, Avriel Goldberger and Karyna Szmurlo (eds), *Germaine de Staël: Crossing the Borders* (New Brunswick: Rutgers University Press, 1991).

—, *Madame de Staël, Novelist: The Emergence of the Artist as a Woman* (Chicago: University of Illinois Press, 1978).

Halpin David, *Romanticism and Education: Love, Heroism and Imagination in Pedagogy* (London: Continuum International, 2007).

Levy, Gayle, 'A Genius for the Modern Era: Madame de Staël's Corinne', *Nineteenth-Century French Studies*, 30:3–4 (Spring 2002), pp. 242–53.

Klein, E. Lawrence, and Anthony J. La Vope (eds), *Enthusiasm and Enlightenment in Europe, 1650–1850* (Los Angeles: University of California Press, 1998).

McMillen, Syndy (ed.), *Sensibility in Transformation: Creative Resistance to Sentiment from the Augustans to the Romantics* (London: Associated University Press, 1990).

Mee, Jon, *Romanticism, Enthusiasm and Regulation: Poetics and the Policing of Culture in the Romantic period* (Oxford: Oxford University Press, 2005).

Moers, Ellen, 'Madame de Staël and the Woman of Genius', *American Scholar*, 44 (1975), pp. 225–41.

Orr, Clarissa Campbell, 'The Corinne Complex: Gender, Genius and National Identity', in Clarissa Campbell Orr (ed.), *Women in the Victorian Art World* (Manchester: Manchester University Press, 1995), pp. 89–106.

Richardson, Alan, *Literature, Education and Romanticism: Reading as Sexual Practice 1780–1832* (Cambridge: Cambridge University Press, 1994).

Simpson, Erik, '"The Ministrels of Modern Italy": Improvisation Comes to Britain', *European Romantic Review*, 14: 3 (September 2003), pp. 345–67.

Sourian, Eve, 'Germaine de Staël and the Position of Women in France, England and Germany', in Avriel H. Goldberger (ed.), *Woman as Mediatrix: Essays on Nineteenth-Century European Women Writers* (New York: Greenwood Press, 1987), pp. 31–8.

Sweet, Nanora, and Julie Melnyk (eds), *Felicia Hemans: Reimagining Poetry in the Nineteenth Century* (Basingstoke: Palgrave, 2001).

Szmurlo, Karyna (ed.), *The Novel's Seductions: Staël's Corinne in Critical Inquiry* (London: Associated University Presses).

Whitford, C. Robert, *Madame de Staël's Literary Reputation in England* (Urbana: University of Illinois Studies in Language and Literature, 1918).

Wilkes, Joanne, *Lord Byron and Madame de Staël: Born for Opposition* (Aldershot: Ashgate, 1999).

Wohlgemut, Esther, '"What do you do with her at home?" The Cosmopolitan and National Tale', *European Romantic Review*, 13:2 (June 2002), pp. 191–7.

Wright, Angela, 'Corinne in Distress: Translation as Cultural Misappropriation in the 1800's' *CW3 Journal*, 2 (Winter 2004), http://www2.shu.ac.uk/corvey/CW3journal/issue%20two/wright.html.

THE

CORINNA OF

ENGLAND,

AND

A HEROINE IN THE SHADE;

A MODERN ROMANCE,

By the author of 'THE WINTER IN BATH', 'THE BANKS OF THE WYE', 'THE WOMAN OF COLOUR', 'LIGHT AND SHADE', &c. &c.

V O L . I .

L O N D O N :

Printed for B. CROSBY AND CO., STATIONERS

COURT, PATERNOSTER-ROW.

M D .C.C.C.I.X

'What Caricature is in painting,' says Fielding, 'Burlesque is in writing; and in the same manner the comic writer and painter correlate to each other. And here I shall observe, that as in the former the painter seems to have the advantage, so it is in the latter infinitely on the side of the writer: for the monstrous is much easier to paint than describe, and the ridiculous to describe than paint. And though, perhaps, this latter species doth not in either science so strongly affect and agitate the muscles as the other: yet it will be owned, I believe, that a more rational and useful pleasure arises to us from it.'[1]

LIFE OF HOGARTH

'When I see such games
Play'd by the creatures of a pow'r, who swears
That he will judge the earth, and call the fool
To a sharp reck'ning that has liv'd in vain;
And when I weigh this seeming wisdom well,
And prove it in th' infallible result
So hollow and so false; I feel my heart
Dissolve in pity, and account the learn'd,
If this be learning, most of all deceived.
Great crimes alarm the conscience, but she sleeps
While thoughtful man is plausibly amus'd.
Defend me, therefore, Common Sense, say I,
From reveries so airy, from the toil
Of dropping buckets into empty wells,
And growing old in drawing nothing up!'[2]

COWPER.

CHAPTER I

'Doom'd from each native joy to part;
Each dear connection of the heart!'[3]
                    LANGHORNE

It was a cold and wet morning, in the month of April, when Mary Cuthbert got into the stage-coach which was destined to convey her many miles from the place of her nativity, and the friends of her infantine days and her juvenile years. Deprived of both her parents at the early age of eighteen, this young and beautiful orphan had felt the heavy stroke of calamity; and though she had sustained herself under affliction, through a firm belief in a superintending Providence, with the resignation of a Christian, yet her whole deportment had evinced that she had greatly suffered – for that she had fondly loved, all who had beheld the dove-like eyes of Mary, when, turned with filial affection on her parents, they swam in 'liquid lustre,' would have given voluntary testimony! Mr. Cuthbert had long been the pastor of a small parish in Somersetshire, where his worth had endeared him to his parishioners; and their respect and reverence had so conciliated his regard, that he wished not to emerge into a more conspicuous walk of life; but, with his gentle and amiable partner, was contented with the small emoluments of his living. Their mutual love, and mutual cares, devolved on their only child, and Mary Cuthbert's improvement had kept pace with their wishes. If perfect happiness resided upon earth, it had surely fixed its residence at Woodberry, till the fading form, the hectic colour of Mrs. Cuthbert told a 'trembling tale' to her fond husband. A cold, taken by walking in the wet to visit a poor woman during the painful hour of labour, laid the foundation of a disorder which baffled all human skill. Mr. Cuthbert never recovered the loss of his wife; from that dreadful moment, he seemed to have lost the elasticity of his mind, with the activity of his body; and even the desolate and orphan state in which his poor girl would be left had not power to stimulate his exertions for life, though the acuteness of his parental reflections contributed to bend him in anguish still nearer to the grave. Too liberal and too generous to lay up from his scanty income, he had only a few hundreds to bequeath to his child: he had no other relations, except a niece, who had recently lost her parents, and, mistress of an affluent and independent fortune, resided in Staffordshire, in a house which her father had purchased a few years before.

Mr. Moreton had carried on an extensive manufactory at Birmingham with great success.[4] He had married the only sister of Mr. Cuthbert, but the wide distance which separated them had deprived the brother and sister of all inter-course, except by letter, for many years preceding the death of the latter; and, on hearing that his niece had lost her other parent, Mr. Cuthbert had contented himself with writing her a letter of condolence, judging that a young heiress, in the full plenitude of wealth, could well spare the personal inquiries of a plain and serious uncle.[5] But when he saw himself daily sinking to the grave; when he looked on his beauteous and innocent Mary; when he recollected the friendless state in which she would be left to struggle with a world, to which she was yet a stranger; all the father rushed to his eyes, and he turned his thoughts towards Clarissa Moreton, as to the future guardian and protectress of her cousin. Of the character of his niece he knew nothing; her mother had been perfectly regu-lar and uniform in her deportment and conduct, and he doubted not, but that her example and instructions had had their proper influence on her daughter. Besides, Miss Moreton was four years older than his Mary; and from eighteen to twenty-two how much experience is learned; how much judgment is acquired; how much consideration is added to the female character? Miss Moreton, too, had been used to the world; she had been born and bred amongst the populous walks of life, whilst the recluse Priory of Woodberry Parsonage had kept Mary Cuthbert as much in sequestration, as though she had been the blooming ves-tal of some time-worn cloister.[6] To Clarissa Moreton then the anxious parent addressed himself with trembling hands and beating heart. Ah! the subject was very near that heart; for was he not pleading for his only child? Miss Moreton's answer was calculated to disperse all Mr. Cuthbert's fears. She accepted the office of guardianship, and agreed, nay, insisted on her cousin's residing with her till she became of age, unless she should marry previous to that period. In two days after the receipt of this letter, Mr. Cuthbert breathed his last in the arms of his beloved Mary.

Thus having, in a general way, placed before our readers the circumstances which led to the long and tedious journey which our youthful traveller was undertaking, alone and unprotected, we will pass over the two first days of it, during which no incident occurred worthy of remark. Her companions in the different coaches had been civil and well behaved; the modesty and simplicity of her demeanour had been her passport to general respect; but, fatigued and tired of such close confinement, she was congratulating herself at having changed her coach for the last time, as the next stage was the city of Coventry, where her cousin's carriage was to meet her, and to convey her to 'the Attic Villa,' (for so was Miss Moreton's residence called) about four miles from that place. On re-entering the coach, Mary perceived that her former companions were gone; a female of decent appearance and a smug round tradesman had made way for two young men of a genteel air; who, having paused for a few moments, to read her blushing countenance with eyes of speaking admiration; and having, through the same channel, mutually communicated their sentiments, now recurred to a conversation (as shall appear in the next Chapter) which seemed only to have been interrupted by the necessary confusion and bustle of entering a stage-coach.

CHAPTER II.

'Even such enraptur'd life, such energy was ours.'[7]
THOMSON.

'Of all things in the world, I shall enjoy the introduction and the visit; of that I am well assured; but, my dear Charles, in the ardour of your regard for me, may you not be stepping a little beyond the verge of propriety? Can you take the liberty of introducing an entire stranger to your fair friend? Surely the customs of the world, and the delicacy of the female character –'

'How often,' said the other gentleman, hastily interrupting his companion, 'how often must I tell you, my dear Montgomery, that your scrupulous conscience, your fears, and your doubts, will always stand in the way of your enjoyments. The goddess of the shrine to which I am guiding you despises the customs of the world, as much as she differs from the rest of her sex. She is a being who stands unique in the scale of creation; it is wholly impossible to define her character; she acts from the impulse of taste – of whim – of what you will please to call it; she delights in patronizing genius – in being known as the liberal rewarder of talent.'[8]

'Genius, talent,' returned his companion; 'but has she discrimination to discover either?' 'Of what material consequence is that, my good friend? She has vanity enough to suppose that she has; and, flattered and courted by all around her, is it likely she should know her own deficiencies? She selects all her acquaintances from those whom she imagines to excel, and –' 'Pray, Charles, may I ask you, for what particular excellence were you placed so conspicuously on the list?'[9]

'Why faith, Montgomery, that question was not wholly unexpected; and you will allow, that to select my follies for the objects of praise was a rare piece of discernment in this fair damsel! You know my predilection for the stage: that, a buskin'd hero, I have frequently strutted my little hour on a theatre of village declamation, y'clept a barn. In one of my random moments, when whim took the place of judgment in my whirling brain, as our company were quartered in the city of Coventry, a company of comedians (I may call them fairly so, for the Tragic Muse must have flown at the first drawing up of the curtain) were entertaining the public; and, pitying the poor devils, willing to draw them a full barn –' 'And willing, too, to show your own theatrical powers,' said the friend. 'Why that is fairly put in, I believe, Montgomery; I plead guilty – but to go on with my story, I volunteered my services, which were gratefully received, as you may imagine, and "the part of Romeo by Capt. Walwyn," was soon blazoned in the bills, and stuck up in every corner of the town. It chanced to meet the eye of the lady of whom we are talking; she honoured the representation with her presence; pronounced my Romeo a chef d'œuvre; though, Heaven knows, it required all my heroism to make love to a fat and brawny Juliet who cried out

> "Wilt thou be gone? It is not yet near day;
> It was the nightingale, and not the lark,
> That pierc'd the fearful *ollow* of thine *hears*.
> Nightly she sits on yon pomegranate tree.
> Believe me, love, it was the nightingale!"[10]

I received a most charming billet from this fair, the next morning, and have ever since been as it were domesticated at the –' 'Does the lady ever exhibit her own powers in the theatrical way?' interrupted Montgomery. 'Oh, to enchantment. She does every thing, or *attempts* it! Indeed, Montgomery, you will not feel any thing like ennui whilst you are a resident under her roof; I defy you not to enjoy the motley groups, and the medley of entertainments and amusements, which will be there offered to you – the strangest, the most eccentric set, to be sure, which were ever huddled together; and I know, my friend, that you have a taste for the *perfectly ridiculous!*' 'But it is a taste which I ought not to indulge,' said Mr. Montgomery; 'I always feel humbled in my own opinion, when I have been *amused* with the follies of my fellow men; but that I have been so too frequently, I will readily confess. There is something very tempting in ridicule; one is generally encouraged to pursue it by the applause, and for the entertainment, of others; and we insensibly forget that we are erring against the principles of benevolence and rectitude.' 'Out, out upon your too tender conscience; I will not stop to hum and to haw, and to consider first causes and secondary effects; I will laugh, I must laugh, where I can and while I can – "Mirth, admit me of thy Crew." But you will go with me, Frederic?' 'I confess that you have raised my curiosity so very high, that, maugre *my tender conscience*, I *must* go!' 'That's my very dear Fred,' said his friend, eagerly shaking him by the hand.

Mary Cuthbert had been a silent hearer of this conversation, and had been congratulating herself mentally at being placed in a more humble situation in life than the lady whose large and independent fortune, and more independent manners, had been so freely discussed in a stage-coach by two young men. She felt curious to know the lady's name; and, Miss Moreton being in the habit of visiting in the neighbourhood, and being likewise in the possession of a large fortune, she doubted not, but that she should have her curiosity gratified, when she reached the Attic Villa. A reflecting and attentive mind derives instruction from the most trivial occurrences. That levity and easiness of access which had been laughed at in the lady who had been the subject of discourse, made Mary

Cuthbert more on the reserve towards her male companions, than she might otherwise have been; and, though she answered every question which they addressed to her, with the most undissembled sweetness, yet was it so chastened by modest reserve, as to draw from them the greatest respect and attention.

The coach soon stopped at an inn door in Coventry, from whence the passengers having alighted, Mary Cuthbert curtsied to her companions; in obliging terms, refused their offers of assistance, and retired to a private apartment to await the arrival of Miss Moreton's carriage, which was to meet her at this place. In a few minutes a waiter announced it, and Mary eagerly rose from her seat and followed him to the door. A handsome landau and four, with postillions in white and silver, saluted her eye. But she had time only for a cursory view; for surprise and astonishment had possession of every faculty, when she saw the two gentlemen who had so recently been her fellow travellers walk out from the inn door, followed by a footman in the same livery with the postillions, who said with the most respectful air, as he addressed the gentleman who had been the chief speaker in the stage coach, 'Miss Moreton, Sir, desired me to present her most particular compliments to you, and to say, that any civility you show this lady she shall consider as an obligation conferred on herself.' 'Such a message must be wholly unnecessary,' returned the gentleman, bowing to Mary, and taking her hand to assist her into the vehicle. She suffered him to do so in silent wonder and confusion. Both the gentlemen jumped into the carriage after her, and it was bowling quickly along. – 'Fortune favours the bold, I have often heard, Charles,' said Mr. Montgomery; '*we*, I think, must just now rank high in the graces of that fickle Goddess; for who could have supposed, when we just now took leave of this young lady, that we should so soon again enjoy the pleasure of her company.' 'Are you acquainted with Miss Moreton, Sir?' asked Mary, in some confusion. 'I am not at present,' said Mr. Montgomery, 'but my friend Walwyn is going to be my gentleman usher.' 'And is it possible then,' (said Mary Cuthbert, lifting up her hands and eyes with the most artless expression of concern,) 'that Miss Moreton is the lady of whom you, Sir, have been talking this morning,' turning herself towards Captain Walwyn for an answer. The hero of the greenroom seemed embarrassed. 'He pleads guilty, you find, Ma'am,' said Mr. Montgomery; 'but you must excuse a great deal in my friend, who is so used to *stage effect*, that he is apt to give himself poetical licence on all occasions.' 'I always speak in the highest terms of Miss Moreton; Frederic, you will give me credit for this at least. – You are a friend of that lady's, Ma'am?' looking at Mary Cuthbert with a painful air of inquiry. 'I am her near relative,' said Mary. Walwyn started; Montgomery was perfectly unconcerned, and laughingly said, 'Trust me, this unwary pleasantry of thine will sooner or later bring thee into scrapes and difficulties, which no after wit can extricate thee out of.' 'I have never seen Miss Moreton,' said Mary, pitying the evident confusion of Walwyn. – 'I know nothing of her character, except that her benevolence has induced her to offer her arms and her heart to an orphan cousin.' 'May Heaven bless her for the deed,' said Montgomery with enthusiasm. The colour crimsoned the cheeks of Mary at the fervour of his aspiration; but, recovering herself, she gracefully turned towards Walwyn, and said, 'Be assured, Sir, that I shall make no unjust use of the conversation which passed in my hearing this morning, and I hope (oh, how earnestly do I hope,) to find that in the warmth of your description you greatly overcharged the picture.' 'And why should you hope so, fair lady,' asked Walwyn; 'surely, you heard me say nothing derogatory to the sterling merit of Miss Moreton?' 'Ah! Sir,' said Mary, sighing, 'self will always be uppermost in the human breast. I have been cradled in solitude; brought up amidst the dear domestic duties of a country parsonage; is it likely then – is it?' – she stopped, she burst into tears. Walwyn appeared as if he did not know what to say, and Montgomery looked as if he could have wept with the lovely girl before him. Ashamed of her weakness, she hid her face with her handkerchief, and tried to rally herself into some appearance of composure, and to collect her thoughts for the introduction to Miss Moreton, but her truant thoughts were taking a review of all she had heard in the morning, and she shrunk from the idea of the miscellaneous group who kept open house at the Attic Villa.

Mr. Walwyn's description must have been partly accurate, for did not Mary at this moment perceive a defalcation from established modes, in the very circumstance of Miss Moreton's having trusted her to the escort of two young men, both entire strangers to her, and one of them equally unknown to her cousin? What had been the first advice of Mary's ever to be regretted mother on the subject of female conduct? – 'My dear child, always avoid singularity; never wish to deviate from the beaten track; never imagine that you show understanding in despising common terms, and those rules of decorum which the world has prescribed to your sex. No situation ought to preclude a young woman from acting in conformity to those laws of custom, and of prudence, which may in some sense be called *her fence of protection*, and the *bulwark of her every virtue*.'[11]

Walwyn soon recovered his presence of mind, and, with much fluency of speech, began to relate many anecdotes to Mr. Montgomery, in praise of Miss Moreton's benevolence and generosity. Mary Cuthbert had discernment sufficient to perceive that these were meant wholly for her ear, hence they failed to make that impression on her mind which had been produced by his unguarded remarks in the morning. But the Attic Villa was now in sight. The heart of Mary bounded at her side; a thousand fearful and humiliating sensations oppressed her; her colour went and came; and she put her head out at the window to receive the freshness of the evening breeze, for she felt gasping for breath. 'A most charming situation,' said Montgomery, putting his head out of the same window, and pretending to be lost in admiration of the villa, at the moment that he watched his interesting female companion; for he could read the 'human face divine,' and he feared the consequences of that excessive emotion so plainly depicted in her countenance.

CHAPTER III

'Here Freedom reign'd without the last alloy;
No gossip's tale, nor ancient maiden's gall,
Nor saintly spleen, durst murmur our joy,
And with envenom'd tongue our pleasures pall.
For why? There was but one great rule for all
To wit, that each shall work his own desire,
And eat, drink, study, sleep, as it may fall,
Or melt the time in love, or wake the lyre,
And carol what, unbid, the Muses might inspire'.[12]
THOMSON'S CASTLE OF INDOLENCE

At length the carriage stopped, the step was let down, Walwyn hastily jumped out: Mary Cuthbert trembled from head to foot as she gave him her hand; but there was no time allowed her for reflection; she was led through the corridor, the door of an elegant apartment was thrown open, Miss Moreton sprang from a sofa, and throwing back a long veil, which half shaded her fine form, she pressed Mary Cuthbert to her bosom, saying 'Welcome! thrice welcome, my dear Mary, to my house and to my heart!' There was something peculiarly grateful to the poor trembling girl in such a reception; she could not speak her thanks, but she smiled through her tears, and when placed at the side of Miss Moreton, she had time to observe her reception of the two gentlemen. Miss Moreton stretched out her hand, in token of amity to Mr. Montgomery, assured him that she had long wished for his acquaintance; and then, turning to Captain Walwyn, said in a style of theatrical declamation, 'Walwyn, at sight of thee my gloomy heart cheers up, and gladness dawns within me!' [13] – 'And this long absence has been to me more tedious than a twice told tale;' said Walwyn, kissing her hand gallantly, and answering in the tragic strain. 'But how comes it, that I see my fair alone?' 'I purposely came hither to receive my cousin,' answered Miss Moreton, 'thinking that our first meeting required not a crowd of witnesses; but now that we are known to each other,' said she, turning to Mary, and taking her hand, 'let me, my dear girl, introduce you to the apartment where my friends are anxiously awaiting us. – Mr. Montgomery – Walwyn – you will follow!' The gentlemen bowed assent, and Mary was led out of the apartment by her cousin.

Mr. Moreton had been a man who had indulged himself in speculative inquiries, and who had professed what he called 'liberal opinions;' he had been extremely fortunate in his mercantile career; and hence his eccentricity had never been tinctured with misanthropy; and he had been held in general estimation by the world, who, if they could not fall in with all his visionary theories and undigested plans, yet all agreed, 'that he was a most generous fellow, that his dinners were excellent, that the company round his convivial board was sure to afford entertainment, and that nobody could envy a man his good fortune, who evinced so much spirit and liberality in the enjoyment of it.'

The commercial concerns of Mr. Moreton had been widely extended, and he had been the peculiar favourite of Fortune, for through the whole of his bartering transactions he had never had a bad debt; and his schemes had generally turned out as he wished; his good luck, as it appeared, usually supplying the place of judgment, for he had outstripped all his competitors; the wary and the prudent had failed where he had been successful; for to *attempt* and to *achieve* had been with Mr. Moreton the same thing.

Clarissa Moreton was his only child; she was her father's idol, for he saw in her enough of his own disposition, and of the traits which marked his character, to make her so. And it was in vain that Mrs. Moreton would have taught her child to walk in the path prescribed to her sex; when her father, proud of her 'superior mind,' and of her 'bold and inquiring spirit,' encouraged her in asserting her opinions, and in deviating in her behaviour and manners from all with whom she conversed. But the superiority of Miss Moreton's talents, like those of her father, were calculated only for display; there was nothing solid or substantial in her abilities or acquirements, no depth of argument in her declamatory harangues, in which she had practised, from the early age of fifteen, to the attentive auditors round her father's table.[14] And while he, poor mistaken man, proud of her shining endowments, looked round for the admiration which, as a 'levy en masse' he expected from all his guests, and which they in some sort were constrained to pay, as the price of their entertainment, Mrs. Moreton's confusion and concern was very apparent, and her motherly countenance would be covered with blushes at the improper confidence of her daughter, and the eccentric propositions, and chimerical absurdities, into which her father's foolish example and blind indulgence, had precipitated her. Miss Moreton's heart might have been rightly formed, but her good qualities were entirely obscured, by the extravagance of her opinions, the pertinacity with which she maintained them, and the most overweening vanity. – Superficial in every acquirement and every accomplishment, she attempted every thing; fond of the new school of manners, and of philosophy, 'philanthropy' and 'benevolence' were words which were constantly jingling in her ears; and, the inflated victim of vanity and self-conceit, was easily persuaded, that she was the succouring angel that was sent to patronise genius and virtue on earth. She had a great tincture of romantic fervour and enthusiasm in her manners, which was called '*energy*,' a word well understood in the new vocabulary of the moderns, and which has been too frequently made use of to require any explanation here; not that Miss Moreton was a modern philosopher, there was not stability enough in her formation to call her any one distinct thing; she was every thing by starts, and nothing long; in fact, a young woman, who, with a showy person, a large fortune, and the most inordinate ideas of her own importance, dared to think and act without regarding the opinion of the world in any instance; and yet expecting not only to receive its general suffrage, but its applause and admiration.[15] If our readers wish to see the contrast between the cousins, we hope they will have patience to follow us through the succeeding pages.

Miss Moreton led Mary Cuthbert into a room, where were seated, in different parts of it, several persons. The tremendous ceremony of introduction being over, Montgomery and Walwyn formed themselves into a group with the two ladies, whilst the rest of the company mixed in conversation, or indulged in their particular amusements, or meditations, as they liked best. Montgomery cast his acute eyes, in a hasty survey, round the spacious and elegant apartment; it was lighted by a number of Grecian lamps, supported by lofty Tripods, while Cupids and Sphinxes, Graces and Gorgons, Hebes and Hydras, covered the walls. Placed at the head of the room was a full length picture of Miss Moreton; there was a fantastic style of drapery, perfectly in unison with her character, displayed in this portrait; a group of Cupids appeared sportively playing at her feet, while the Muses and the Graces were all crowning her with votive wreaths. The furniture of the room was correspondent to the various taste of the owner, books and exotics, globes and battledores, telescopes and skipping ropes, old china and dancing dolls, were strewed round it in elegant confusion; while a grand piano forte, a harp, a tambourine, a violin, a violoncello, flutes, and hautboys, were huddled promiscuously in one corner, and enveloped by music books.[16] From inanimate, Mr. Montgomery recurred to animate objects: a highly rouged and most extravagantly dressed female was reclining on a sofa; she had made only a half inclination of her body, on being introduced to Miss Cuthbert; the greatest ease and most perfect assurance seemed to pervade her manners; and she was now employed, 'sans ceremonie,' in picking her teeth and arranging her eye-brows, at a little glass which she had taken from the 'ridicule' attached to her side. This lady appeared nearly forty years of age; and, by the glances which she cast from her large dark orbs on the male part of the company, Montgomery judged that she had not 'numbered these years in vestal purity.' A gentleman sat near her, whose well-powdered whiskers reached his mouth on either side, and whose shrugs, whose grimaces, and whose perfumes, bespoke the insignificant coxcomb; he seemed very attentive to the lady. Indeed, the Signora Grosera and the Monsieur Myrtilla were excellent companions; her voice was the only attraction which she possessed;

and the sweet tones which he drew from his Cremona were the only claims from which he could derive either favour or sufferance, as his manners were completely ridiculous, and his morals were most licentiously depraved. A plain dressed and very quizzical-looking man had drawn his chair in a direct line before Mary Cuthbert; and pursing up his thick lips, was pursuing a whistle, with his eyes intently fixed on her countenance, and very dexterously twirling his thumbs, as his hands met on his well-stuffed waistcoat. As Montgomery saw the heightening colour of Miss Cuthbert, as he watched her retreating eyes, and increasing confusion at being so obviously singled out from the company to be whistled at; he was on the point of asking him what he meant by such impertinent behaviour, when he felt himself tapped on the shoulder by Walwyn, who said in a whisper, 'Come, I see I must be your Cicerone, for else you will be liable to some devilish mistakes; come with me under the veranda, and I will give you the professions, as well as the names of the company.' 'What! and leave that fellow to insult Miss Cuthbert by his lawless gaze?' asked Montgomery. 'My dear fellow, if she were an automaton Mr. Copy would regard her just as intently: he does not examine Miss Cuthbert as a creature of flesh and blood.' 'She looks more like one of celestial mould, certainly!' said Montgomery. 'Nor that either, my good friend,' said Walwyn; 'he is merely thinking how she will look on canvass; he has not an idea beyond his art, which is that of a mere copyist; he is one of the most stupid and tedious animals I ever saw; absent beyond description, all his senses are engrossed by his profession; and he can talk on no other subject.' 'Why do I see him here, then?' asked Montgomery. 'Because he painted that portrait, which is thought a great likeness,' said Walwyn. 'And did he design the Muses and the Graces too?' 'No, these were copies of copies, introduced at the desire of myself and some other of Miss Moreton's friends, who judged them symbolical and appropriate.' Montgomery shook his head. 'Those two you know,' said Walwyn: – 'The Signora sings, and the Monsieur plays the fiddle, when Miss Moreton likes to have music; but, to say the truth, this is not the hall of song very often, for music disturbs Mr. Copy; the Signora Grosera is frequently subject to the head-ache, when she is asked to sing; and it interrupts Mr. Germ in his botanical researches; you observe him sitting there, in green spectacles, looking over his different specimens of thistles?' 'But in such a spacious house as this, why are there not apartments appropriated for each particular pursuit?' 'Because Miss Moreton has fixed on this for 'the Lyceum,' and that she is the undisputed mistress of her own mansion,' Montgomery was answered; Captain Walwyn continued, 'the gentleman whom you see there has been for some time an inmate of this house; I understand that he has been very unfortunate in his own country (France); but it must be confessed, that he has experienced the entire reverse here, where his pathetic story of emigration touched the heart of Miss Moreton, and from the moment that the Chevalier D'Aubert became known to her, he became a resident at the Villa.' 'How very imprudent!'

said Montgomery: 'has not Miss Moreton one friend who will speak the language of truth, and tell her of the impropriety of her behaviour?' 'Do you recollect that independence of sentiment and action form the leading traits of her character? Frederic, believe me, that opposition only adds fuel to the fire, as Mrs. Deborah Moreton, an old maiden aunt, who resides in the village half a mile distant, finds to her cost every day that she takes a walk here, to rail at all which meets her eyes and ears!' Montgomery sighed; it was a sigh of the most pensive cast; he foresaw a thousand dangers, a thousand evils in store for the young and inexperienced Mary, under a roof where all the rules of propriety were invaded, and where a promiscuous and depraved throng found easy access. Even his friend Walwyn was by no means a man with whom a woman of strict virtue and modesty should be on intimate terms; his manners were lively and pleasant; his person was prepossessing; but, under this engaging exterior, Montgomery was well aware that he entertained a very indifferent opinion of the female world, and that his success with the weaker part of it had contributed to strengthen him in it, and that he sought their society only as they contributed to his gratification, or were likely to be instrumental to his advancement. That, under a semblance of frank gaiety, he entertained the idea of carrying off the rich heiress, Montgomery easily perceived; and there was a peculiar poignancy of expression and acerbity of manner when he mentioned D'Aubert, which evinced that the sentimental Frenchman was the rival whom he most dreaded. Captain Walwyn was the second son of a very respectable family; he was generally received as a pleasant companion; his fondness for the stage rendered him desirable in most of the gay circles, and his purse often failed in supplying his extravagancies; for his indulgences extended far beyond a younger brother's allowance, although that was not scantily allotted. The Walwyns inhabited the manor-house of the parish, where the father of Montgomery had been pastor for many years. Mr. Montgomery and Mr. Walwyn had been early acquainted, and had lived in terms of the strictest friendship; their difference of situation had been no barrier to their intimacy; Mr. Walwyn loved his friend for his superior sanctity and virtue, and Mr. Montgomery never thought the wealth of Mr. Walwyn entitled him to any portion of that respect, which he voluntarily yielded to his benevolence and goodness of heart. Two sons and a daughter were all the family of Mr. Walwyn, whilst a large tribe sprang up round the parsonage table. Early habits and early associations, rather than any similarity of character, had continued an intimacy between Captain Walwyn and young Montgomery. Frederic Montgomery was the eldest of the family; his conduct had hitherto been exemplary; he was intended for the Church, to which profession his wishes had always bent; and he had kept his last term in Oxford previous to his ordination, when, meeting with Captain Walwyn, he was induced by his friend's earnest entreaties, and his own curiosity, to while away a few days at the Attic Villa.

CHAPTER IV

'Whether he measure earth, compute the sea,
Weigh sun-beams, carve a fly, or split a flea,
The solemn trifler, with his boasted skill,
Toils much, and is a solemn trifler still.'[17]
                    COWPER'S CHARITY.

When Walwyn and Montgomery returned into the room, they perceived that the Chevalier D'Aubert had seated himself between Miss Moreton and Mary Cuthbert. Mary understood none of the half English, half French phrases, which were from time to time addressed to her cousin, accompanied with a sigh, or a look of languishment from the pensive orbs of the young Frenchman; but she saw that they were received by Miss Moreton with much satisfaction, who answered him so much in his own strain, and with an air so expressive of tender interest and feeling, that Mary felt embarrassed at being a disengaged spectator of the scene; especially as Mr. Copy still kept his eyes on her face, and had drawn his chair, the last time he resumed his whistle, rather nearer to her. She was ordered to sit in the seat she occupied, by Miss Moreton, and she had not courage to desert her post, though she felt very awkward in retaining it. In this dilemma, she recollected that she had her knitting in her pocket, and observing that the Signora had fallen asleep, and Monsieur was arranging a new crimson and silver cane string, she judged it to be no breach of politeness to take it out, which she accordingly did. 'What a picture of Industry!' said Miss Moreton, with something rather sarcastic in her exclamation. 'A picture! where?' said Copy, rubbing his eyes, and starting up from his seat in a moment. 'There,' said Miss Moreton, pointing towards Mary. 'Why, Mr. Copy, you are more absent than ever. I thought you had been studying it this half hour!' 'In the character of Penelope,' said Copy, muttering to himself, 'in the absence of Ulysses – Let me see, Penelope is generally drawn with blue eyes.' Mary Cuthbert's eyes were fixed on the knitting. Leaning his elbows on his knees, Copy very coolly looked up in her face – 'Yes, yes, I see, hers are blue too.' 'But Penelope wove, you know, Mr. Copy,' said Walwyn; 'this Lady's employment is of a different kind.' 'Very good attitude too,' continued Copy; 'head, a little too much recumbent – fingers displayed to advantage by the knitting – Penelope in character – the matron style of drapery, veil pendent from the left side.' 'But she did not knit – I tell you she wove, my friend,' said Walwyn – Copy paid no attention. Mary Cuthbert took out her scissors to cut her thread. – 'Or the fatal sister,' said he. 'Mista, black terrific maid!' said Walwyn, with a most hideous expression of countenance, looking towards Copy, and laughing: Copy whistled out the new idea and heard him not.

> "'Join the wayward work to aid.
> 'Tis the woof of victory.'"[18]

said Montgomery quoting from the same Poem. 'There are five sorts of spiders,' said Mr. Germ, who had caught the words woof and weave, these had fallen within the compass of his studies; and eagerly wetting his thumb and finger at his mouth, and turning over the leaves of an octavo volume which he drew from his pocket, he continued – 'first, the house spider, who hangs her web in neglected apartments; secondly, the garden spider, who weaves in the open air a little round web, the centre of which is her situation in the day time; thirdly, the black spider, to be met with in cellars and the cavities of old walls; and, fourthly, the wandering spider, who has no settled nest like the others; fifthly, the field spider, which they call the long-legs.' – Aha, aha, Monsieur Germ, aha, me think you be much like von gentilhomme, called Monsieur Long-legs,' said the fiddler. 'And perhaps the wandering spider, who has no settled home, may apply to you, Mr. Myrtilla,' said Germ, coolly resuming his former studies.

> "'The spider's most attenuated thread,
> Is cord, is cable, to man's hold on bliss!'"[19]

said Walwyn; but he was sorry that he had made the quotation, when he perceived the sentimental Chevalier strike his hand on his forehead with emphasis, and heave a deep drawn sigh, which was gently echoed by Miss Moreton. The Chevalier walked to the veranda; Miss Moreton followed him in great appearance of agitation, and took his hand, as if beseeching him to compose himself. Mary Cuthbert was heartily glad, when she could with any propriety, retire for the night; and, though laid on a bed of down, and surrounded by all the splendid elegancies of life, she gave way to her full heart in a burst of sorrow. She contrasted all that she had seen at the Villa, to all which she had been accustomed to see at Woodberry; there her duties had been her delights, and a series of useful and rational employment had enlivened every hour; there regularity and social order had presided, and no invasion on propriety or custom had taken place. It was by the express, the dying injunctions of her father, that she had sought her present asylum; destitute of friends, low in fortune as he had left his child, it was natural for him to wish that she should be sheltered by her only remaining relative, when she lived in a state of affluence, single and independent. By introducing the cousins to each other, he had hoped to render them mutually useful, and thus to have bestowed a mutual benefit: and he had frequently given Mary Cuthbert rules of behaviour, on her becoming the guest and companion of Miss Moreton, in which he had instructed her to comport herself with sweetness and gentleness of manner, and to make her company useful and agreeable to her protectress; 'never flatter her foibles, or nurse her weaknesses, my dearest Mary; always consult your own dignity of character,' continued the kind parent. 'You must remember that you are to be accountable for your actions at the tribunal of your Heavenly Parent, and that while you continue to mould your conduct by that law of right which has been transmitted to you from above, you may rest secure in your own integrity, and the silent plaudits of a good conscience!'

Mary Cuthbert's talents and acquirements were not of the brilliant cast; her understanding was good, her perception lively and acute; but her natural modesty and reservedness of disposition, added to her secluded education, and the retirement in which she had lived at Woodberry, had given to her whole demeanour and behaviour, an air of timidity and *mauvaise haute*, which, though it did not diminish her natural and peculiar attractions in the eyes of those who had discernment and understanding to appreciate them according to their value, made her appear to the followers of art and fashion as an awkward bashful girl, calculated neither for ornament or amusement. In the presence of Miss Moreton and Miss Moreton's circle, Mary had felt the most unaccountable embarrassment, and a restraint which was wholly foreign to her nature; for, open in her disposition, she was prompt in expressing her sentiments, although they were tempered by true modesty and diffidence. Yet at the Attic Villa she seemed to feel that every word she should have uttered would have been laughed or carped at by her hearers, as being in utter contradiction to their habits and sentiments; and for her own part, hers were in as direct opposition to theirs. Miss Moreton was very much pleased with her cousin; her modest behaviour and diffident manners were the passport to her favour; for a rival under her roof, one whose conversational powers outshone hers, or whose flights of fancy had been as brilliant; one too possessed of youth and loveliness, could not have been suffered; for the *genius* of *philanthropy* and *benevolence* upon earth, the arbitress of *wit* and of elegance, had hitherto possessed her high situation in *absolute power*; she had scarcely known what envy was, as the women who approached her had been her fawning sycophants, the men her slaves.[20] Mrs. Deborah Moreton, indeed, daily poured *plain truths* into the ear of her niece; but opposition and advice from a woman of rough manners, of coarse voice, and of an *unenlightened* mind, was received in the most disdainful manner by Clarissa; she generally on these occasions, adopted a cool and contemptuous silence; but, to show the notice she took of the advice in her future conduct, if Mrs. Moreton had endeavoured to dissuade her from any half formed project, from that moment she determined to put it in execution; and, on the contrary, if Mrs. Moreton recommended her to adopt any particular mode of behaviour, she contrived to be the exact reverse to the thing proposed. So proud was she of her fancied superiority; so vain of her own independence. Mrs. Deborah Moreton was a woman of common stamp; but she entertained very good and wholesome notions concerning the proper behaviour and the conduct of women, and they had been grafted in her mind, nearly fifty years before the *age* of *reason* and of *sentiment*; and had they been tempered with mildness and suavity of manners, they might have been of great use to her niece; but, unhappily, this good lady's temper was of a most irritable and hasty kind; ashamed of the repeated and daily increasing extravagancies of her niece, she no sooner heard of any thing she had done, or was about to do, than she sallied out in her long waisted sack, and with her ebony crooked cane, to give vent to her disapprobation; and as this was done in pretty harsh terms; as she so frequently had seen the consequences which had been produced, it would have been politic, if she could have put a check upon this effervescence of wrath; but she never attempted it. And if, over a sixpenny pool with her village friends, any anecdote had been related of the *Antic* Villa, (as not very inaptly it was called by the sober set at Marlow,) the next morning Mrs. Deborah Moreton was sure to be seen walking off; and as she passed some of the sisterhood, she would put in her sharp nose at their open windows, and say 'You see I am as good as my word; I am going to give her a good round lecture!' We have informed our readers how these lectures usually turned out; but nothing discomfited the old lady; at her return she greeted her curious friends with, 'Well! I have done *my* duty, I have told her a piece of my mind; now she may choose whether she will hearken to it!' How seldom is the language of truth heard by young women in Miss Moreton's situation! her aunt might be said to be the only one who had ever spoken it to her; and, coming under so homely and ungraceful a garb, no wonder that she turned from it with disgust and disdain to the more fascinating tones of falsehood!

CHAPTER V

'Stern rugged nurse! thy rigid lore
With patience many (an hour) she bore!'[21]
                                    GRAY.

After a restless and uncomfortable night, Mary Cuthbert left her pillow; and having taken a survey of the park, and the surrounding country, from her windows, and made a little arrangement of her wardrobe, she stole down stairs, intending to taste the morning air by a short stroll. All was quiet in the house, and she found her way to the corridor, and the door of the Lyceum being open, she saw a house-maid busily engaged with her duster and brushes. 'Are none of the family stirring?' asked Mary. 'Oh dear, no, Miss,' said the servant with a curtsey. 'Does Miss Moreton breakfast in this room?' 'Oh no, Miss, she do breakfast, most common, in the *Boy doer*, with the French *Caviller*; only sometimes she gets up *earlyish*, when the Captain be here, because they spouts a bit together, before breakfast, with the pebble stones in their mouths, out there in the park, because they do make plays in there, in the theatre, together.' 'Has Miss Moreton a private theatre in the Villa?' 'Yes, that's what she have, Miss – t'was a chapel in old times, but now 'tis *convarted*, you see!' Mary Cuthbert shuddered at the perversion of her cousin; when a tall figure, in a blue worsted dressing-gown and scarlet night-cap, crossed the gravel-walk, outside the windows; she started. The maid, who was a simple uninformed creature, burst into a loud and hearty laugh; 'I'fegs, Miss, I don't wonder at your being a little *gushed*; what a *quare* figure he do cut, to be sure! he is really terrifying to behold!' 'Is the poor creature beside himself?' 'Oh law's me, no, Miss, he be only one of the *Floss-all-overs*, as they call 'em; 'tis Mr. Germ; he as you seed last night; he gets up early to *snailing*!' 'What is that?' asked Mary. 'What, don'tee know, Miss? Why, he've been a gathering of snails, and slugs, and caterpillars. Oh law! he's a most *enauseous* old gentleman, to be sure; and you little know the work I've a got to clean after he; he brings it all into the house; as Joseph said, t'other night, he makes his room like Noah's ark, for he hath got creeping things *numerable* as the sand upon the sea shore, *sexing* and *dissexing* of it; look at 'en now, Miss, he is galloping away, long-legs, spectacles and all, after a drumble drone! What an old fool 'tis!'[22] Mary perceiving the servant to be very much inclined to volubility, now took up a book, and returned to her own apartment, not wishing to encounter Mr. Germ, by going out in the park, for she perceived that his race was not yet run. The book that she had taken was an English translation of a German play; it did not suit her taste; the language was bombastic; the sentiments were too lively drawn to do more than meet the ear; there was no depth of thought, no soundness of principle, and no invention in the fable; the catastrophe was unnatural and horrible. She had just concluded it, when the following note was put into her hand: –

'My dear Coz! – As I heard you say, last night, that you did not understand the French language, I will not inflict on you the misery of being present at my déjeune, which I shall have in my Boudoir this morning, as the dear Chevalier is good enough to read to me a most inimitable novel, the work of one of his own country-women. Such a novel! oh! my dear Mary, could you but read Delphine, or rather could you but hear it read by the Chevalier, with *my* feelings, you would receive a gratification almost celestial.[23] I shall not be able to see you till near dinner time, having appointed a little rehearsal with Walwyn, when D'Aubert shall have left me. I have ordered breakfast for you alone, as the Signora and the Monsieur have usually a morning's tête-a-tête, à la Françoise, in her room, and Mr. Germ's speculative and free inquiries into the wonders of Nature do not in general render him a very desirable companion for the repast of the morning; and I fear poor Copy might whistle you out of countenance. The two friends will probably lounge over their coffee together, while Walwyn gets himself perfect in his part, previous to meeting with me. This is Liberty-Hall, so pray amuse yourself as you like whilst under the roof of 'CLARISSA MORETON.'

Mary Cuthbert smiled at the various ways in which Miss Moreton's visitors were disposed and dispersed, though her heart sickened at the romantic and extraordinary stile of the billet, and the unblushing ease with which Clarissa admitted men to a tête-a-tête in her private apartment. Breakfast was prepared for Mary in a snug little parlour; which was more in unison with her habits and occupations, than Lyceums or Boudoirs. Supposing herself free from interruption for some hours, she employed herself in altering some white dresses, previous to throwing off her deep sables; and she had been reverting to the times when she had worn them last; when she had been the happiest of the happy; blessed with the fostering protection of both her parents, and sheltered in the parsonage of Woodberry; tears of irrepressible sorrow forced their way at the recollection. Her back was towards the door, when she heard it open, and a loud and discordant voice said, 'For *once*, then, I see my niece employed as I could wish. So, you have at last learnt how to handle your needle; Miss Moreton, I sincerely congratulate you.' Mary Cuthbert rose from her seat, and turned her tearful eyes on an old lady of stern and harsh physiognomy, who stood in an erect posture of surprise, as she earnestly surveyed her. That this old lady was Mrs. Deborah

Moreton, the aunt of her protectress, Mary instantly perceived, and hastily wiping her eyes, and placing her a chair, with a graceful, yet modest curtsey, she desired her to be seated, and that she would ring, and order the servant to acquaint Miss Moreton of her arrival. 'No, child! no!' cried the old lady, detaining her by stretching out her long cane, and laying the end of it on her arm. 'No, pray sit down, and go on with your work. My niece, Miss Clarissa Moreton, minds me just as much as she does you. Your name is Cuthbert, I suppose?' 'Yes, Ma'am.' 'You are very much like your aunt Moreton, child; if you wore your hair combed straight over a toupee, and had a fine taper waist, I should almost conceit that I saw her again, when my brother first brought her into Coventry. When did you come, child?' 'Last evening, Madam.' 'And is it true that the ranting, raving Captain is here again, and some other young scrape-grace?' 'Captain Walwyn is here, Ma'am, with a Mr. Montgomery.' 'Oh fie, fie!' said the lady, holding up her stick, and lifting up her eyes; 'here are doings with a witness! Book-worms, painters, fiddlers, and Frenchmen, an't enough, it seems, but the rake-hellish red coats must come forth. Oh, if your aunt was alive, she would mourn these days, these dissolute days, in sackcloth and ashes; but she, poor woman, was taken from the evil to come! Miss Cuthbert, you seem to be like your aunt in character, as well as in person. She was a regular, a modest, and a well-behaved woman!' 'You are very good, Madam, to entertain so favourable an opinion of me. I hope I shall conduct myself so as to deserve it.' 'Why, in truth, child, I am not apt to pay compliments; Honest Blunt is the name I go by, and if I would retain my character, I can speak no smooth words in times like these. The whole world is turned upside down, now-a-days. I am confident that it will very soon be at an end; for wickedness is come to its highest pitch! In *my* days, if a young woman was seen to be speaking to a man, unless he happened to be her father, her brother, or at least her cousin-german, he was set down as her betrothed admirer, and it generally turned out that he became her husband; but now 'tis hoity-toity, higgledy-piggledy, fiddling, racketing, acting, a parcel of fellows kept and maintained in the house of a young woman, for no earthly purpose, that I see, but to make her the talk and the scandal of the whole neighbourhood. Here is the mischief and folly of leaving young girls to their own guidance. Talk of fortune and independence, forsooth; in God's name, let her enjoy her fortune and her riches; who is to prevent her? who wishes to prevent her? I ask; but then, let her enjoy it like a reasonable being, and like a Christian, and use it with moderation; let her visit the poor; let her work for them; let her make baby-linen for the honest wives; let her have a good piece of roast beef, and a handsome pudding of a Sunday; let her give amply at the altar, and never turn away her face from a poor man in distress; and in God's name let her chose some respectable man of character, and a steady age, and after a reasonable time, a year or two spent in the proper formalities of courtship, let her marry, and so secure to herself a protector. I have no objection to these things; I do not wish her, I do not want her, to live single, nor to hoard up her money: but to spend it on lazy rattle-trap vermin, who do not care one farthing for her, it makes me almost frantic!' 'Miss Moreton seems very good humoured and amiable, Madam,' said Mary, now interposing a word, as Mrs. Deborah Moreton literally stopped to draw breath. 'I think that she would attend to any advice which came from so near a relative, and which was so well intentioned.' 'You would not think her so, if you knew her,' said Mrs. Deborah; 'she always acts in direct opposition to me, as if she studied the rule of *contrary*, for no other end, but to tease and provoke me; but no matter, I do my duty, I always have spoken my mind, and I always will, let what will come of it. She is my own niece, and if I don't speak out, who else will? I don't mince matters – no, not I. The blacker she looks, the more I talk; and if I think my company is not wanted, I will come the oftener, to see how things are going on. It shall never be said that her own aunt deserted her, though I may have hurt my own character, for aught I know, by continuing to come here; for, except myself, I believe she cannot reckon a truly *chaste* and *virtuous* woman in the whole range of her acquaintance.[24] And indeed, Miss Cuthbert, I am glad to see that she had the grace to accept the guardianship of your person, though I believe your father would as soon have thought of sending you to Jericho as here, had he known what a sort of a daughter his poor sister had left behind her!' Mary thought so too: her heart sickened at the description of Mrs. Deborah Moreton; for, however exaggerated, that she was placed in a most awkward and extraordinary situation was very apparent. 'Who have you seen this morning, child?' 'Nobody, but the servant who has attended me, Ma'am, or those who I have met in the apartments as I passed.' 'And that is as it should be, let me give *you* a word of advice, the less you are with the pack who are assembled here the better – much the better will it be for you.' 'Indeed, Madam,' said Mary, 'I am so wholly unacquainted with the world, that I feel very awkward in such a mixed party.' 'I know a good deal of the world,' said Mrs. Deborah, raising her head and her cane at the same time. 'But, as you rightly say, this is a mixture, and that too of its very scum and dregs – of all countries too; and now in the time of war, when a true-bred Englishwoman should avoid a Frenchman, with as much care as she would a serpent! For is not one the *natural* enemy of her country, as the other was in old times of her sex? Now are these doors opened to as many of 'em as will come, and the more they jabber and chatter their monkey nonsense, and kick their maccaroni heels, the more are they applauded and caressed!'[25] At that moment entered Monsieur Myrtilla, in a chintz robe de chambre, lined with pink garnet, red and sharp pointed slippers, with high green heels, and about fifty strings of light blue ribbon at the knees of his flesh-coloured muslin small clothes, while his hair was rolled up in as many papillions; his violin was slung round his shoulder, and tied by a bunch of the same blue ribbon on the top of his shoulder. 'Ah! me demand pardons, Ma'amselle, me thought you were all alone, so brought my fiddle, thinking to entertain a Ma'amselle, with one, two, pretty petit ariettes.' 'I believe, Sir, neither Miss Cuthbert or myself could derive entertainment from your *airs*,' said Mrs. Deborah Moreton, 'although it must be confessed that they are very extraordinary.' 'Madam, you do me much, ver great honneur, by de compliment,' said Monsieur, making several bows, and skipping off with the most assured and unembarrassed countenance. 'You may say what you will to this herd of parasites and sycophants,' said Mrs. Deborah, 'they will not be offended, they pretend to take it all in the way *coom-plee-maung*, as the French monkey calls it; and as a dog returns to the vomit, so do they resume their grimaces and contortions; my niece must see the contemptible insignificancy of this animal, but she countenances him merely because he can play the fiddle, as if the scraping a stick to and fro on a few strings to tickle the ear could make up for the want of every thing besides.' How long Mrs. Deborah Moreton might have pursued her harangue, is uncertain; but the first dinner bell sounding, she said to Mary, 'I suppose, child, you will want to make some little alteration in your dress, though you are mighty well, for aught I see, *clean* and *decent*, which is more than you will be able to say of all your companions; however, don't mind me, I shall look about me; but I mean to stay to dinner, I generally do so about once or twice a week; to put some little restraint on the company, by the presence of one of my respectability. I make it a point of conscience, for I assure you, I feel no pleasure from the visit.' Mary Cuthbert folded up her work preparatory to leaving the room. 'Aye, aye, your guardian may learn a little tidiness and order of you, I see, if she *would*. Ah, child, you have been well brought up! I see you have been well brought up; I dare say your mother was a clever notable woman!' Mary's heart was full; she longed to speak in praise of her mother, but her tongue refused its office. So, making a silent curtsey, she withdrew.

CHAPTER VI

'Vain is the tree of knowledge without fruits.'[26]
THOMSON

Mary was soon arrayed; and, perceiving that the parlour had been vacated by Mrs. Deborah Moreton, she followed her into the Lyceum, which she understood to be the general sitting room. At the top of the apartment, on a large chair, sat Mrs. Deborah Moreton; her head was erect, her unbending brows exhibited a picture of stern severity; her hands were folded before her; and, neither turning to the right or to the left, there was a magisterial dignity and *hauteur* about her, which was calculated to intimidate, and to awe all those around her; but, perfectly easy and free in manners, as in morals, none of the company appeared to regard her, except Copy, who had placed himself as directly opposite to Mrs. Deborah, as he had been to Mary Cuthbert on the preceding evening, only that, instead of advancing gradually towards the old lady, as he had done towards the young one, he made a retrograde motion, as he perceived the curve on the forehead become stronger, and the lines more deeply marked over the rest of the features; and from time to time, he muttered to himself – 'yes, stern, and unrelenting; these are the characteristic marks of her countenance; something of a Popish hat on her head, the cross, and the rosary. – The centre picture for the other two: Gardiner at the right hand – Bonner on the left – Queen Mary in the middle, the best I ever saw; not a smile, not the smallest relaxation of muscle – three quarters length – she will do, yes, yes, she will do!' and he began a long and uninterrupted whistle, as the rest of the company, engaged by their own amusements and pursuits, looked not at the ideal painter.

Miss Moreton was recumbent on an Ottoman; near her stood Walwyn, while the humble Chevalier, in all the flow of sentiment, had sunk on the carpet at her feet. Mr. Germ had a large folio of coloured plates before him, and was comparing his specimens with their descriptions; while his pockets were stuffed out like wallets; and he had books piled on each side of the carpet as he sat. Montgomery stood at a window; the Signora had not yet made her appearance; Mary Cuthbert felt a little awed at the unbending stiffness of Mrs. Deborah Moreton, and at being thus obliged to make her *entreé* before the company; but Miss Moreton immediately beckoned her towards her, and taking her hand, would have seated her at her side; while Captain Walwyn and Mr. Montgomery eagerly advanced, and, in the politest manner, made inquiries after her health.[27]

'You received my billet this morning, my dear Mary,' said Miss Moreton; 'I was sorry to be obliged to leave you entirely to yourself, but should have been quite *au de despoir*, if the Chevalier had not read to me an hour or two, in the divinest work which ever issued from a Parisian press!'

'You had *much* better take a seat by me, child,' said Mrs. Deborah Moreton, calling to Mary; 'here is *much* the fittest place for you.'

'Don't think of leaving *us* Mary,' said Miss Moreton. 'Mrs. Deborah Moreton is, you see, quite deserted,' said Mary: 'and as she has been so kind as to give me her company this morning, I must not neglect her now.'

'Oh, by all means, go,' said Miss Moreton, Mary obeyed; and though the disappointed look of Montgomery might have told her, had she taken notice of it, that he wished her to remain in her former station, yet she felt gratified in showing some attention to the old lady, when she saw her entirely neglected by the rest of the company.

Dinner was at length announced. 'The Signora is not ready,' said Miss Moreton, 'let the Signora know;' and she remained on the Ottoman, while Mrs. Deborah Moreton rose from her chair, and sailed with slow movement into the dining room; Germ seemed to understand her meaning, and hastily pocketing his specimens, he strided after her. 'We *must* go, I perceive,' said Miss Moreton, giving one hand to Walwyn, and helping the Chevalier to rise with the other; as if by an involuntary movement, Montgomery took the hand of Mary to lead her into the dining room; and Monsieur Myrtilla, skipping away, said, 'Where can ma chere Signora be all this great long time? She vas finish de rouge and de patch, ven I saw her last!' and all the way up the stair-case, he danced, calling, 'Ma Signora, Ma Signora – dinner be quite ready; dinner be waiting for you, Ma chere Signora!'

At the right hand of the table *stood* Mrs. Deborah Moreton, waiting for her niece to head it, and to hear grace. '*I* go to the side *to-day*,' said Miss Moreton; 'Mr. Germ be so good as to help the fish.' Mr. Germ obeyed. 'Indeed, Walwyn,' continued she, 'my spouting has nearly incapacitated me for any more exertion to-day; there is a great deal of violent action in that last scene!'

'Who says grace, Miss Moreton?' asked Mrs. Deborah, still standing. 'Who is the chaplain, niece?'

'My dear Madam, it is entirely out of fashion, quite exploded; it is never attended to when said.' 'It is a custom more honoured in the breach, than the observance,' said Walwyn. 'And the fish is spoiling,' said Germ. 'Can't *you* say grace, child?' asked Mrs. Deborah Moreton, turning towards Mary Cuthbert. '*I* can, Madam,' said Montgomery, with the utmost promptitude. He said a short grace, in a distinct and serious tone.

'Thank you, Sir,' said the old lady; 'here is a chair at your service, between me and this young lady.' Miss Moreton was seated between Walwyn and the Chevalier; Mr. Copy was at the bottom of the table; but, instead of carving, he was whistling, and taking the character of Germ's face *ideally* on canvass.

The Signora at length entered, led by Monsieur. 'It vas all of von obstinate little lock, which so cruelly detained the Signora,' said he; 'she has been one, two, tree, whole hours in disposing to her wishes.' The Signora scarcely noticed the party; but, seating herself, called for a glass of Madeira, while the attentive Monsieur kept tempting her palate, by praising the numerous dishes of which he ate. Montgomery was pleasant, and well bred; he paid Mrs. Deborah Moreton proper respect and attention, whilst he did not overlook his fair neighbour; and insensibly, the old lady's countenance relaxed a little of its accustomed sternness, at meeting with such unusual politeness at the Villa; and, on her re-entering the Lyceum after dinner with Mary Cuthbert, she declared that she had never dined so decently with her niece before. 'That Mr. Montgomery is a civil, well-behaved young man,' said she; 'and I only can wonder what can have brought him here?'

On Mrs. Deborah's rising to leave the gentlemen, the Chevalier D'Aubert had taken the hand of Miss Moreton, it never being his custom to sit after dinner; and the Signora Grosera had re-filled her glass, it not being hers to leave the Monsieur Myrtilla to a solo over his wine.[28]

After a sentimental tête-a-tête between the Chevalier and Miss Moreton in the viranda, the Chevalier quitted the room. 'Pray, niece,' said Mrs. Deborah, 'is that Mr. *Dobbert* a married or a single man?' 'Heavens, Madam! do you think I ever asked him the question?' 'I should think it a very natural one, Miss Moreton, admitted as he is, upon such very familiar terms in your house; and to tell you the truth, which you know I am very fond of doing, I have heard that he *is* certainly married, and that his wife is now in England, and in the utmost distress.' 'Poor man! I pity him!' 'Poor man? – Poor woman, you should say,' said Mrs. Deborah, 'to be deserted by her husband, and that, too, in a strange country!' 'Dear Ma'am, what is *country*? a mere local distinction: to a truly benevolent and liberal mind, this or that tract of land makes no more difference than this or that potato.'[29]

'Poor D'Aubert! joined, but not matched! How, how is my sympathy excited in your melancholy fate!' 'Miss Moreton – Miss *Clary* Moreton –' 'How often, Madam, have I desired, nay conjured you not to *Clarify* me!' 'Fie, fie, Miss Moreton, are you determined to act for ever in opposition to all the world? Will you still permit this wicked diabolical Frenchman to intimacies which I blush only to think of, and, *knowing* that he can never become your husband?'

'Husband! What an idea! Madam, I never *thought* of him as my husband!'

'*Not* as a husband? what then, child? – Miss Cuthbert, you had better quit the room, before she confesses what you ought not to hear!'

'Madam, the whole world, which *you* are so afraid of, may hear my sentiments. The friendship which exists between D'Aubert and myself is of a nature which common and vulgar minds may not comprehend, nor do we desire they should. To level it to every-day understandings, and to every-day practice, would destroy all the charming privacy of its nature. Friendship, like ours, Mrs. Deborah More- ton, is the sweet confidence of kindred souls. Benevolence and philanthropy first impelled me towards the suffering Chevalier; but these feelings have long ceased to actuate me. In the prosecution of our delicate and refined interchange of sen- timents, I find all that can interest my heart, and touch its softest emotions; and I glory in saying that the Chevalier D'Aubert is the very sweetener of my exist- ence.'[30]

'Oh, monstrous, monstrous!' cried Mrs. Deborah. 'You glory in your shame, child; and if, as you say, you are really so wrapt up in this *Dobbert*; for what earthly purpose have you brought back that rattling Captain again?'

'For my amusement,' said Miss Moreton, with the utmost *non chalance*; 'While D'Aubert is the friend of my soul, Walwyn is the companion of my lighter hours!'

'Why, child, one would think, to hear you talk, that you had yielded yourself up, a shameless wanton!' 'That *one* must have very *gross* ideas then, Madam, and a most depraved mind!' 'And who is Mr. Montgomery, that sat by me; and who, to say the truth, appears to be the best of the whole bunch; what is HE, I pray you? Is HE the *friend* of your *soul*, or the *companion* of your lighter hours?'

The crimson mounted to the cheeks of Mary uncalled for, as she heard this question; Miss Moreton, she thought, seemed a little confused as she answered; 'He is, at present, neither the one or the other – if I was inclined, indeed, to choose a companion for my *heavy hours*, he might perhaps suit me; for he seems vastly grave, and wonderfully solemn – however, *heavy hours* are best passed alone, I believe.'

'Then you are likely, one day, to have a very *solitary* time of it, child,' said Mrs. Deborah; 'for when you shall reflect, how you have abused the talents, and slighted the bounties, which have been given you – how you have perverted the blessings of Heaven, and wasted your fortune on the profligate and the unde- serving; – when your flatterers shall have left you, and old age shall approach –'

'Pray, Madam, do not talk of old age,' said Miss Moreton; 'it is time enough for *me* to think of that some years hence. I act up to the impulsive movements of my own heart; I glory in being the protectress of the unfortunate, the fosterer of the distressed, and the friend and patroness of genius – and, in the proud emo- tions of this moment, how strikingly true do I feel the truth of the axiom, that, 'virtue is its own reward!' 'What vain, what proud self-boasting, do I hear?' said

Mrs. Deborah. 'Virtue! it is known to you only by name; you have got a little high-sounding jargon by rote, and you use it like a parrot on all occasions. The fosterer of the distressed, indeed! what humanity is there in separating a husband from a wife, and feeding him on the fat of the land, while she probably is starving for want of food? – Where is the merit of patronising men and women, who are below the attention, and even the notice of all respectable characters? – Oh, Miss Moreton, Miss Moreton, would you but learn a little Christian humility, it would better become you than all the benevolence, the philanthropy, and the genius, about which you rave so much. The only part of your conduct which I can commend, was your accepting the office of guardian to this poor child. God grant that your example may not operate to her destruction! *There*, now I have given you a piece of my mind, you may take it as you like.'

'Just as usual, Madam,' said Miss Moreton, 'the conscious mind is its own awful world!' Nothing shall ever induce me to give up *my* friends to the antiquated and strait-laced dogmas of the old school, which must be utterly exploded by all the proselytes of refinement and sentiment.'

'I wish that word had never been uttered in England,' said Mrs. Deborah Moreton; 'but I have done – I have spoken my mind!' 'You have indeed,' said Miss Moreton, as rising from her seat, folding her arms, and lifting up her eyes, she began an invocation, which was meant to appear as involuntary, but she was well aware, that the company were all returning into the Lyceum, and that she had numerous hearers.

CHAPTER VII

'Would you (blest) Sensibility resign?
And with those powers of Genius would
you part?'[31]

                    LANGHORNE.

'Oh, ye immortal Spirits of Sentiment!' cried the impassioned Clarissa; 'Hear, oh! hear, the profanation which has been offered to your Muses! Divine Petrarch! where, if Sentiment had not existed, where would have been found those heart-piercing notes, which, like the harmonious trilling of the nightingale, were wafted on the evening breeze, in soft murmurings, through the woods of Vauclusa? In the absence of Sentiment, where, oh! where had been the immortality of Rousseau? The genius of his inspiration flown, in vain should we have sought for those polished periods, which will melt the heart to tenderness and affection – Eloise – St. Preux – Unfortunate Lovers! your sorrows would not have been excited by him; hearts of sensibility would not have known the pause of exquisite rapture; they would not have shed the tear of exquisite, of refined sympathy. Goethe too, then beloved writer! I call on thee! Where would have been the ray of light, which illumined thy pen, if Sentiment had been unknown to thee? Was not the affection of Werter the offspring of Sentiment *alone*? Was it not the refinement of passion, acting on the soul of sensibility? Oh! immortal and beatified lover of Charlotte! how often have I melted over your virtues, your passion, and your melancholy fate! – How often have I contemplated on the soul-harrowing picture of thy death! – How often in imagination descended with thee to the tomb!

'Sterne, too, thou genius of Sentiment, thou friend of all created beings, was it not Sentiment which warmed thy heart, when the oath of Uncle Toby blotted thy immortal page? And is it not to Sentiment, to Sentiment alone, that we owe the life of our souls, the most precious of our existing moments.

'For me, for Clarissa, she avows it,' (and she gracefully extended her right hand, and then pressed it emphatically on her breast.) 'Clarissa glories in the avowal, that when she ceases to be actuated by Sentiment, she ceases to think herself a reasonable being!'[32]

The different sentiments of the company, during this wild rhapsody of Miss Moreton, as expressed by their gestures and countenances, were worthy of observation. The brows of Mrs. Deborah Moreton were curved into a tremendous frown. She moved to and fro in her chair, as if she had lost all patience; and when Clarissa had finished, she said, 'The Lord be good unto me! Miss Moreton, all the world must think you have lost your *reason* now!' The Chevalier had placed himself very near Miss Moreton, in an attitude expressive of 'wrapt attention;' while, as if catching the very impulse by which she was directed, his whole countenance marked that he, too, was the devoted worshipper of Sentiment.

Walwyn stood in the door-way of the Lyceum, the living statue of stage-struck astonishment; and as the last fall of Clarissa's voice struck on his *charmed ear*, he clasped his hands together, saying, 'Is she not more than painting can express, or youthful poets fancy when they love?' 'Oh no, by no means, by no means,' said Copy; 'I have taken her, I have taken her several times myself, and I think I might succeed again. Miss Moreton's eye and figure are just the thing!' 'Miss Moreton's be very fine tones of voice, don't you think so, Signora?' asked Monsieur. 'They be so fine, so silvery sweet!'

'Oh, yes,' said the Signora, yawning; 'and they take in such compass – and her action is so tragic!' Mary Cuthbert looked at her cousin with wonder, fear, and pity; and her features expressed all she felt.

Convulsed by laughter, Montgomery could not repress his risible feelings, till, turning his head towards that part of the room where she sat, he observed her sorrowful air, and, at one view, entered into her thoughts. Then, the most bitter look of severity was to be seen on his countenance, as he turned towards Germ; who, as usual, with spectacles on nose, was poring over a large heap of books, and had continued his studies during the whole effusion of sentiment, with perfect composure:

'Did you ever trouble yourself, Sir, to examine the history of the Queen Bee? It is a study well worthy your attention, I assure you,' said Germ. 'I have,' said Montgomery, with some asperity of voice, 'and have vainly endeavoured to find out the character of the *drones*, who attended her; for I find she is always followed by a *swarm* of them.' 'They are useless insects, Sir,' said Germ – 'Entirely so,' said Montgomery, 'and I admire the discernment which enables the Queen Bee to discover this, and expel them from her society!'[33]

Mrs. Deborah Moreton soon walked off; little notice was taken of her departure; indeed she paid no parting compliments to any of the company, except a 'well – God bless you!' to her niece, a nod to Mary Cuthbert; and a formal curtsey, and, 'I wish you good night, Sir,' to Montgomery, as he opened the door of the Lyceum to let her pass.

In all the wild wanderings of Clarissa Moreton, her *heart* had hitherto taken no part. Borne away by vanity and self-confidence, she fancied that every new eccentricity, into which she ran, was a new proof of discernment, of talent, and of pre-eminent merit; or rendered her more interesting, and more graceful, in the eyes of her beholders. She liked the attention of the men, and welcomed the fulsome adulation of every coxcomb (whom she chose y'clep a *genius*) as a natural homage; but she had hitherto felt no particular preference in favour of any individual; and, though her fortune was daily suffering from the crowd of worthless beings, whom she drew around her, yet she never appeared likely to become the *exclusive* prey of one, frequently declaring, that she would not resign her liberty for the best husband in Christendom.

While these strange and volatile opinions deterred the regular and the well-principled from pursuing her, it rather emboldened than intimidated those of a contrary stamp; those who were acquainted with the instability and the capriciousness, of the female character, and *those* who, having nothing to lose, would make a bold venture in pursuit of fortune. Amongst these were Walwyn and the Chevalier.

Walwyn had seen enough of the frailty of the ladies, to know that he had great advantages on his side. The musty studies of the antiquated Germ were not calculated to *warm* the imagination, any more than the frivolous Monsieur, or the absent Copy were to *interest* it.

His own pursuits gave him a decided advantage over them. There was so much to be expected from the scenes and the situations of the drama, and he had there the greatest opportunities of prosecuting his suit with all the enthusiasm of passion: – that passion was there depicted in words the most forcible, tender, and yet warmly coloured. Miss Moreton herself, by turns the soft Monimia; the interesting Belvidera, hanging with fond affection on her Jassier; the voluptuous Cleopatra; the frail Calista, mourning her fault! – Surely he had *every* thing to hope, if Clarissa's heart had but the smallest preference in his favour. And this he would have suspected, if he had not perceived, that the sighing, the sentimental Chevalier D'Aubert, was admitted to all these liberties in *propriâ personâ*, which he had never attempted, but as the hero of the tragic tale.[34]

The Chevalier was artful and designing. Under the semblance of misfortune and distress, he hoped to bend Miss Moreton's principles to his own base purposes. A needy adventurer, he had already taken advantage of the distresses of his own country, to be received and commiserated in *this*; and he had left his wife to earn a precarious subsistence in London; by making flowers, and by other ingenious little devices, whilst he tried to work on the feelings of Miss Moreton, by representing himself as the most wretched of all created beings; as wedded to a woman without *a soul*, without an *existing sentiment*; and, by poisoning Clarissa's ear with the impure and sophisticated tenets of the French school of philosophers, and by putting their productions into her hands, he endeavoured to weaken her small deference for established laws and for revealed religion.

But, while Clarissa was enraptured with the insinuating manners of the Chevalier, and her fancy was taken captive by the flowery style, and the specious arguments of his favourite authors; she did not conceive the idea of forming any connection with him, but that of the most unlimited friendship. Indeed, neither the form or the face of the Chevalier, were calculated to kindle another flame, in the breast of a young lady who made any use of her eyes in her choice of a partner for her heart; the one not being moulded in the harmony of proportion, and the other being deficient both in hue and comeliness.

But a Frenchman, it is universally known, has a good opinion of himself; and the little Chevalier would not have yielded the palm of manly beauty to the Apollo Belvedere, although he had an air of negligence and of melancholy abstraction, which appeared wholly unconscious of his attractions.

Yet while he feared Walwyn, and Walwyn feared and hated him, there was *now* a third, more to be dreaded by each, and on whom neither of them had yet cast a thought; and this was Montgomery!

Montgomery had come to the Villa at the entreaty of Walwyn; who, knowing that he could not fail of being amused, and being fully aware that the principles of Montgomery would secure him from being his rival (as they were in direct opposition to those of Miss Moreton) he thought he should be adding to the gaiety of the Villa by this addition to the party.

But here he was mistaken. Montgomery had never felt himself so reserved – so silent – so inclined to be petulant, as since his introduction to the Villa. He looked at Miss Moreton with something very little short of horror. He had the highest opinion of the female character; and any defalcation from the standard raised in his own mind, gave him a disagreeable sensation. But Miss Moreton's conduct was most unusually opposite to any thing he had ever seen or formed an idea of.

The imposing air of conscious superiority, which was apparent in her demeanour, at the moment when she was rising to the very acme of folly and indiscretion, filled him with disgust; and his feelings were more strong, because his pity was excited, in no common degree, for the interesting Mary Cuthbert. And though, as a cool spectator at the Attic Villa, Montgomery might have been entertained, and contributed in his turn to amuse; though his lively gallantry, and ready wit, might have delighted the mistress of the mansion, and his sarcastic humour would have given an edge to the gaiety of his friend Walwyn; yet these were all lost to him, in contemplating the peculiar situation of the young orphan; whose modest sweetness of manners, and the bewitching *naiveté* of whose countenance, could not be contemplated by him without the utmost melancholy and regret. Indeed, so forcible was the impression made on his mind, that to be again at ease, he would have flown from the Villa almost as soon as he had entered it, if he could have resolved to quit that lovely object for whom he felt so much.

To a serious mind, such as Montgomery possessed, one in whom education and situation had both encouraged habits of reasoning and reflection, there were a thousand dangers to be apprehended for Mary Cuthbert. She seemed, indeed, to fear them for herself; but with the helpless apprehension of an infant, who yields itself an affrighted victim to the devastating flames.

Yet how to warn – to caution – to save her! Alas! Montgomery could only pity, in silence pity her! He had no friends, no connections, who could put out their fostering arms to this poor girl. His parents were compassionate and humane; their tender hearts would ache to hear of the distress which they had not the means of alleviating; for, struggling with a narrow income, and a numerous family, they were but just removed from a state of poverty. How, then, could they extend their protection to her?

Such also was the strict import of Mr. Cuthbert's will in this respect; and so entire, so implicit a deference did his daughter pay to it, that he questioned if any inducement would prevail on Miss Cuthbert to quit her cousin till she became of age. Three years of trial! thought Montgomery; oh! if Mary Cuthbert passes through this frightful ordeal, her manners unsophisticated, her morals pure, she will be pre-eminent in merit as now in loveliness! – but the heavy sigh which concluded this mental soliloquy, seemed to proclaim, that the wish could never be realized.

CHAPTER VIII

'Now while the drowsy is lost in sleep.'[35]
THOMSON.

Miss Moreton saw that she had a new guest in Mr. Montgomery. In Walwyn's friend she had expected to behold the prototype of himself; one who could rattle, rant, spout, rave, and sigh, and laugh in a breath, and be just what the humour of the moment should require. How, then, was she surprised at seeing that she must condescend to talk to him, if she would hear his voice; how was she astonished at seeing him retire to a distance, whenever an opportunity offered of approaching her; and sit in sombre silence during those bright effusions of humour, which set her 'table in a roar!'[36]

This peculiarity of behaviour, rendered him at first an object of no common curiosity, which was heightened, perhaps, at perceiving that his dark eyes beamed with intelligence; and that, whatever might be the cause of his taciturnity, she could not for a moment impute it to a 'deficiency of soul.'

'Perhaps,' thought Clarissa, 'dazzled with the emanations of my superior genius, he fears to approach me, lest the refulgent scintillations of my wit should be too much for his faculties. Perhaps he too painfully remembers the different situations in which we are placed by the world. He may be awed by the customs of society; he may not rightly estimate my notions of mental equality, which contemn all customs that would place barriers to sentiment and genius!'

So reflected Clarissa on her pillow; while the animated countenance, the fine form of Montgomery, as he had leaned over Germ, when she concluded her invocation to Sentiment, danced before her eyes; for, though she had not heard a syllable that he uttered, yet, from the warmth of his manner, and the bright sparkle of his eye, she was sure that an eulogium on herself must, at that moment, have involuntarily escaped him; and, surely, at such a moment, he must have been more than mortal to have restrained it!

'Such a character,' thought Clarissa, pursuing her ruminations, 'wants encouraging and emboldening. I must draw him out; Montgomery's is the *extreme* of sentimentality. Enthusiast as I am for Sentiment, I like to hear her votaries *talk* of her. Oh! if the *words* of the Chevalier were poured from the lips of Montgomery,

I should then have an opportunity of regaling my *eyes* and ears with harmony! D'Aubert is refined and tender, but his person is against him. Walwyn has fire and vivacity, but he is too energetic – too fervent.'

Miss Moreton sighed – It was seldom that she sighed, except whilst hearing the Chevalier read, Walwyn recite, or to fill a pause in one of her rhapsodical effusions. Perhaps this was the most deep drawn sigh, which had escaped her for some time; and she rocked her wild brain on the pillow, while forming numerous plans for drawing out this *kindred soul*!

On Mary Cuthbert she did not bestow a moment's consideration; for she had perceived, at the first view, that she was quite of the common stamp; a good sort of yea and nay girl, who seemed to suit aunt Deborah, but who had most unblushingly avowed her entire ignorance of the French language: 'le pauvre Chevalier had quite laughed when she had told him of it; and D'Aubert seldom laughed!'

That a girl who said little, and that little in a diffident manner; who used no action, and was quite deficient in attitudes and energies; that such a girl could ever rival Miss Moreton in the favour of any individual, was quite out of her calculation. She allowed that Mary Cuthbert had a pretty childish face; but she was quite under size, and had not the least grace or *dignity*.[37]

A variety of sensations accompanied Mary Cuthbert to her chamber; none of them of the most pleasing cast. The moon shone with mild lustre into the window; and, folding her arms, she stood before it. She surveyed the beautifully wooded park by this softened light; and a sigh issued from her bosom at the contrast, which the quiet and peaceful scene from without displayed to the interior of the Villa.

How happy, thought she, might my cousin be in this elegant retirement, if she would but resolve to perform the duties allotted to her station; and be contented to be esteemed and beloved! Of how much use would that fortune be, which is now wasted on the profligate and designing? Alas! she little imagines, that she is ridiculed and despised by those very beings, who now crowd around her, and pour their nauseous flattery in her ear!

Mary Cuthbert lifted up her heart to Heaven with meek resignation. She acquiesced in all its dispensations. She acknowledged, tearfully acknowledged, that she had enjoyed many years of undisturbed happiness; and that it was her part to meet her present difficulties with unrepining patience. She was walking in the path prescribed to her by her father. 'Then why,' sighed she, 'do I fear any evil, for thou, O God, art with me: thy rod and thy staff comfort me?'

At the moment when this devout aspiration issued from the pious bosom of Mary, she was alarmed by a loud and instantaneous noise at her window; the glass gave way; something fell on the floor, with a violent noise. She started to the other end of the room; and, in making her retreat, threw down her candle, and extinguished it.

All was again quiet in the room; yet poor Mary had not courage to walk to the shattered window, or even to look towards it. She knew that the cause of her alarm still lay on the floor; and, with palpitating heart, and trembling limbs, she seated herself on the bed, behind the drawn curtains, till a voice at the door, which she knew to be the house-maid's, whom she had seen in the morning, aroused her attention with 'Miss, Miss Cuthbert; be you asleep, Miss?' Mary immediately answered in the negative, and unbolted the door, though in doing so, she walked over the fragments of glass, which were plentifully scattered over the floor.

'Lah, Miss,' said the maid, 'I *warnest* you must have been mainly frightened; you looks as pale as a ghost, pretty nigh. To be sure the noise were enough to wake the dead, but you'll be used to us in time,' giving a knowing wink.

'What is the meaning of this? Who threw it at my window?' said Mary, picking up a large battledore, and blushing to think that she had feared to approach it. 'Surely, Miss Moreton could not countenance an insult like this?' 'Lah's me, Miss, why Miss Moreton knows nothing at all about it. Mr. Germ was entirely by his own self.'

'Mr. Germ!' repeated Mary, 'A man of his advanced age to play so boyish a trick; you surprise me!'

'Yes, yes, Miss, he does; and 'tis an even chance that he doesn't go to his bed till day-break, for he told me to ask your pardon, and to fetch un his *battledoor* again.'

'Lah's, Sir,' says I, 'now do'e please to call un battle-window for the future.' He said I was a silly wench, and bid me go along, but I don't mind the *Floss-all-over* much.'

'If he means to repeat his attacks, I had better wait for day-break too,' said Mary, calmly assisting the servant in picking up the pieces of broken glass. 'Oh! he mayn't come along this way again for the night, Miss; he's only *batting* and *owling* hood now; and so he went with his battledoor, to knock down one of the *leather-wings*, just as he went flap, flap, against your window; and then it all went crash, crash, and off flew the bat. And I declare for my *partickler* part, I thought the whole house was coming down about our ears.

'But, lah's me, Miss, I must run to old Germ, for he's had no sport this blessed night; not one bat or screech owl has he caught. I'll come up again directly, Miss, to make the window shutters fast, and then you'll be safe, and then I'll make you comfortable; and to-morrow we'll have the glazier; though if I was *somebody*, and mistress of the Antic Villa, I wou'd know who should pay for the mending.'

Quite recovered from her affright, and reconciled to the occasion of it, now that she found that it had proceeded entirely from accident, Mary was inclined to smile at the vulgar simplicity of the girl; but she was careful not to encourage her in her loquacity, and she readily saw that Kitty did not want it, for on her return to the apartment, she resumed her discourse.

'Well, the old gentleman is as pleased as punch, and he's gone into the shrubbery, *batting* and *owling* again; such a rare *curious* sight! 'Sir,' says I, 'I'm afeard you'll catch cold in pursuing them *enauseous* beasts.'

'Beasts,' says he, 'they are no beasts.'

'Lah's, Sir,' says I again, 'dont'ee say so, for you must remember what a beastly mess the last owl as your honour catch'd made about the little dressing-room where you kept it.' He turned upon his heel, for he couldn't well answer to this; and away he ran, with his *battledoor* in his hand, his green *specticles* on his nose, and a red *handkercher* tied under his chin; a body would think he was crazy as did'nt know his ways. Well, Miss, I must *wish'ee* good night, and hope as how you will have *nothink* to *disturb'ee* no more to-night.' Mary hoped so too, and, glad to be rid of her talkative companion, she resigned herself to the influence of sleep.

CHAPTER IX

'Ah, little think the gay licentious proud,
– How many drink the cup
Of baleful grief, and eat the bitter bread
Of misery.'[38]

                                    THOMSON.

Mary Cuthbert awoke early; and, perceiving that it was a very fine morning, she determined to indulge herself with a walk, being assured that she should not be liable to meet any of the inmates of the Villa, unless it was Mr. Germ; and she guessed that even the philosopher would be more inclined to seek sleep than *snails*, after his nocturnal rambles. Mary strolled round the park, and was delighted with a lovely and richly variegated prospect. She seemed borne out of herself, and her own concerns, whilst wandering over these new and luxurious scenes; and whilst lifting up her heart, in gratitude and praise, to the Fountain and Giver of all Good, her spirits seemed strengthened and exhilarated.

Following as fancy led, she got beyond the precincts of the park, and found herself on the verge of a common, skirted by a wood. A neat little cottage was in sight; she walked towards it; and when she had reached it, her curiosity was greatly attracted, at seeing a very lovely young woman standing at the door, and holding an infant in her arms, apparently in great distress, as her tears, and the agitation with which she continually folded the innocent to her bosom, plainly bespoke.

Ever ready to sympathise with the unfortunate, Mary gently inquired what was the matter? The young woman started at hearing the voice of a stranger; having been too much occupied in her own reflections to perceive her approach. 'Is it possible for me to be of any assistance to you?' asked Mary. Her soft voice spoke to the heart; the tears of the young woman could no longer be restrained; they forced their way in torrents down her pallid cheeks. But this was a momentary affection; for, turning half aside, as if ashamed at discovering her feelings, a bitter and harsh expression overspread her countenance, as she said, 'No, I thank you, Ma'am, the *rich* and the powerful have no *right* to be troubled with grieves that they know nothing about.' 'I am neither rich or powerful,' said Mary, 'and after acknowledging this, you may perhaps think my curiosity wholly impertinent, as I cannot be essentially useful, but the *will* to alleviate distress is mine.'

'You come from the Villa, I suppose, Madam?' said the young woman, with an incredulous look. 'I do,' said Mary; 'I have been there two days; I am quite a stranger in this country, but Miss Moreton will, I make no doubt, exert herself to relieve your distress, if you will make it known to her!' 'You *are* a stranger, I perceive, Madam. Ah! Miss Moreton wouldn't hear of *my* distress; 'tis of a *common* kind: My husband's long illness, his consequent loss of work, four helpless little ones –' she stopped and wiped her eyes. 'What is your husband's business?' asked Mary. 'A carpenter, Madam; and in Mr. Moreton's time he had constant employ at the Villa.' 'And has he never worked for his daughter?' asked Mary. 'Oh, yes, Ma'am, and it was there that he got his hurt.'

'He had an accident, then?' 'Oh, yes, Ma'am; and, acting against his conscience, as I may say, he has sometimes thought that it was a judgment upon him; but William was only working in the way of his occupation, and, as I have often told him, if he had not done it, another would; but he cannot make himself easy, though he told his mind, broad plain to Miss Moreton, in the beginning, and that is more than many of them do that are about her. 'Tis a thousand pities; for if she had not been spoiled, she might have made a nice young lady, and been the glory of the country.'

'But your husband,' said Mary; 'speak of his accident,' willing to hear the story rather than any remarks on Miss Moreton. 'Will you condescend to sit down, Madam?' and Mary walked into the cottage, and sat down in a room where neatness appeared struggling with poverty, and where one child was spreading the breakfast on the lowly board, whilst two smaller ones were looking on.

'These are my four babes,' said the mother, still holding the infant in her arms; 'my poor William is not able to get up to breakfast this morning.'

'I fear, I shall interrupt you,' said Mary; 'I would not retard your meal.' 'Oh dear, no, Ma'am, we shall not breakfast till William has had his nap; he had but a troublesome night of it, and so fell into a little doze this morning; but grief is wakeful, I could not rest, so, as soon as he was fast, I stole from his side to stand at my door, and to think of all that is likely to befall me. For, I thank God!' wiping her eyes, 'I still contrive to carry a cheerful face before poor William, although my heart is pretty nigh breaking!'

Mary sighed at the sight of the genuine distress, depicted in the countenance of the young woman, as she uttered the last words. 'Ah! Madam, forgive me; but you seem to feel for the unhappy; to be good and kind; and there is so little of this to be met with, that one is apt to be too bold; but I will go on with my story.

'William's father, Madam, was a carpenter, and bred his son to his own business; they were born and bred in this very cottage, and father and son always worked at the Villa. But in the days of my husband's father it was not called a Villa, no, Madam, it was Rutton Court; the family of the Ruttons were known centuries back in this country; they always lived in the great house, and were beloved and respected; they never raised their old tenants, or discharged their old servants; they had a chapel in their own house, and any body who liked might attend service there twice every Sunday. And the chaplain would visit all that wished it, and give comfort to the souls of their poor neighbours; while the Squire would take care that their bodies were in no want. The last Squire Rutton died without a will, and childless; the property went amongst a plenty of distant relations very far off, so there was a sale of Rutton Manor, and every thing belonging to it, and Mr. Moreton, you see, Ma'am, being a very lucky man in the trading way, came into the country and bought it, and retired from business, and came to live here.

'Mr. Moreton was a different man from the Ruttons; not that he was hard-hearted or tyrannical; but he was fond of every thing new, and old customs were laid by and forgotten, and new-fangled ones were taken up, and the duty in the chapel was gave over, and it was shut up, though I have heard that his Lady, Mrs. Moreton, was very sorry at this. My William, however, had constant work, in turning the old court to the new Villa, and had very good pay, and very well content he was; and then, when Miss Moreton came to be mistress of it, he was had again, to beautify and alter, and all very well; for who have a right to follow their own inventions if the rich have not, Ma'am? and how would the workman get employ, if there was not a time for pulling down, as well as building up. But then such alterations as Miss Moreton made, Ma'am! 'twas too bad certainly to convert the house of God into a – William did call it a den of thieves; but no, Madam – but no, Madam – no, it was to be a theatre; William spoke his mind, for it went to his heart, who was always brought up in the fear of the Lord, to see the old paintings, and the angels, and the ten commandments, torn down, from what used to be the Altar Piece, to make room for the naked gods and goddesses; for William had heard many and many a good sermon in that place, and it sorely went to his heart, and he did speak, and that too in Miss Moreton's hearing.

'She said it was her wish to get over all superstitious notions; and that the chapel had been quite useless to her, as her servants had refused to sleep there; and that she was delighted at having such a good theatre raised to her hands, with such a fine caned roof to speak in; and William said, Ma'am, he saw her get up in the pulpit, and speak a long speech from a play-book, to try how her voice would sound. Well, to work they all went, to beautify the theatre; and William, in taking down a piece of carved wood from the ceiling, to put up Fame blowing her trumpet, fell from the high scaffolding, and broke his thigh near the hip bone.'

Sarah Jarvis stopped in her narration to wipe her eyes; and walking to her dresser, she opened a drawer, and taking from it a small tablet of wood, with the letters I.H.S. emblazoned in gold on it, and surrounded by a Cross and Glory, she said 'this was the piece of carving which poor William displaced, Madam. He brought it home with him, and he has often said, that, if he were a Roman Catholic, he should have said his prayers before it, over and over, and asked its pardon.' 'And surely, Miss Moreton, who is all benevolence,' said Mary, 'surely, she stretched out her arm to succour and to help you!' 'Ah! Madam, that benevolence is a fine word for talk; but one grain of old-fashioned active charity is worth a mint of it.'

'Miss Moreton was not very well pleased with William for speaking about the chapel at first; and then some of the servants and the work-people talked about his accident, and said it was a judgment for daring to pull down God's house. So then, Miss Moreton was fretted and vexed, and a new carpenter was sent for from London; one as they called a right proper play-house carpenter; and so poor William took to his bed, and I lay-in soon after of this poor baby, and with one thing and t'other, we were brought low enough, as you see us now!'

'And has Miss Moreton done nothing for you?' asked Mary, in a tone almost amounting to incredulity. 'Oh! yes, Ma'am, she walked to our cottage herself one morning, with one of the Frenchmen; and she asked for my husband; and indeed I was very near laughing outright, in the midst of all my troubles, when I saw that she had brought him a present of a fine worked cushion to put his maimed limb upon; and she gave him likewise a white dimity gown to fold about him. It was all very well meant, I suppose, but, to be sure, they were not the sort of things which William wanted; however, nothing would serve but Miss Moreton must place the cushion herself, and help on the gown with her own hands! The *Civilear*, as they call that French gentleman, was lifting up his eyes, and clasping his hands together all the while, as though he had been saying his prayers; and he called her a ministering angel, and the tears were to be seen standing in his eyes. But somehow, I did not please either of them; for very unfortunately for the nice nose of the *Civilear*, I had been frying a little cabbage and potatoes for my children's dinner, and so the house smelled of it of course. The gentleman eyed me, and sniffed, and sniffed again; and he shrugged up his shoulders till they fairly reached his ears; and going out, I heard him tell Miss Moreton, that he plainly saw I had neither *sentiment* or feeling, and was a woman of most gross ideas, to entertain myself with *fryed meat*, whilst my husband was so ill! Miss Moreton seemed to be of his opinion, and from that moment to this I have seen no more of *the lady*.' An emphasis was laid on the two last words. 'Nor of the gentleman, I should suppose!' said Mary, rather quickly. 'Ah! Madam! I soon saw the cloven foot; but though I am poor I am honest; and no man in *England* should tempt me to wrong the poor man above stairs. But the *Frenchman*! only to think of his impudence. Ah! my very blood boils at the bare mention of it; however,' said she, after a few moments pause, 'I never breathed a word of this before, even to my own dear William, but somehow, Madam, you looked so good and so kind, that I was fain to tell you all.

'You need not repent your confidence,' said Mary; 'indeed, you have conferred an obligation on me, by letting me into the character of this foreigner. I hope he has ceased to annoy you!'

'I hope so, Ma'am; I showed him that I had some share of spirit, and that I could feel an insult, although I was only the wife of a poor carpenter. And I declared that, if he persisted in molesting me, I would go to the Villa, and complain of him to Miss Moreton. – This had a good effect; it is only virtue that is bold, Ma'am. If you could but have seen how he shrunk down, and fawned, and, spaniel-like, was for licking my hand, by offering hush-money! – I thank my God, with only a few shillings in the house, and not knowing where to look for more, I had the grace to refuse it; he has never been here since, and I hope he never will again.'

'I hope not,' said Mary, rising; 'your story has deeply interested me, and I sincerely wish it was in my power to be of real service to you, but I am an orphan relative of Miss Moreton, placed under her care till I become of age. I hope I shall be able to call on you frequently, and that I shall soon hear of your husband's entire recovery; you have my best wishes;' and, modestly putting half a guinea into the little hand of the infant, Mary waited not to see Sarah Jervis's looks, or to hear her thanks, but ran out of the cottage, and across the common, and glided, like a sylph, into the park, where, slackening her pace to take breath, she mentally reviewed the simple story which had just been recited to her.

CHAPTER X

'And as he view'd her ardent o'er and o'er,
Love, Gratitude, and Pity, wept at once.'[39]
                                        THOMSON.

ALL that Mary Cuthbert had just heard had but confirmed the fears which she had previously entertained of Miss Moreton's character; though she could not have suspected that her eccentricities were carried so far, or that she had utterly discarded all that was regular and respectable, and had so widely out stepped the modesty of nature.

The licentious and unprincipled Chevalier was at once the object of her fear and her abhorrence; and she shrunk within herself at the idea of associating and being on terms of apparent intimacy with a being of his stamp.

"'Along the cool sequester'd vale of life
To keep the even tenor of my way"[40]

is no longer allowed me,' sighed Mary. 'I am drawn from my humble retirement; and, though I am still in a subordinate station, yet am I exposed to all the dangers and the unpleasantries of a promiscuous society; but let me trust in thee my God. –

"Then, though thou should'st wrap me in clouds,
And threaten the hill with a storm;
Yet the sunshine of peace shall break forth,
And the summit reflect its last ray."*[41]

This pious quotation seemed to infuse new cheerfulness over her mind; and she was again regaling her eyes with the beauties of nature, when she was startled at hearing a small gate fall of a shrubbery, which led towards the house; and the next moment Montgomery appeared before her.

'Miss Cuthbert,' said he, 'how I rejoice at this accidental encounter! I will not say, I am surprised at it; but I am flattered at thinking that a similarity of sentiment has led us both to admire the beauties of such a morning as this.'

'This park is very delightfully situated,' said Mary, returning Montgomery's compliment by a modest curtsey; 'if I was Miss Moreton, I should spend a great part of my time in it.'

---

* Miss. Bowdler's edition of poems, by a young lady deceased.

'Suppose then,' said Montgomery, 'that you were to lengthen your walk a little, and return by the shrubbery, which is a more circuitous route than the one
you were taking – You will then be soon enough for breakfast; for Miss Moreton
herself is to favour us with her company at that repast, and had given an hour's
grace to all the slothful, at the moment when I quitted the house.'

'I think some of the party require a little indulgence after their late vigils,' said
Mary, laughing.

'What do you mean?' asked Montgomery, with quickness. 'Only, that Mr.
Germ, in the pursuit of owls and bats, invaded my territories a little last night,
and broke my window with a large battledore.' 'And he frightened you, of course?'
said Montgomery. 'I am almost ashamed to confess how much,' answered Mary;
'my spirits were in an agitable state, I believe. However, laughter succeeded apprehension, when a light was brought me, and I recognised the imbecile instrument
of my fear lying on the floor, and heard the simple and ludicrous account which
the house maid gave of Mr. Germ's nocturnal pursuits.' – 'It is almost incredible,'
said Montgomery, 'that man, who is formed with faculties which capacitate him
for a wide field of study and investigation, should thus confine himself to the
contemplation of a moth and a spider. He neglects the admiration of the great
universe, for the dissection of a butterfly; and stifles all the social and compan-
ionable qualities, in dry dissertations on the dry shell of a cockle. Such is the
mischief of a ruling passion! for except with regard to his insects and his reptiles,
Germ appears to me the mere drone of his own hive, and one of the most stupid
and absent creatures that I have ever seen!'

'Except Mr. Copy,' said Mary, with some archness.

'I will not except even Copy,' said Montgomery, with equal archness; and,
looking at her, 'in as much as I consider the contemplation of the '*human face
divine*' to be a sublimer study than that of the gnat or the flea. Painting is a noble
employment – it speaks to the soul – it moves the passions – it warms the heart!
When we behold generous actions portrayed on canvas; when we see the benign
countenance of an hero; he seems to live again; he is brought to our mental as
well as to our corporeal vision, and we feel as if we were participating in his emotion, whilst we are only looking at his mimic resemblance!'

'But Mr. Copy,' said Mary, 'appears to have none of that warmth of imagination, which you are describing.' 'Your observation is very just,' said Montgomery,
laughing; 'and I have wondered how it was possible for him to be a painter, till I
recollected that he was only a *Copyist*. He has no mind, no fire; he merely paints
from what he sees, the only sense, by which ideas of his art can be brought to his
comprehension; and I have seen an automaton painter in a piece of mechanism
which would exactly give you my idea of Copy.

'How much preferable is a little general knowledge to such an unlimited predilection for one pursuit, unless that pursuit forms the means of existence? But I am

now speaking of it merely as forming agreeable companions; and I think I could have picked out persons, who, though not so clever, as it is called, would have been much more amusing and instructive to Miss Moreton, than the group at present assembled at the Villa.' 'I dare answer for it you could,' said Mary, 'and I greatly fear, that neither the taste or the benevolence of Miss Moreton are quite correct. I have no right to speak of her conduct; and, most probably, I might be equally unthinking and credulous, if placed in a similar situation; but with respect to *amusement*, I think I should never select the gentlemen we have been talking of to contribute towards it, any more than I should the Chevalier D'Aubert for an object of charity.'

Mary spoke the last words with more emphasis than was common to her, for the story she had been hearing at the cottage was yet fresh on her mind.

'Nor to me, either, does the Chevalier D'Aubert appear an object of compassion,' said Montgomery. 'That noble patriotism which led the nobility of France to prefer emigration to becoming the subjects of an usurper; that constant attachment to a dethroned and murdered sovereign, which led them to relinquish their fortunes and to confiscate their estates, to prove their fealty and allegiance; which taught them to brave the horrors of want and penury in a foreign land; was worthy of the highest applause, and the benevolent exertions of all good men. But, when we see these misfortunes made the pretext for introducing into this country all the frivolity, the false philosophy, and the licentiousness of France; when we see the promulgation of such sentiments received and cherished here, merely because they call themselves emigrants; we must naturally feel the most irrepressible disgust; and I think, in my whole life, I never met with a being towards whom I felt it in so great a degree, as the Chevalier D'Aubert!'[42]

'He strikes me as a most artful and dangerous character,' said Mary. 'He certainly is so:' returned Montgomery. 'The frivolous coxcombry of the fiddling Monsieur is seen and laughed at; but the sighing sophistry of D'Aubert has more serious effects; for, under the mask of pensive sentimentality, he would sap every principle which can make us happy here, and take from us every bright prospect of an hereafter!' – Montgomery paused; he seemed startled at his own seriousness; for, turning towards Mary, he said, 'I might apologise to you for talking in this sententious strain; but indeed, Miss Cuthbert, I feel greatly interested for you – I seem to have acquired a right to converse with you in the language of friendship and sincerity, from having been privy to the amiable emotion, excited in your bosom, when my friend Walwyn, so unintentionally, let you a little into the character of your protectress. Believe me, when I tell you, that it is with no little anxiety, on the account of her protegé, that I have, since I came to the Villa, employed myself in scrutinizing the character of Miss Moreton!'

'And what has been the result of your investigation?' asked Mary, looking up with undissembled earnestness into the face of Montgomery. 'Ah!' said he, shaking his head, with a desponding expression, 'where there is so much confidence, so little judgment, and such a boundless thirst of praise, what can be expected but selfish and capricious conduct? Miss Moreton just now believes, that she may do any thing; that she is the object of universal attention and admiration; and that notoriety and applause will incessantly follow her steps. Poor young lady! she is to be pitied for entertaining such fallacious and extravagant notions; but she has too much self-conceit to be undeceived. I have been studying your character a little, likewise,' said he, his voice lowering, and seeming almost afraid to trust himself to look at Mary. Neither did Mary examine his countenance with the lively earnestness that she had before displayed; the crimson suffused her cheek, as she said, 'Indeed! *my* character! pray give it to me, Mr. Montgomery?'

'I have been examining it, as it relates to Miss Moreton,' said he; 'and I confess that the timidity, which prevents Miss Cuthbert from unfolding the graces of her mind and the charms of her conversation, in indiscriminate society, and which has been a severe mortification to me, since I have resided under the same roof with her, is yet the best promise that I perceive of her continuing on tolerable terms with her guardian; and will, at the same time, shield her from the bold and unlicensed attacks of *her* associates!' 'Oh! may I ever feel constrained and awed in their society, if it will be a prevention from danger,' cried Mary, clasping her hands together –'Yet may I always fearlessly speak at the command of Virtue!'

'That, I am confident, you ever will,' said Montgomery, taking her clasped hands tenderly, yet respectfully, in his – 'charming Miss Cuthbert, you are most peculiarly situated; Providence has thought fit to place you, where your patience and your forbearance must be exerted; but, while you follow the pious rectitude of your own heart, you will have nothing to fear! you will go through the path of duty with cheerful magnanimity!'[43]

'You are very good to embolden me,' said Mary, releasing her hand to wipe off the starting tear. At that moment Walwyn appeared coming towards them, and, gaily kissing his hand to Mary, he said, 'Miss Moreton in the Lyceum waits,

> "The banquet spread, and all her guests assembl'd,
> For thee, sweet maid, and for thy *charm'd* companion,
> She now the tardy moments chide,
> That keep thee from the light repast.
> Haste then, fair Mary, haste,
> And *tea* and *butter'd muffins* taste.
> With *sugar* sweet as thy own lip,
> The balmy sweets of India sip!"[44]

Sorry to be late at the breakfast-table, Mary hastened into the Lyceum, followed by the two gentlemen; she flung off her hat, as she passed through the Corridor; her fine brown tresses parted on her white forehead, and her cheeks glowed with the freshness of the morning, and she afforded a pretty striking contrast to some of the assembled group.

CHAPTER XI

'They represent vices as frailties, and frailties as virtues.'[45]

FORDYCE.

The veil of Miss Moreton half shaded her face, as she reclined on a sofa, at the head of the long table, on which the breakfast was spread; bouquets of flowers were placed at every plate. Germ and Copy were already seated; the latter was holding a moss rose at a short distance from him, and whistling at it, as if in the act of portraying it on paper; while Germ, with green spectacles, was examining a leaf on which he had found the aurelia of a butterfly. Miss Moreton was studying, and did not, (or pretended not to) hear the entrance of Mary Cuthbert, or her morning compliments. Walwyn took his seat at her right hand, and, understanding its motion, immediately began to pour out the tea; when the Chevalier glided into the room, pressed the disengaged hand of Miss Moreton to his forehead, and to his heart, and, partly enveloping himself beneath her veil, leant over her shoulder to become a participator in her studies. Montgomery and Mary seated themselves; and Monsieur Myrtilla, skipping in, in the dress in which Mary had seen him the preceding morning, said, 'One, too, tree million pardons vor de chere Belle Signora; she has not leave her toilette yet, so I just promise to make'a coffee vor two in her *apart-ment*. *Bon jour*, Mademoiselle Moreton;' and away he ran.

'Do you know this flower,' asked Germ, addressing Walwyn. 'Can you tell me what an egg is?' said Walwyn, smiling, as he took one. 'Certainly, certainly,' answered Germ; 'let me see this little book – No, hang it, this is my Essay on Crocodiles. I have, though, somewhere certainly' – searching his left hand pocket. 'No – wrong again, that is the History of the Horned Owl. Ah! here, here it comes at last; let me see – Eggs! page one hundred and sixty-three. Now, Sir, we have it.' 'I have *had* it, Sir,' said Walwyn, crashing the empty shell in the ear of the philosopher.

'Pish, pish!' cried Germ, starting and settling his spectacles. 'The egg you have had, but not its history; Willoughby, in his Ornithology, says, page one hundred and sixty-three – Willoughby says 'we may easily distinguish the yolk in the heart of an egg, as likewise the first white substance that surrounds it, and a second white in which the mass in the middle swims."

'For Heaven's sake, Mr. Germ,' cried Miss Moreton, 'let us not dissect as we are breakfasting!' 'Be dumb for ever! Silent as the grave!' said Walwyn, giving Germ a cup of tea. 'Take this beverage, Sir, it will wash off the *mass* of crudities which are collected in your brain!' 'Tea is nothing more than the leaf of a tree, which grows in China,' said Germ, not vastly well pleased to have been stopped in his dissertation on eggs. 'The leaves, when steeped in warm water, and corrected in their bitterness by a *small* quantity of sugar –'

'Twenty lumps,' said Walwyn, 'is *your* usual number, I think, Sir,' putting sugar into Germ's cup. Germ nodded his head and proceeded: 'The leaves diffuse the scent of a violet, and a volatility which, in some measure, refreshes the brain; and, besides these qualities, it has the reputation of being an asperient.'

'I will trouble you for another cup of coffee,' said Montgomery, who thought Germ had proceeded quite far enough with the medicinal properties of tea. 'Coffee – I have that in page two hundred and ninety-three,' said Germ; 'it is a little berry, gathered from a tree in Arabia-Felix, towards Aden and Mocha, and they now begin to cultivate it with success in the parts adjacent to Batavia.'

'What precise time do you mean by *now*?' asked Walwyn, who knew that Germ was speaking in the words of an obsolete author; 'Coffee has been cultivated in Batavia long ago.'

'Let me reflect, Sir,' said Germ. 'Why, yes, 'twas then; it might then, be as far back as Anno Domini one thousand seven hundred and thirty.'

'That is a great way back, indeed,' said Walwyn, 'to prove that in those days coffee was a *little* berry!'

Germ saw that the laugh was against him, and began to butter his roll with great eagerness and attention.

'I am enchanted with your book, my dear friend,' said Miss Moreton, laying it down and sipping her tea; 'and I declare to you, if there be a woman in the world whom I envy, it is the divine Madam Stael – what pathos – what feeling does she not display!'[46]

'As a writer, and a composer, she is certainly very great,' said Montgomery; 'Delphine is an interesting production; but there are sentiments of a most pernicious and blameable tendency interspersed throughout the work, particularly *pernicious*, as, with many readers, imagination would usurp the place of judgment, and, captivated by flowing language, and impassioned descriptions, their interest would be too much excited to stay to examine its intrinsic merit.'[47]

'Do tell me where you can discover errors in this sublime composition,' said Miss Moreton; who, spite of her admiration of the book in question, felt a secret pleasure in having at length called forth the interest of Montgomery.

The Chevalier probably wished to evade the discussion. 'You read it in English, Sir, of course,' said he. 'Ah! many of the finest sentiments, many of the most melting touches, are lost, are annihilated in your language; they are harsh and incomprehensible in an English translation, and to an English ear. Miss Moreton reads it with the taste of a Parisian, and in the original diction and *purity*!'

'In a grammatical sense, that word may perhaps be properly applied,' said Montgomery, 'but in no other: *our* language would indeed, Sir, convey *harsh* meanings to many of the specious sentiments contained in that production!'

'I wish you would point out your objections,' said Miss Moreton, reclining towards Montgomery, and stretching out her white arm to give him the book.

'I read it just as it appeared, and before its translation,' said Montgomery, 'and my treacherous memory will scarcely serve me as to the names of the characters, or the incidents of the story; but I well recollect many, *very* many, exceptionable parts, though I do not know where to look for them, neither should I like to be at the trouble of again turning over six volumes in such an unprofitable search, as the time spent in it must be lost, to say no worse of it.'

'Mr. Montgomery does not seem able to point out the faults,' said the Chevalier, 'although they are so very glaring;' and he turned an expressive look towards Miss Moreton, which Montgomery understood.

'I can yet remember general principles which are pernicious and immoral,' returned Montgomery; 'for instance, the very little deference paid to the marriage vow, and conjugal fidelity. All the *particular* friends of the heroine; all the married ladies, for whom we are to be the most interested, have tender attachments, independent of their husbands! On the subject of divorce, too, Madam Stael delivers her sentiments very freely for a female writer; and Delphine, the heroine of the work, suffers a passion for Leonce de Mandeville to take possession of her heart, knowing him to be the plighted husband of her cousin; and, after his marriage with her *cousin* and *her* friend, maintains a correspondence with him, that cousin, too, an exemplary character!'

'Is it possible,' cried Miss Moreton, 'that you, Mr. Montgomery, can really call Matilda de Vernon an exemplary character? a cold-hearted prude, and a rigid devotee as ever professed Catholicism; and as chilling, and as forbidding in her manners as – as Mrs. Deborah Moreton!'[48]

'I think the character a regular and a good one,' said Montgomery, 'bred up in the strict regard of a religion which maintains a good deal of formality in devotion, and following its strict letter, from principle and a pious disposition; as a *catholic*, I think her character is an amiable one, and I pity her constant mortification and humiliating trials, seeing her rival shining before her eyes in those attractions, which she does not possess, and stealing from her the affections of her husband.

'Delphine, too, so impetuous in her feeling, so hasty in her resolves, so regardless of the customs of the world!'

'Oh! Mr. Montgomery, you are quite a cynic,' said Miss Moreton; 'I cannot, *will not*, have my fascinating favourite Delphine abused; what sensibility! what feeling! does she not display? In what interesting situations is she not placed? and how enchantingly does she conduct herself through them!'

'Enthusiasm and romance form the ground-work of her character,' said Montgomery; 'and these naturally draw her into those situations which you mention, from which a *common* character would have been exempt.'

'Delphine's is no *common* character, certainly,' said the Chevalier. 'It is a character not to be found with *us*, I believe,' said Montgomery. 'And *can* you think so?' asked the Chevalier, turning his languishing little orbs, with melting meaning, towards Miss Moreton. 'I think so, I had almost said (pardon the affront to your heroine, Sir'), said Montgomery, as if not understanding his allusion, 'I *hope* so. – Our atmosphere is too foggy for such volatile spirits; it is not composed of such inflammable materials; the imagination of *our* ladies (bating a few exceptions) is not so vivid; and the genius of the nation yet makes the prudent conduct of our women its peculiar care!'[49]

Miss Moreton knew not how to keep her seat; the matter of Mr. Montgomery's speech was not at all pleasant to her; but the *manner*, the sparkling of his brilliant eye, the graceful action, the mantling colour on his manly cheek! she was rivetted to the spot by the warring sentiments with which her fancy was teeming; and, prone to translate every thing as her own vanity wished, she immediately concluded, that the warmth of his manner proceeded from a secret jealousy which he felt towards the Chevalier D'Aubert. This had roused his indignant spirit; this had urged him to speak in so decisive a tone; and impelled by this feeling, surely nothing could be more natural than his disapprobation of any book which his rival had recommended.

It was the Chevalier, then, and not Delphine, which Montgomery had condemned; and at that moment, he was in her eye the personified image of Leonce de Mandeville. Turning towards him with a most insinuating smile, Miss Moreton asked Montgomery if he would accompany her in the landeau round the environs of the Villa. Montgomery, though surprised at the invitation, could not refuse, and bowed assent. Walwyn looked rather disconcerted at not being included. The Chevalier re-opened Delphine, and sighed over its soul-harrowing pages! – Mary did not expect to be admitted of the party; but the *perfect amiable* was the humour of the moment; she also was invited, and went to prepare herself.

CHAPTER XII

'The lovers of a tune urge no severe inquiries concerning the heart of a fiddler. If he be a mercenary, while he teaches female pupils, he is watched; and if he performs in concerts, he is paid. If above pecuniary gratifications, he is rewarded with hyperbolical compliments. Articulate or inarticulate sounds is ample retribution.'[50]

Biographical Anecdotes of WILLIAM HOGARTH.

Mary had soon put on her bonnet and cloak; a trouble which Miss Moreton had deemed unnecessary, for her hair and veil floating on the breeze together, she sprung into the vehicle, in her morning dishabille, reclining negligently on one seat of the carriage, whilst the one opposite was occupied by Mary and Montgomery. Four swift horses carried them through the park. Miss Moreton had all the conversation; Montgomery seemed very well contented to be a patient hearer; and Mary's monosyllable, of an affirmative or negative, was all which was required of her by her protectress.

Miss Moreton appeared to take no little pride in pointing out the extent of her demesne to Montgomery; and she talked of her improvements and plans with very great satisfaction. – 'There is,' said she, 'so much pleasure in feeling one's self above the world; I mean, its customs and its foolish notions, and in having had spirit to break from its iron thraldom, that I only wonder there is any one left, who will comply with its arbitrary dictates! Don't you think, Mr. Montgomery, that every one is at liberty to do as they please?'

'Not knowing to what latitude you extend your question,' said Montgomery, 'I am at a loss to answer you; but if you mean, that people are always at liberty to follow their own inclinations, surely not. And think, if they were to do so, what a countless number of ills would ensue!'

'You take things in too serious a light,' said Miss Moreton; 'I am merely talking of those little gratifications of whim, taste, (*caprice*, if you will) which the tyrant world, and custom, would forbid our sex to enjoy; and which are perfectly harmless in their nature. To overstep these, is surely praise-worthy. In a mind, which has the capacity of thinking, to soar above trifles is laudable.'

'It depends on circumstances, whether even these may not be better observed than infringed on,' said Montgomery; 'in as much as things which are, in their nature, inoffensive, by encroaching too near the boundaries of decorum, break down those fences which she has raised for the safety and security of morals and manners.'

'Decorum is so like my aunt Deborah,' replied Miss Moreton, 'that I declare to you, Montgomery, I think if you were but to use it in her presence, you would stand a good chance of becoming her heir – Apropos! I will take you to call on her; she will be delighted to see you.'

They were arrived at the entrance of the village or the little town of Marlow, where Mrs. Deborah Moreton resided. As a plain but elegant chariot appeared at a little distance to be coming towards them, Miss Moreton ordered her drivers to stop at a little public-house, where the sign of the Red Lion was meant to attract the attention of the passing traveller.

Neither Montgomery or Mary Cuthbert could divine her business at this humble house of entertainment, till they heard her order the man at the door to bring her a half pint of cider.

'I am very dry,' said she, turning to Montgomery, as she put the cup to her lips. The chariot at that moment passed the landeau; a young lady of a very interesting appearance was seated in it. *Cup in hand*, Miss Moreton saluted her *en passant*. The lady returned the recognition with a stiff yet civil bow – 'Thank Heaven!' cried Clarissa, 'I have quenched my thirst, and given that notorious prude, Miss Davenport, a topic for a month. Miss Moreton *drinking* at an alehouse door in a morning! Oh! what a delightful incident to circulate through Marlow! Now drive on to Mrs. Deborah Moreton's.[51]

'You look surprised, child,' said Miss Moreton, turning to Mary; 'but you will know me in time. This is a little gratification, which the unfeeling world would have denied me. Now tell me, Montgomery, was there any harm in it?' 'Most assuredly, no serious harm,' said Montgomery; 'but as *Miss* Moreton's example may be brought as a precedent for others to do the same; as an *alehouse* is certainly not a proper place for females of delicacy to frequent; as evil reports are frequently raised from slighter foundations than this; and as Mrs. Deborah Moreton's residence is so very near, where you might have taken any refreshment you wished – I must confess that *I* think you might as well have driven by the Red Lion!'

'I can't be angry with you; for I asked for it,' said Miss Moreton; 'and yet in the whole circle of my friends, not one of them save yourself would have given me such a lecture!' Mary Cuthbert felt grateful to Montgomery for giving his opinion so freely, as she hoped it might have some influence on her cousin's conduct; for she saw, with the deepest concern, that she prided herself on setting all the common decencies of life at defiance. Montgomery felt that he had no right to talk in this manner to Miss Moreton, as neither his age, his sex, or the length of his acquaintance with her authorised it; but he found that his style, though novel, was not offensive to her; and, while his whole soul recoiled at her eccentricities, he felt that it was for the lovely Mary alone that he was interested in the conduct of Miss Moreton.

Mrs. Deborah Moreton received her visitors with some ceremony; but, notwithstanding her old fashioned formality, it plainly appeared, that she approved of the present companions of her niece.

Miss Moreton threw herself on an old settee, covered with tent stitch, and flinging off her slippers and gloves, declared that she was expiring from heat and fatigue.

'Then do take something, Clary,' said Mrs. Deborah. 'Oh, no, I thank you, I took a draught of cider at the Red Lion, at the entrance of the village.'

'Clary – Miss Moreton – do I hear right? have I lost my senses; the Red Lion, a pot ale-house – my niece – no, you are only joking; or I must be mistaken. Pray, Sir, did you have any cider at the Red Lion? or is my niece tormenting me on purpose?'

'I had none certainly, Ma'am,' answered Montgomery.

'There, there, I am really revived again!' said Mrs. Deborah, 'how can you be such a tormenting girl!'

'But Mr. Montgomery only answered for *himself*, Ma'am; and I only spoke of *myself*; for, upon my honour, I stopped there to quench my thirst; and, if you will persist in discrediting me, ask your friend Miss Davenport, who passed in her carriage at the very moment that I was drinking it, and holding the cup in my hand. I dare say that puritan will answer for me, if you ask her; or rather that she will tell it you the first time she sees you; for surely the spirit will move her to tell of so *uncomely* an action.'

'It will never move Miss Davenport to say any thing which will give another uneasiness,' said Mrs. Deborah; 'and she has too much respect for my family, to hurt the reputation of one of its members!'

'My dear aunt, *my* reputation is perfectly safe, believe me; though I cannot but be wonderfully indebted to you, for the prodigious fuss you make about it.'

'*You* obliged to *me*, indeed! Ah Clary, Clary, I wish you *meant* what you said, for then you might pay a little more attention to my advice. Indeed, indeed, child, you are going the very way in the world to be the general talk!' A pleased expression on Miss Moreton's countenance seemed to infer that this was precisely what she aimed at, as, turning to her aunt, she said, 'Dear Madam, you must be surely complimenting me!' 'I say, complimenting,' said Mrs. Deborah; 'I believe there are few persons who would accuse me of complimenting – If I can do any good, by advice and by plain speaking, I am very ready; but as to complimentary, fawning civility, 'tis Frenchified, and finical, and I hate it! What's become of the Chevalier, and the fiddler, and your Italian Madam?'

'All safe at the Villa, my dear Madam, thank your kind inquiries; which I will not neglect to repeat to them.'

'My inquiries, niece, extended just as far, as to know if you had sent them a packing yet, and this is the only information with respect to them, which could give me any kind of satisfaction. How long do you intend to maintain them?'

'Maintain them? what a question! Oh! Madam, when will you learn to expand your ideas, and dilate your mind?'

'When I become the tool of the whole world, and call myself a Sentimental Philosopher,' said Mrs. Deborah, and turning up her lip, and frowning with acrimonious severity; 'I would not care, if the *fidler*, the *squaller*, and the *whiner* were to hear me this minute; for I speak my mind, when I say, I think they are not proper associates for a young woman, and that they are a disgrace to you!'

Miss Moreton rose from her reclining posture; and, making a mock curtsey, was leaving the room – 'O, stop a minute,' cried Mrs. Deborah, 'I will put on my hat and cloak, and go with you; I intended to dine at the Villa to-day, if you had not come, and now I can have a seat in the carriage!'

'If you please, Ma'am, I will let it return again for you,' said Miss Moreton; 'for you must recollect, that I have already two companions, and that I always engross one of the seats myself.'

'Pray, Mrs. Moreton, take my seat, and suffer me to walk to the Villa,' said Montgomery. 'Or me,' said Mary, with earnest simplicity.

'Neither of you shall stir an inch for me,' said Mrs. Deborah.

'Oh! by no means,' said Miss Moreton.

'No, no, we will see if you can't for once sit upright, like a human being,' said Mrs. Deborah. '*I* will be your supporter!'

'What! in that odious red damask, Ma'am? You will give me a fever fit!'

'Perhaps it may do you good, child,' said Mrs. Deborah, pinning up the train of her gown, with great *non chalance*; and, having put on her hat and cloak, and made a curtsey to her niece and Mary Cuthbert, saying, 'I will follow you ladies,' she accepted the proffered civility of Montgomery, and held by his arm, as she walked to the door, where the carriage was in waiting.

The respectful politeness of his manner seemed to have some effect on Miss Moreton; for she suffered her aunt to take her seat very quietly, and, putting Mary Cuthbert by *her*, she got into the vehicle herself, and, notwithstanding that Montgomery several times requested to be allowed to walk, she insisted on his sitting next to her.

'I am glad you are coming to the Villa to-day, Ma'am,' said Miss Moreton, addressing Mrs. Deborah; 'as, perhaps, the Signora may be in tune to give us a song; and she is going to leave the Villa very soon, and the dear Monsieur likewise; they are engaged to attend a music-meeting at Lord —. I am sure I think myself in high luck, to have retained them so long; for they are in general requisition in the musical world.'

'Now that's what I think so very improper in the customs of the present day,' said Mrs. Deborah; 'every thing is carried to an excess, and *music* in particular, as if that word was an incantation, which bound up every sense but *hearing*.'

> "Music has charms to soothe a savage breast,
> To soften rocks, and bend the knotted oak!"[52]

said Miss Moreton, in the true pathos of tragedy.

'It seems, indeed, to be a magical art,' said Mrs. Deborah, 'and to have the power of transforming every thing. The difference of rank, and the different classes of society, are entirely overlooked in the pursuit of this tweedledum and tweedledee; and my lord is to be seen walking, arm in arm, with his fiddler; a *bishop* has been known to sing Goosy-gander with a shoe-black, if he had but a voice; and a *young lady* is on terms of intimacy with an abandoned courtesan, merely because she can pitch her pipe to an Italian bravura.

What the world will come to at last, I know not; for it is not that people are fonder of music than they were formerly, when the 'Dusty Miller,' 'Farewell Manchester,' and 'Lady Coventry's Minuet,' were as much as a young lady, in *your* station,' addressing herself to her niece, 'was expected to know of it; and these good old tunes she kept herself in constant practice of, by playing them on her spinet at least *once* a week.'

'Charming, charming!' said Miss Moreton. 'You really, my dear Madam, draw a most accurate description of the *taste* and the *talents* of *your* century. The spinet, the hurdy-gurdy, and the jew's harp! what an harmonious combination of sounds!'

'You may laugh, Miss Clary Moreton, but every thing was done decently and in order in those days. There was some method, some regularity, let me say, some *modesty* observed; a young woman would as soon have thought of flying to the moon, as of asking two profligate foreigners to come and stay in her house, merely because they could squall and squeak.'

'What words for expressing the most celestial melody,' said Miss Moreton.

'I do not stop to consider my words, when I am speaking my mind,' said Mrs. Deborah; 'and I am heartily glad that you are likely to be rid of two such disgraceful inmates; their shameful intimacy is very generally spoken of; and I have been told that they live like man and wife, even at your house, and I believe you can't deny it.'

The whole countenance of Mary Cuthbert was suffused by crimson at this coarse speech of Mrs. Deborah Moreton, but more so at the disgraceful information which it contained; and, without daring to look at Miss Moreton, she painfully waited to hear a refutation of the charges which were brought against her favourites.

Montgomery looked at the prospect; whilst, with the greatest *sang froid,* Miss Moreton said, 'Dear Madam, I never troubled myself as to the exact nature of the intimacy which subsisted between these souls of harmony; but, if to live like man and wife, is to have a perfect concordance of sentiment, of similarity of idea, and of unison of taste, *then* most certainly, do the Signora and the Monsieur resemble a united couple; *then* have you paid the highest possible panegyric to the married state, for it must be a state of undisturbed harmony and love!'

Mrs. Deborah lifted up her hands and eyes, and heaving a bitter sigh, she said, 'this comes of my brother's giving you what, poor infatuated man! *he* called liberal notions!'

'It does, Madam,' said Miss Moreton; 'I must ever honour the memory of that parent who saved me from the narrow opinions, and the circumscribed and illiberal notions of most of my sex; who, valuing themselves on one single virtue, give reins to all the acrimonious spleen, with which their minds are fraught.'

The landau, at this moment, drove up to the door of the Villa; Montgomery handed out the ladies; Mary was the last who wanted his assistance; but he held out his hand in a mechanical *distrait* manner, and hurried to the shrubbery; where, flinging himself on a rustic chair, he gave loose to reflections the most painful. All the pride of his soul was roused at the idea of staying longer the guest of a woman, whose principles and whose conduct he held in such low estimation as he did Miss Moreton's. The blunt speeches of Mrs. Deborah Moreton had wounded him to the quick. Might she not have asked him when *he* meant to leave the Villa; and had *he* even the excuse of scraping the fiddle to allege as a reason of his stay? Must he not be classed with the herd of Miss Moreton's sycophantic dependants? and could his visit be interpreted into any thing else, than a design on her person and fortune?

No! he would leave the Villa the next day; he would fly from a place which had afforded him uneasiness instead of entertainment; he would offer up prayers for the happiness of Mary Cuthbert, and then try to forget that such a being existed.

But of all created beings, the gentle Mary seemed the one whom Montgomery was the least likely to forget. There was such a touching sweetness in every thing she said; such a blended look of intelligence and of timidity, that he should continually bear her image in his mind's eye, and not want the talents of a Copy to pourtray it on canvass! – He must leave – he must go to-morrow; – but that to-morrow was *Sunday*, and to travel on a Sabbath-day was what Montgomery had never done, so of necessity he *must* remain *one* day longer at the Attic Villa.

He did not take into his calculation the practicability of walking over to Coventry the next morning, and of spending the Sunday, both publicly and privately, in an observance of its duties; he reasoned a little sophistically on the subject, it must be allowed; but which of my female readers will refuse to plead for him?

Montgomery determined, however, on leaving the Villa on Monday; and, having dressed himself, sought the company in the Lyceum, where, as usual, in stately effect, as Censor-General of the group, sat Mrs. Deborah Moreton.

The Monsieur was trying his cat-gut, and squeaking it, and tuning it, most scientifically (but not very harmoniously) at her ear; at every shrill tone, the old lady's brow became more deeply indented, but she observed an inquisitorial silence, as though something might escape her observation, if a word issued from her mouth.

The Signora lounged negligently on a sofa, with her fat and naked back turned towards Mrs. Deborah Moreton; Mary Cuthbert, in a corner, was quietly pursuing her netting; whilst the mistress of the mansion, as if determined to redouble her civility to Signora Grosera, after the conversation which had passed between herself and Mrs. Deborah Moreton in the morning, said, 'Dear Signora, I shall be quite *au de despoir*, when you and the Monsieur leave the Villa; I shall pant for your society, for your soul-subduing strains, which touch the heart to rapture and to love!'

'You do us ver great tres honneur,' said Monsieur, bowing, grinning, and taking more than half the compliment to himself and his Cremona; 'we shall often, ver frequently, talk of de plaisir, de felicité ve both enjoy at de Villa Attic – shall we not, Ma Signora?'

The Signora gave an assenting nod and smile; for the trouble of conversation was too much for her, and she generally gave up her sex's prerogative to the officious Monsieur.

The rest of the gentlemen soon entered the room; the pensive Chevalier seemed not to have recovered the disappointment of the morning; his sighs and his looks, when turned towards Miss Moreton, were evidently intended to upbraid her with cruelty. Not so Walwyn; – his light heart soon forgot a transient mortification, and, with renovated spirits and hilarity, he addressed Miss Moreton.

The day went off much as the preceding one had done; Montgomery kept his ground in the good graces of Mrs. Deborah, by again officiating as chaplain at table; and Mary retained hers by the undeviating modesty and sweetness of her behaviour.

At the accustomed hour Mrs. Deborah got up to leave the room; and in the exact precision which she had observed the evening before, Montgomery attending her to the door.

Mary Cuthbert saw that she was considered as a perfect cipher by Miss Moreton; this did not hurt her, for Mary had no undue ideas of her own importance; and she felt that her sentiments were so little in accordance with Miss Moreton's, that it were better that she should withhold them, than to excite useless argument and disputation, from which the peaceful breast of Mary recoiled.

But Mary had her doubts, whether a residence at the Attic Villa would be compatible with female delicacy and propriety; yet where, and to whom, could she go? Could she at once act in direct opposition to the will of her father? – a will so binding in its injunctions, so express in this point, that in Miss Moreton's hands were already placed the few hundreds which were to form her future subsistence, and which she had orders not to relinquish, till Mary should attain the age of twenty-one, or should marry.

Mary found that it would require much forbearance and fortitude, to sustain her present situation; but there was something consolatory in the approbation which would follow her good conduct; and the words which had fallen from Montgomery on this subject sounded yet sweetly in her ears.

The Signora and the Monsieur were going from the Villa; they might not renew their visit for some time. If the Chevalier D'Aubert would but take his leave also, Mary would feel more comfortable; for the knowledge which she had unexpectedly obtained of his character, made her feel an unconquerable repugnance towards him.

CHAPTER XIII

'It is difficult to say, whether the instrumental duties of religion, as they are usually termed, have been more misrepresented by superstition and hypocrisy on one hand, or by vicious *refinement* and *vain philosophy* on the other. By the *former* they have been extolled, as if they were the whole of religion; while the *latter* have decried them as vulgar, unavailing, and insignificant.'[53]

FORDYCE.

Sunday morning arrived. The inhabitants of the Attic Villa appeared to hold it in general observance, by keeping their apartments an hour or two later than usual. And this observance extended even to the domestics; for when, at nine o'clock, Mary descended into the little apartment, where she had usually sat when alone, she found it just as it had been left the preceding day; and presently the house-maid appeared, rubbing her eyes, and saying, 'Lord bless'ee, Miss, I didn't think as how you would be up yet, as 'twas Sunday.' 'That was the very reason which impelled me,' said Mary; 'I thought I would walk to Mrs. Deborah Moreton's, and go to church with her, if Miss Moreton does not go herself.'

'Oh no, Miss Moreton never goes,' said the maid; '*she* doesn't much hold with church-going; and the company as visits here be most of 'em *Meetingers* and *Romans*, I believe, for they never goes none of 'em to church.'

'But surely the servants go,' said Mary. 'Law, Miss, how can us? Now think if the family is all of 'em in bed, how is it possible to be done?'

'But in the afternoon?'

'Why, Miss, just as evening prayers goes in, cook must set about getting her dinner; and we be well worked all of us in the week; and we likes a little rest *one* day in *seven*; though, for my *pertickler* part, I should have no objections to go to church once a day myself, for I'm a church of England, born and bred to it all my life; I don't hold with the Methodists at all.'

'You appear to be a zealous church-woman,' said Mary; 'but if you never enter its sacred walls, I fear the mere profession of religion will not avail.'

'Oh! I ben't at all fond of Professions, Quakers, nor *Floss-all-overs*, nor *Byterians*, I stand fast by the Church, and always will to the last!'

'As one of its *outside* props,' thought Mary, who found it was useless to try to argue with such unparalleled ignorance. 'Alas!' sighed she, 'if *such* only were its supporters, how soon would the venerable fabric fall; but firm is its foundation, for it rests on the Rock of Ages!'

Mrs. Deborah Moreton's house was very near the parish church. Having taken her solitary breakfast, Mary set out to call upon the old lady, and to ask her leave to accompany her to it. Mrs. Deborah Moreton received her young visitor with much formality; but good humour might easily be discovered under her ceremonious politeness; and though her manners were reserved, and her appearance stiff, yet her words were in direct contradiction to them.

'You did right, child,' said she, 'to make your escape from the tents of ungodliness, to visit the house of your God! I shall always be happy to see you; the family pew is large enough – *too* large,' said she, lifting up her hands and eyes, 'for I only make use of it. Miss Moreton *never* comes; *she* lives without God in the world!'

There was much to interest Mary Cuthbert in Mrs. Deborah Moreton; under all her peculiarities, she discovered warm affection for her niece, and deep sorrow for the eccentricities of her conduct. A near and beloved relative going so far astray from every thing that was right, was surely a painful subject of contemplation. And Mary's respect and attention insensibly heightened towards Mrs. Moreton, as these reflections passed in her mind. With surprise, not unmixed with satisfaction, Mary Cuthbert distinguished Montgomery amongst the congregation assembled in the church; and when the service was ended, and she was moving slowly along with Mrs. Deborah Moreton through the crowd, in order to leave the church, he joined them, and his compliments were most graciously received by the old lady, who insisted on both her companions resting themselves at her house before they returned to the Villa. This invitation they did not refuse; and, on entering the house, Mary recognised Miss Davenport sitting on the sofa, not without a suffusion of crimson at the recollection of where she had last seen her.

In the most unaffected and prepossessing manner, Miss Davenport advanced towards Mrs. Deborah Moreton, who welcomed her with much satisfaction; and introduced her particularly to Mary Cuthbert, as to the ward and first cousin of Miss Moreton, and then to Montgomery.

Miss Davenport immediately inquired after Miss Moreton, and said, 'had I known she had so near a relative at the Villa, I should have made a point of calling; but I shall certainly not fail in paying my respects very soon.' Mary curtsied, and Mrs. Deborah Moreton said, 'Do so, my dear Miss Davenport, you will find this young lady one of the right sort, one of the old school; and I shall take it as a particular favour done to me, if you will visit a little more frequently at the Villa, for your example may do wonders.'

Miss Davenport seemed confused, and turned the conversation, by saying 'It was in my way to church that I heard of Miss Cuthbert; I accidentally called on a poor woman, whose husband has been very ill, and she spoke to me in warm terms of the goodness and sympathy of a young lady lately come to the Attic Villa.' Mary turned towards the window.

'I knew you would suit exactly; I said so from the first; I said that you would do exactly for one another,' said Mrs. Deborah, a pleased expression gradually softening the asperity of her harsh features. – 'One turns away from hearing her own praises; the other always calls *accidentally* on the poor objects of her bounty – I said so, I said from the first, that you would do exactly for one another!'

Montgomery followed Mary to the window, and while his eyes flashed intelligence, he said in a low voice –

'"Do good by stealth, and blush to find its fame!"'[54]

So grateful is praise from characters whom we have reason to respect, that perhaps Mary Cuthbert had never felt more happy than at this moment. The reserve incident to her disposition seemed to fall off; and she joined in a general conversation with readiness and spirit; which the good sense of Miss Davenport, the vivacity of Montgomery and the quaint remarks of Mrs. Deborah Moreton rendered very agreeable and animated.

The two young ladies seemed equally reluctant to separate; but Miss Davenport had an indispensable engagement, and Mary found it time to retrace her way to the Attic Villa.

Montgomery was but too happy in the prospect of being her escort; but, when he took leave of Mrs. Moreton, and mentioned his intentions of leaving the Villa the succeeding morning, that lady loudly expressed her regret; Mary Cuthbert was silent, and her eyes sought the carpet.

'I do not wonder at your going; I cannot say that I do,' said Mrs. Deborah; 'for a man of sense and understanding must feel himself in a very awkward situation, in that temple of folly! – I had hoped that my niece – I was in hopes that she might have had discernment to have – but you are going, Mr. Montgomery?' Mrs. Deborah Moreton, paused again, and curtsied slowly to Montgomery, as she bade him farewell.

For some minutes the walk was pursued in silence. Mary Cuthbert was the first who broke it, by saying, 'Miss Davenport appears a charming young woman.'

'She does,' said Montgomery, 'and much do I rejoice in your introduction to her; for, deeply interested as I must ever feel for you, my dear Miss Cuthbert,' (and the dear Miss Cuthbert was expressed with unwonted emphasis), 'I must consider the countenance of Mrs. Deborah Moreton, and the friendship of Miss Davenport as great ameliorations to your situation.'

'You are very good,' said Mary, 'I think I feel them so; I am grateful for the kindness and sympathy of every human being, and to you, Mr. Montgomery, I owe a great deal, for the consideration and attention which you have manifested towards me!'

'Grateful! grateful to me! Oh Mary,' said Montgomery, and he paused and looked in her speaking face; but, checking the instantaneous impulse of his feelings, by remembering their respective situations, he said, 'I should have been unworthy the name of a *man*, Miss Cuthbert, if I had not been interested by your introduction here, being privy to all the circumstances of it; and had my dearest sister been thus situated, I could not have wished her to deport herself in a more becoming and exemplary manner than you have done!'

Mary tried to vary the conversation; but she did not find her ideas very prompt. Montgomery was not peculiarly brilliant in his remarks, and made none but indifferent ones, till they had nearly reached the house; when, hastily turning, and taking Mary's hand with emotion, he said, 'this may be the only moment allowed me of saying, that I must always feel interested for your happiness; and that, though my lot in this world may throw me at a wide distance from you; yet shall I ever fervently pray for your felicity, and bear about me the remembrance of your wondrous sweetness; even though I should never meet you more – God bless you, farewell, Miss Cuthbert!'

The last words were spoken with peculiar emotion; they forced the tears to the eyes of Mary; but, luckily, Montgomery saw them not; for, relinquishing her hand, he fled from her, and turned by another path into the shrubbery, instead of accompanying her into the house.

Mary's full heart overflowed at her eyes; and she was glad to escape from the observation of the family, and to gain her own room, where she tried to restrain her emotions; emotions for which she could not account, as her acquaintance with Montgomery had been too short, she thought, to justify them. 'To be sure, his manners were particularly pleasing; his respectful attention to her had been peculiarly grateful; and I feel it now,' thought Mary, 'because the loss of my dear parents has left me a forlorn and isolated orphan on the world!'

Mary soon gained her accustomed composure, and went into the Lyceum to seek Miss Moreton, not having paid her compliments to her for the day; – but Miss Moreton was not there. Mr. Germ was employed in sorting shells, and designating them under their respective classes, as he put them into little paper boxes; while Copy, with his pallet and easel before him, had sketched the outline of Superstition, and a Gorgon front he had given her; notwithstanding that, it bore a slight resemblance to the harsh features of Mrs. Deborah Moreton. In the viranda was seated the Monsieur in his morning robes, his hair 'en papillot,' with his Cremona on his shoulder scraping, 'Go to the Devil and shake yourself;' and several other dances which bore equally elegant appellations.

Mary was leaving the room again, when the Monsieur cried out, 'Oh now, Ma'amselle, now don't leave us, me pray you, Ma'amselle Cuthbert, do not leave us – we be only little *tranqueel amusement*, just to pass away little time in absence of les belles Damoiselles.' 'Where is Miss Moreton, Monsieur?' asked Mary, 'I was come to seek her.' 'Oh she be gone with Monsieur Walwyn or the Chevalier – Oh! you would have been delighted, if you had been here just now; we look all about, but we could not find you; 'twas ver fine, ver fine, indeed. She perform in one tragedy the character of one *Madame Caleesta*, and the Monsieur Walwyn was *Lothario*, the grand hero of the piece; one ver fine man, ver great man, indeed! – we look all about for you, Ma'amselle, and for Monsieur Montgomery, but they said you vas gone to church – he he! he! he! varm weather for church, Ma'amselle, ver warm weather, indeed! Oh! Ma'amselle Cuthbert!' and he tapped her cheek with the end of the fiddle stick, 'what beautiful, ver fine colour in your cheeks, they look like the Provence rose!'[55]

At this moment, the Signora's large person passed through the door of the Lyceum; and, in a louder key, with more vivacity, and in better English, than she generally used, she said, 'Monsieur, where have you been? I have been waiting for you this half hour; and here I find you fooling with your fiddle-stick! do come and braid my hair!'

'Oh, Ma chere Signora, why did you not ring your bell, *den* I fly to execute your commands!'

The Signora said no more, and without noticing Mary Cuthbert, returned to her apartments; whilst the agile and light-heeled Monsieur skipped after her, practising the newest cotillion step all the way.

The remainder of this day was passed like any *day* but Sunday.

Miss Moreton cast a hasty glance of inquiring scrutiny on the ingenuous countenance of Mary, when she heard that Montgomery had been to church; but reading nothing there, she returned to her own easy and conscious superiority.

The Signora thought it right to be obliging on the eve of her departure, in order to ensure herself an invitation to repeat the visit; and some of the amatory effusions of the Italian poets were sung by her, and accompanied by the Monsieur, with expressive attitudes and gestures.[56] The Chevalier appeared to be heart-struck, Miss Moreton was charmed, and every moment turned to Montgomery for his approbation; who rejoiced at hearing Mary Cuthbert say, she had not the slightest acquaintance with the Italian language. Her ears at least were not offended, though he perceived that the extravagant gestures of the large and half clothed warbler; and the fantastic attitudes of the Monsieur were not calculated to give her satisfaction.

Before Miss Moreton left the room for the night, Montgomery advanced towards her; and, gracefully thanking her for her politeness and hospitality, he mentioned his intention of quitting the Villa in the morning.

Miss Moreton was surprised and hurt to hear him announce his departure. She tried to dissuade him; but, not being able to prevail, she extended her fair hand, and gave him a most pressing invitation to renew his visit. Mary Cuthbert received another fervent farewell, as he quitted the room, and soon retired to her own apartment; where her best wishes were offered up for the safety and welfare of the amiable Montgomery.

Miss Moreton retired also, but not to rest! She had been foiled in her dearest wishes, 'the cold, the insensate Montgomery was going to leave the Attic Villa!'

'And is he then cold? is he insensate?' asked she. 'Ah no, no; it is the very magnitude, the warmth of his passion, which drives him from me; he fears to stay, he fears to trust his own heart in my presence!'

This was a more pleasant idea than the first; and, prone to construe every thing as her wishes would have it to be, Miss Moreton had soon resolved that this was actually the case. She was really charmed with Montgomery. The eloquence of his manners; the manly beauty of his person; had raised a passion in her bosom, which she had never felt before. But vanity was still the ruling feature of her mind. It was not according to her disposition to let Montgomery know the progress he had made in her affections at present; nor, till she should have acquired yet greater influence over him, and enveloped his whole soul, as it were, by the irradiation of her talents and her virtues. Then, when he should have worshipped her at a distance, as do the Persian idolaters the Sun, she would beam resplendently upon him, and raise him to life and happiness![57]

A perfect Machiavel in art, nobody guessed at her secret sentiments; and, when she met her company in the morning, the softened voice, in which she addressed Walwyn, the sentimental effusions which she poured forth to the Chevalier, led each to imagine that he was the favoured object of Miss Moreton's preference.

Montgomery had quitted the house at break of day. The Signora and the Monsieur took their departure about noon.

END OF VOL. I.

THE

CORINNA OF

ENGLAND,

AND

A HEROINE IN THE SHADE;

A MODERN ROMANCE,

By the author of 'THE WINTER IN BATH', 'THE BANKS OF THE WYE', 'THE WOMAN OF COLOUR', 'LIGHT AND SHADE', &c. &c.

VOL. II.

LONDON:

Printed for B. CROSBY AND CO., STATIONERS

COURT, PATERNOSTER-ROW.

M D .C.C.C.I.X

'What Caricature is in painting,' says Fielding, 'Burlesque is in writing; and in the same manner the comic writer and painter correlate to each other. And here I shall observe, that as in the former the painter seems to have the advantage, so it is in the latter infinitely on the side of the writer: for the monstrous is much easier to paint than describe, and the ridiculous to describe than paint. And though, perhaps, this latter species doth not in either science so strongly affect and agitate the muscles as the other: yet it will be owned, I believe, that a more rational and useful pleasure arises to us from it.'

LIFE OF HOGARTH.

'When I see such games
Playd by the creatures of a powr, who swears
That he will judge the earth, and call the fool
To a sharp reckning that has livd in vain;
And when I weigh this seeming wisdom well,
And prove it in th infallible result
So hollow and so false; I feel my heart
Dissolve in pity, and account the learnd,
If this be learning, most of all deceived.
Great crimes alarm the conscience, but she sleeps
While thoughtful man is plausibly amusd.
Defend me, therefore, Common Sense, say I,
From reveries so airy, from the toil
Of dropping buckets into empty wells,
And growing old in drawing nothing up!'

COWPER.

CHAPTER XIV

'Happy, beyond the common condition of her
sex, is she who has found a friend indeed; open
hearted, yet discreet; generally fervent, yet steady;
thoroughly virtuous, but not severe; wise and
cheerful at the same time!'[1]

FORDYCE.

The absence of Montgomery was deeply felt by Mary Cuthbert; but she received
some consolation by a visit from Miss Davenport, who came, unannounced,
into the little parlour where she was sitting at work; and taking out her netting,
remained with her two hours. Mary was delighted with her new acquaintance.
She found her a most sensible and well-informed young woman; her manners entirely divested of self-importance and conceit; her heart teeming with
benevolence and charity towards the whole world. No romantic effusions; no
bombastic exaggerations, fell from the lips of Miss Davenport; her words came
from the heart; they did not evaporate in expressions; and her conversation was
marked by sincerity, yet a sincerity chastened from offending by the obligingness
of her manner.

Miss Moreton was studying with the Chevalier, and, as she was never interrupted from pursuing her interesting researches by morning visitors, Mary had
the pleasure of an unrestrained conversation with Miss Davenport, who pressed
her to spend the ensuing day in the same friendly manner, at Heathfield Cottage.

Mary said, 'she would gladly avail herself of the invitation, if Miss Moreton
would permit it.'

'She will permit it, I am confident,' said Miss Davenport; 'you must not be
too obedient at first, my dear; but I am sure you will be allowed to visit me, for I
have never been one of Miss Moreton's rivals in any shape. She has always been
very civil to me; but we think so differently on most subjects, and our pursuits
are so dissimilar, that you cannot wonder at our not being very intimate.'

Heathfield Cottage was about two miles from the Attic Villa. Mr. Davenport, the father of the young lady, who inhabited it, had been a respectable

manufacturer in the city of Coventry; and, having acquired a fortune to satisfy his moderate wishes, he purchased Heathfield Cottage, with twenty acres of land, and retired from business with his infant daughter.

Mr. Davenport was a man of strict principles, both of morality and religion. He had a taste for reading; which, though it had lain dormant for many years, whilst engaged in the active scenes of life, was now suffered to revive again. His choice of books was judicious. He carefully discarded all which were calculated to dazzle by their brilliancy, and to blind the judgment; and he selected those alone which referred every thing to the *laws of right* and the *precepts of morality*, which were deducible from the Christian religion.

Such being the bent of his mind, no wonder that his daughters was formed in the same model; and that she caught those truths, which came mended from the tongue of her father.

Gentle and affectionate in her disposition, with an accomplished and a perspicuous mind, and a prepossessing person, Miss Davenport was left sole mistress of herself and a fortune of fifteen thousand pounds, at the early age of nineteen. Her conduct in this situation had been strictly prudent and highly meritorious. No ostentation, no show, was observable in her mansion; the chaste simplicity of her manners gave the tone to her whole household, and decorum and propriety reigned throughout. – Prudent and economical in her own expenses, the charities of Miss Davenport were diffuse and extensive; and though, in accomplishing some of her plans of benevolence, she was obliged to appear to the world in her true character of benefactress to her fellow-creatures; yet where it lay in her power, she scrupulously adhered to the scripture injunction of not letting her right hand know what her left had done.[2]

Conforming to the customs of the world as far as they were reconcilable with her duty, there was nothing precise or eccentric in her manners or conversation. There was not indeed as much gaiety, as in most young women; but this was caused by some foregoing circumstances; for, previous to these, Clara Davenport had been the gayest of the gay!

Mr. Davenport had been dead three years. When Miss Davenports independence was first made public, many had been the pretenders to her hand; but a Captain Walsingham, then quartered in the city of Coventry with his regiment, was the only one who had any chance of success. To the rest Miss Davenport speedily gave a polite but gentle refusal; and her mildness and modesty secured her their friendship and esteem, even while she put an end to the hopes of the lover.

Lesly Walsingham was handsome in person; elegant and insinuating in his manners; he possessed a genteel fortune; his family was superior to Miss Davenports; and his character was held in general estimation by the world: and that world universally applauded the choice of Clara, when they saw Captain Walsingham received at Heathfield Cottage as an accepted lover.

Miss Davenport was of a tender and affectionate disposition; and the preference which she felt for Walsingham was very great. In his turn he was deeply in love, and thought that in the whole created universe there was not such another amiable being as his Clara.

At the end of twelve months, after the death of her father, Miss Davenport had promised to become his wife. The marriage settlements were made; the day was fixed; and the lover was all hilarity and transport. Thrown off his guard by the impetuous emotions of happiness which he felt, he gave the reins to his sportive imagination; and, conversing amongst a party assembled at the Cottage, let fall some expressions which Miss Davenport thought wholly irreconcilable with a belief in the Christian revelation.

She had too much prudent consideration to notice this at the moment; but Walsingham's words had impressed her mind, and stirred up an uneasy sensation there, which an explanation with her lover only could remove. That explanation came! Too sincere, and too candid to dissemble or conceal his sentiments; what was the horror of the amiable Clara, when she found that the object of her fondest affections was a professed disciple of the new school of philosophy, and a disbeliever of Christianity!

To cease to love Lesly Walsingham, was impossible. To make him her convert, was now the sanguine wish of her heart; but, obstinate in error, proud in fancied knowledge and sceptical opinions, he resisted all her fond, her pious arguments, and received her last farewell!

It was only the comforts of religion, and the sweet consciousness of having acted with propriety, which could have reconciled Miss Davenport to this great disappointment. She nobly took upon herself the stigma of the world, declaring that she had broken off the match; and not assigning the reason, that the character of Walsingham might receive no injury from the discovery of his sentiments, and hoping that the day would yet come, which would behold him abjure his dangerous errors. Walsingham was honest enough to give the real reason of their separation.

But few people credited his story, as the '*religious* creed of a *husband* was of so little consequence in the *matrimonial connection*, that all the ladies *were sure* this was only the *ostensible* cause of Miss Davenport, and supposed that she had seen somebody whom she liked better, which was a very fair reason for breaking off with the Captain.'

But time rolling on, and no new lover being received at Heathfield Cottage, it was at length decreed, *nem. con.* that 'Miss Davenport loved her liberty and independence, and meant to live and die in single blessedness!'

And this did appear very likely; for Miss Davenport would never suffer a declaration of love since she had discarded Captain Walsingham. Disappointed, so cruelly disappointed in the object of her youthful affections, her heart did not seem inclined to 'own another lord.' And, in the active duties of life, in extensive benevolence, in social and frequent intercourse with a few estimable friends, she evinced that disappointment had not soured her disposition, although it had obscured her prospects.

Mrs. Deborah Moreton had always been on intimate terms with the Davenport family; and whilst she loved her niece from a feeling of relative affinity, her affection for Miss Davenport flowed spontaneously from the heart. She would have given worlds (had those been in her power) to have seen Clarissa Moreton such as Clara Davenport; but, unfortunately, she mistook the way of bringing this about, for, by praising and applauding Miss Davenport to her niece, by repeating anecdotes of her charity and active usefulness, of her propriety of conduct, and economical arrangements, Miss Moreton took yet greater distaste to what she called, 'the sober regulations of common, *every day* kinds;' and she always acted in direct opposition to Miss Davenport, merely because her conduct was praised by her aunt Deborah, and held up to her for a model.

When she occasionally met Miss Davenport, she was barely civil to her; never entered into any thing like conversation, from an idea that Miss Davenport could only have an inferior understanding, and the most precise and confined notions; while, in her turn, Miss Davenport felt a timidity and reserve, foreign to her character, when in the presence of Miss Moreton.

Miss Moreton made no objection to Mary Cuthberts spending the day at Heathfield Cottage; and she was received with the most unaffected hospitality and pleasure by Miss Davenport. Insensibly the hours stole away in the pleasant and ingenuous interchange of corresponding sentiments and remarks. With an improved and highly cultivated mind, Miss Davenport was yet fond of those works of ingenuity and industry, which peculiarly belong to females; and while Miss Moreton disdained to handle a needle, lest she should depart from the dignity of her character, and rank only with a *mechanical seamstress*, Miss Davenport was always engaged in some piece of useful or entertaining work of invention or fancy; and carefully concealed that she had pursuits of a higher nature from the eye of common inquiry, lest she should be thought to have strayed from the path prescribed to her sex.[3]

It was impossible to find a pleasanter companion than Clara Davenport; yet it was not her wit, it was not her vivacity, it was not her language, which was her secret charm; but it was the indescribable sweetness of her manner, and the good humour and candour with which she conversed on every subject!

The new friends separated, with a promise of meeting frequently. 'I do not ask you to neglect Miss Moreton on my account, my dear girl,' said Miss Davenport; 'but recollect that when she is pursuing those pleasures and pursuits which are independent of you, if you find your time go slowly by, or that your spirits droop, you will always find a welcome reception here; and that you will afford me great pleasure by your company.'

'On Miss Moreton's account I am rejoiced at your residence with her; but, prone to be selfish, on my own I am still more so. I regret the peculiarities of Miss Moreton's character; but I should hope, that they will never lead her to do any thing flagrantly wrong; and, harsh and censorious as the world is in most cases inclined to be, it yet makes great allowances for a young woman placed in her independent situation. Wealth has a great influence on public opinion; and when youth and beauty are its concomitants, the judgment receives a stronger bias in its favour.'

Mary Cuthbert returned to the Villa, her heart filled with sentiments of respect and affection towards Miss Davenport, and with gratitude towards Mrs. Deborah Moreton, for promoting their intimacy.

CHAPTER XV

'A few only can be expected to act alone,
But millions are formed to follow others.'[4]

SAUNTERER.

Nothing very material occurred at the Attic Villa for some weeks, except the secession of Walwyn, who, *maugre* his love-torn Romeos, and his gay Lotharios, was obliged to leave the fair lady of his adoration, and to join his regiment, which was ordered to the barracks, at Horsham in Sussex; and the absence of his superior officer rendered his immediate return absolutely necessary.

With many a sigh, a vow, and pathetic adieu, he left the Villa, and the entire field open to the Chevalier; who luckily had, at this period, a most skilful auxiliary in the shape of a French novel of wonderful celebrity, which had recently issued from the press.[5]

Germ intended to hunt butterflies at the Attic Villa, while there was one left on the wing; as he liked the dainties of Miss Moreton's table much better than the *dry collections* which he should most probably 'pick clean teeth' over, when he returned to his lodgings in town.

Copy, too, had one particular month for going to the metropolis; for, while the town was empty, he should have no one to sit to him; and he wisely thought, that he might search very far before he could meet with such good and such cheap accommodations as the Attic Villa; so he kept his ground.

But the painter and the philosopher were too much engrossed by their separate pursuits to interrupt the Sentimentalists; and Mary Cuthbert was suffered to run about the house like a domestic animal, or to visit Heathfield Cottage as frequently as she pleased; for Miss Moreton and the Chevalier D'Aubert could not be interrupted, whilst they were studying *Corinna*! It was the very work to suit the taste of Miss Moreton; for though she had neither judgment or knowledge to appreciate the beauty or the truth of the historical remarks, in which Madam Stael has certainly displayed great genius and learning; yet her imagination was enamoured of the character of Corinna.[6] The lengths which she ran in pursuit of Lord Nelville; the fervid passion which she felt for him; her rejection of all common forms; her enthusiastic disposition; and her extemporising faculty, were all beheld by Miss Moreton as the reflected image of her own character. And, when she had read one or two of the improvisatories of Corinna; when the Chevalier, observing her flushing cheek and flashing eye, had remarked the similarity of her genius to that of Madam Stael's heroine, and, turning to her, had called her 'The Corinna of England,' the sickly brain of Miss Moreton became inflamed, and she resolved to imitate the inimitable Corinna, whenever opportunities should offer of discovering her genius to the world, or her passion to Montgomery.[7]

Yes, reader! *he* was still the Lord Nelville of her imagination. And whilst, from his sombre turn of mind, the pensive cast of his sallow countenance, and his gloomy and reserved turn, the Chevalier had guessed that in Lord Nelville's character Miss Moreton could have seen his image alone; *she* was busily personifying the handsome and interesting Montgomery, and fancying him as suffering from the pangs of absence, and the uncertainty of his passion, as the English nobleman had done.

Mean while, Mary Cuthbert was in utter ignorance of all that was passing in the mind of her protectress; but, from her heightened intimacy with the Chevalier, she feared that he was trying to secure her hand and fortune, and to procure a divorce from his wife.

As this was only conjecture, Mary did not mention her fears, even to Miss Davenport, with whom her intimacy increased, and in whose society she passed many happy hours. She sometimes thought of Montgomery as of a dear friend; whom it was not likely that she should soon meet again; and, whilst she heaved a sigh at the idea, a pleasurable sensation stole over her soul at the recollection of his amiable and endearing qualities.

Mrs. Deborah Moreton frequently spent a day at the Attic Villa, and loudly spoke her mind on the subject of the Chevalier. Seeing all the rest discarded, and that his intimacy continued, she naturally concluded that he was the gentleman most in favour with her niece; and she loudly inveighed against the criminality of continuing such a disgraceful intimacy with a *married man, and a Frenchman*!

The lectures of her aunt had no power over the inflexible Corinna (as she now called herself), except in making her more attentive; and, to all appearance, more fond of the Chevalier. *His* vanity was easily persuaded to believe what he hoped; and, if he could once bring Miss Moreton to consent to give him her hand, a sum of money would soon silence the clamour of his *ci-devant* wife, and send her back to her own country again.

It has been said, that Miss Moreton's heart had never heaved a sigh but for Montgomery. But the Chevaliers society was pleasing and delightful to her; and, while he marked the course of sentimental reading, and, with melting pathos, turned each flowing period, he '*taught the young idea how to shoot*;' but its attacks were always levelled towards Montgomery!

Miss Moreton's model, the heroine on whose character her own was from henceforth to rest, in order to acquire that acme of popularity and eclat, which it so eminently deserved, the Corinna of Italy, had encouraged the addresses of numerous admirers, and had apparently favoured the pretensions of a *train* of lovers.[8] The Count, the Marquis, were only the prototypes of the Chevalier and of Walwyn. And how would the whole soul of Montgomery dissolve in the full tide of rapture, when he should discover that the soft throbs of affection had been reserved for him alone; when he should find that the *Corinna* of England – she, whose talents, and whose virtues had been borne on the *blast of Fame* through the extended dominions of Great Britain; that *she* had elected *him*, to be the partner of her fortune and of her glory![9]

In such wild and chimerical rhapsodies did the visionary enthusiast indulge herself, and pant for the opportunities of discovering her talent as an *Improvisatore* (though the musical abilities of *Corinna*, not keeping pace with her oratorical powers, perhaps this title was somewhat improperly applied). She practised attitudes and extemporaneous declamation in her private theatre, with no spectator or hearer save the designing Chevalier, who was frequently melted into *tears* at her sublime effusions; and flattered her with such skill, that he led her to believe, that her talent for extempory composition surpassed any thing which he had ever heard of![10]

Mary Cuthbert became every day more enamoured of Miss Davenports character; and, if ever she suffered a wish for affluence to escape her contented bosom, it was when she beheld the noble use which her new friend made of riches. She was the patroness of a Sunday School, and likewise of a School of Industry; and, while she daily visited her little cheerful scholars in the week, to inspect their improvement, she never neglected on a Sunday to inquire into their still more momentous improvement in religious knowledge. And all this was done with so unconscious an air, with such benignity of manner, and with so little display, that she appeared as if she had been receiving obligations herself, instead of conferring them.

The poor carpenters family had found a friend in this general benefactress. She had procured the best medical assistance for the invalid, who was daily mending, and was supplied with wholesome and nutritious diet from Heathfield Cottage. Two of the children had been taken into Miss Davenports schools; and the poor woman received at proper periods those helps which her distress required.

Thus were a whole family lightened of its cares, and relieved from the extreme of penury, by the timely intervention of a person, with ability to relieve, and a heart ready to succour; and whilst Sally Jervis poured out blessings on the head of Miss Davenport, she forgot not the kind visit, and the heart-consoling sympathy of the amiable Miss Cuthbert, who had helped according to her ability, and whose pious wishes had been so amply fulfilled.

Pleased as was Mrs. Deborah Moreton at the intimacy which now subsisted between Miss Davenport and Mary Cuthbert, she yet had not the satisfaction of seeing, that it had any influence on the conduct of her niece; and though the frequent visits of Miss Davenport to the Attic Villa might deceive the world into a belief of her being on close terms of amity with Miss Moreton, and be advantageous to her in this respect, by giving her the credit of a respectable acquaintance; yet in no other shape did it appear likely to benefit.

Many a useless walk did Mrs. Deborah Moreton take to the Attic Villa, 'to tell a piece of her mind;' but the Chevalier was still in high favour with the lady of the mansion; *Corinna* in her hand and in her head, and the unconscious Montgomery in her heart!

The absence of this favoured object of her affections; her entire ignorance concerning him, would have given *any other* heroine great anxiety; but Miss Moreton had not a doubt with regard to a reciprocity of sentiment existing between them; and her busy memory was constantly employed in retracing his behaviour at the Villa; and at every succeeding retrospection, she became more secure of the heart of her lover, while her vivid imagination as frequently portrayed his hours of solitary meditation; his impassioned addresses *to the Moon*; and the tumultuous emotions of his soul, at hearing the fame of her genius and her talent sounded in his ears; and the ecstatic rapture which would be his, when, raised to the very acme of popularity, at once admired and adored, she should resign the glorious independence of her situation to make his fortune, and to become his wife.[11]

From these delightful ruminations, Miss Moreton often tore herself to take lessons from the Chevalier on Sentiment and Platonism, and to improvisatore before him. The Chevalier declared, that she every day exceeded herself, and that she wanted only a proper opportunity of displaying her wonderful talent to be followed as a prodigy!

Corinna (as she now always termed herself) was now become the complete victim of vanity; and, seeing every thing that she said or did through this medium, she believed all the D'Aubert told her, and much more which was whispered in her ear by this subtle deceiver. She was ever on the watch for an opportunity of displaying herself; her action daily became more strong and more animated on the most common subjects; her countenance daily acquired a more daring character (if such an expression be allowable in describing a female), and her manners became more decided and more energetic.

Such was the *Corinna of England*, when accident first gave her an opportunity of displaying her oratorical powers in public and to a very numerous audience.

CHAPTER XVI

'Bare was her throbbing bosom to the gale:
Loose flow'd her tresses.'[12]

THOMSON.

It was a fine morning, when Miss Moreton mentioned her intention of taking a drive in the barouche; and, contrary to her general custom, she invited Mary Cuthbert and Mr. Germ to accompany her, as well as the Chevalier D'Aubert. Mary would not refuse; for so seldom had she been of their party, and so frequently had the Chevalier gone *tête-a-tête* with Miss Moreton, that she very prudently thought it would be serving the character of her protectress to be seen with her, as frequently as she had an invitation; and, ever happy to benefit another, though in the remotest way, she readily prepared for the airing. Mr. Germ did not think it politic to refuse the proffered civility; and the party soon ascended the open barouche, drawn by four horses, with the drivers in their gayest liveries, and two outriders following.

A large bonnet shaded the face of Mary Cuthbert, and a mantle was thrown round her shoulders. Loose and negligently attired, Miss Moreton's hair was loosely waving over her forehead, and decorated on the crown of the head by a bunch of bay leaves, which she had selected from a heap of flowers and evergreens that lay on the corridor table as she passed, (for flowers were sent there every morning by the gardener, according to his mistress's order, that she might choose, as fancy or taste might lead;) the corner of a long veil was carelessly hung at the back of her head, and shaded her neck and shoulders, while her bosom was bared to the air and sun, and shaded only by a large parasol of pink Persian, which the Chevalier held mutually over them, and which, though it might give an interesting suffusion to the features of Miss Moreton, had no apparent effect on the sallow visage of her companion.

Mr. Germ wore a large straw hat, which flapped at the ears, and partially obscured the profile of his face, though his lanthorn jaws were still very apparent, and his large green spectacles, when illumed by the sun-beam, exhibited some of the prismatic hues of a rainbow.

Thus arrayed, the equipage of Miss Moreton was seen passing through the ancient city of Coventry. Always an object of attraction, she was not surprised at seeing many curious eyes from doors and windows as she passed; but she presently perceived that an unusual throng seemed to precede the vehicle, and that with every step the horses took the concourse increased, till a mob of people, assembled in a narrow street, prevented the drivers from proceeding.

Beckoning to one of her outriders, Miss Moreton ordered him to go on, and inquire the meaning of the tumult, and the confused noise. – The man obeyed, and was presently in the thickest of the ranks, whilst the horses in the barouche, eager to follow, pawed and snorted, and could scarcely be reined in by the postillions. Mary Cuthbert was frightened and intimidated, but she had presence of mind sufficient to conceal her feelings by silence, and, shading her features more closely by her bonnet, she sat with patient calmness. Miss Moreton seemed to enjoy the scene; she looked around her, from time to time, with an air of triumphant majesty, her mind seemed labouring with some hidden meaning, which it was on the point of giving utterance to, when her servant returned with difficulty through the mob, and said, 'Tis the first day of the fair, Ma'am, and so the Lady Godiva be a riding about, to make a little bit of diversion for the people here in Coventry.'[13]

Miss Moreton leant her cheek upon her hand for a minute, in an attitude of meditation; and, perceiving that her carriage was now effectually wedged in by the crowd, and that she had to the full as many followers as her *Ladyship*[14]: seeing also that the windows of the narrow street were well lined on each side of her with attentive spectators, she began to think that it would be highly impolitic to let such an opportunity pass without displaying her rhetorical powers; and softly whispering to the Chevalier, 'I must not let this glorious minute slip,' she slowly arose from her seat in the barouche, and beckoning to her astonished servants, she ordered them to command silence from the multitude, and to give audience. The trembling and half-fainting Mary Cuthbert knew not the meaning of what she saw, and began to conceive that a sudden paroxysm of frenzy had visited the sickly brain of Miss Moreton – Germ stared through his spectacles; he lifted up his hat, and looked, then on the mob, and then on the lady, as if to ask for an explanation. Even the Chevalier was at a loss to know in what manner Miss Moreton meant to proceed; though, after a pause of a moment, and her motioning to him to stand at her side, and to guard her with the parasol, he guessed that a declamatory harangue was about to ensue, especially when he found her hand laid on his shoulder with impressive earnestness, as she first broke silence.[15] Miss Moreton's address began –

'Citizens of Coventry! My Countrymen, attend!' – She spoke these words in a distinct and loud tone of utterance; her face was fully turned towards the mob, one arm was extended, and her veil was expanded with it, whilst the other leant on the Chevalier as a pillar of support. Acclamations, huzzas, peals of laughter,

'Hear, hear her, – 'tis a preachment – silence – attention!' sounded from all sides.[16] Overcome by affright and emotion, Mary Cuthbert hid her face in her handkerchief on the shoulder of Germ, and thus, unconsciously, added to the ludicrous appearance of the scene. – It was impossible for her to have escaped from her situation; the torrent of people became more strong; the horses grew more restive, and every instant seemed to threaten mischief and destruction. – With much presence of mind the outriders had placed themselves on each side of the barouche; and thus, in some measure, the people were kept from pressing near the sides of the carriage, though many jumped up behind it, in order to be nearer Miss Moreton, who, nothing daunted, made a graceful bend to the multitude, on hearing their tumultuous shouts, and then again began her address.

The first impulse of surprise having ceased, curiosity was the general feeling,

˙ 'And the quelled thunder died upon the ear' as *the Corinna of Coventry* again spoke – [17]

'Citizens of Coventry! my countrymen, attend! Accident has led me hither to be a pleased witness of your spectacle of this day, and of the patriotic enthusiasm which is excited in your bosoms! Though centuries have rolled by, and have been lost in the lapse of time, since Leofric, Earl of Mercia, the first Lord of this city, loaded your sires with heavy burdens, and the fair and illustrious Godiva so nobly signalized herself to loosen the bonds of your ancestors; gratitude yet lives in your breasts, and you immortalize the memory of your heroine! – Ye Citizens of Coventry, free men of an ancient city, behold this day *another* woman speaks! *another* woman asserts the glorious prerogative of her sex, the bold freedom of thought and of action, hitherto so exclusively, so unjustly confined to men alone! – People of Coventry, and do I then behold you sunk to a state of effeminacy and servitude.' The cry of 'hear, hear, hear her,' resounded from all quarters; a gentle hissing was faintly distinguished, but it was borne down by 'hear, hear.' 'People of Coventry! *Men*! possessed of capacious minds, of soaring genius, of depth of intellect; how do I behold you engaged? In what manner do I see the energies of youth, the judgment of manhood, the experience of age, employed? Is it in any one thing noble or praise-worthy? You are silent, you dare not – cannot answer me!' A pause of the Corinna was here followed by, 'In providing bread for ourselves and our children – in honest industry – in weaving for our employers – hear her, hear, hear, hear,' was the prevailing cry, and Corinna was suffered to proceed. – 'In providing bread for yourselves and your children! you say – How? By the labours of your hands; but what is your labour? – the weaving of a few gaudy ribbons, which ought to be prohibited in an enlightened country. – Is the manufacturing these tasteless, useless ornaments, a worthy object for men – men, who have arms to chisel out the hero's form, and eyes that with Promethean fire can animate their work? Vain, vain do you complain of hard labour and scanty pay – for what is the intrinsic use of your achievements? – The attenuated thread of blue! The soft and silky ribbon to catch the eyes of childhood and frivolity! – Shame, shame on these inglorious occupations! Was it for people such as these, that the fair, the chaste Godiva, adventured her beauteous form, unclothed, uncovered, through your narrow streets? Was it for ribbon-weavers alone? No! she fondly prophesied that a race of painters, poets, heroes, should spring up in after times, burning with her patriotism, fraught with her enthusiasm, and glowing as her own sanguine fancy! – Rally, rally yourselves, ye citizens of Coventry! Escape from the delusion by which you are enthralled – seek for more noble pursuits, more glorious occupations. – *I* ask no other boon than to be remembered as the *humble* being who pointed your talents to a higher aim than that to which you now direct your labours.[18] – People of Coventry, farewell! – Adieu!'[19] And, gracefully curtseying, and folding her arms emphatically on her breast, Miss Moreton meant to have sat down again, but this was not allowed; her carriage was encircled by the wild mob; they jumped on every part of it, with the cries of 'Down, down with the Frenchman, democrat, Jacobin – more wages, more wages – Moreton for ever, huzza, chair her, chair her, huzza.' – 'Hiss, hiss, tear down the carriage,' was now continued with the most riotous excess, and intermingled with the most blasphemous and indecent expressions.[20]

Poor Mary sunk into a swoon at the feet of Germ, who seemed insensible of *her* situation, but fully aware of the disagreeableness of his own, he looked on all sides, but there appeared no escape. His appearance being rather extraordinary, he was also taken for a Frenchman, and his spectacles were readily snatched off, and thrown amongst the rioters; this caused such good diversion, that his hat and wig succeeded, and how far the populace would have proceeded in forcing all the party to adopt the costume of Lady Godiva is uncertain, for there was now a new tide in the affairs of things.

It was proposed by one of Miss Moreton's admirers, to take out the horses of the carriage, and to draw her to the Villa. This was eagerly seconded, as the minds of the mobility once inflamed, they were ready for any mad exploit, and were a great many of them anticipating a reward, from the known liberality of Miss Moreton. – Delighted, enchanted at this proof of public devotion, Miss Moreton curtsied from side to side, like a hero making his triumphal entry.

The horses were presently taken out; men usurped their places; and the gratified *Corinna of Coventry* was drawn along, the idol of the people, while poor Mary Cuthbert was luckily insensible to all that passed.[21]

When arrived at the Attic Villa, Miss Moreton descended, amidst the acclamations and plaudits of a crowd, made up of all the dregs of population in Coventry. – They followed her into the elegant corridor of the Villa, and a hogshead of strong beer was soon emptied to her health in the park, whilst her money was as freely bestowed in return for their praises. The day was too short for their rejoicings; and night came on whilst the park still rang with their tumultuous mirth and wild revelling.

CHAPTER XVII

'E'en the lewd rabble, that were gather'd round
To see the sight, stood mute when they beheld her;
Govern'd their roaring throats, and grumbled pity;
I could have hugg'd the greasy rogues: They pleas'd me.'[22]

OTWAY.

Mary Cuthbert had been conveyed to bed by some of the servants, and when she had recovered her senses, the horrid recollection of the scene which had deprived her of them, recurred with such force to her mind, that it required all her resolution to prevent herself from being again overcome; her whole frame was unhinged, and she was glad to be alone in her chamber, though it was in vain that she courted sleep, for the noise from without would have effectually precluded it, even had her reflections been of a tranquillizing nature.

The Chevalier D'Aubert was not a little rejoiced at being again returned to the Villa with a whole skin, as some epithets had reached his ears, which led him to believe that he had been in a dangerous situation. *Now* he appeared as the ready Mercury of Miss Moreton; and, in distributing her rewards to the almost 'countless multitude,' he came in for no small share of their favour.

Germ was very much hurt at the loss of his *summer* hat, and the demolition of his *green eyes*; he could get no glasses to suit him nearer than London, where his optician resided. 'The Spectacle de la Nature' was no spectacle to him now he had lost those assistances of vision; and he determined to leave the Attic Villa as soon as possible; besides he had been taken for a Frenchman – a stigma which he felt very severely; though, knowing Miss Moreton's sentiments, and how highly the Chevalier stood in her favour, he wisely kept his mortification on this account to himself.[23]

Copy stared, and whistled at Miss Moreton's florid account of the public adulation which she had received. – He thought of a picture of Jack Cade preaching at Smithfield, which he had remarked in a collection of paintings that he had recently seen; whilst Miss Moreton finished her description with turning to the Chevalier, and saying, 'My friend, nothing ever equalled it, except when

Corinna was crowned at the Capitol in Rome – it reminded me of that; my mind, my heart was full; and I then attained a new era of my existence!'[24]

Corinna then relapsed into a fit of melancholy, yet ecstatic musing. – She thought of Montgomery – of the *Lord Nelville*, who should have beheld her triumph, who should have witnessed the acclamations which had followed *her* steps, who should have participated in *her* glory and *her* fame![25]

Fatigued and tired after the exertions which she had undergone on the preceding day, Miss Moreton had not quitted her pillow, when her aunt Deborah arrived at the Villa. Mary Cuthbert had just taken her breakfast in the little parlour; she was ill both in mind and body, and felt a sensation of satisfaction when she saw Mrs. Moreton enter the room, though this was succeeded by apprehension, when she observed her ruffled countenance. Sitting down in a chair, and, as if panting for breath, the old lady began – 'My patience, help me, child! is all true that I have heard? Did my niece raise the riots in Coventry yesterday? Tell me the truth – tell it me all – tell me every syllable you know of the matter, and that directly; I know not which way I got along; my blood curdles to think, that ever a niece of mine should so have misbehaved herself. – I see that you are frightened, child, and well enough you may; but speak out, and tell me all you know about the matter!'[26] Mary obeyed, and gave a narration of what had passed the foregoing day, as far as she could remember it. – She extenuated Miss Moreton's conduct as much as she could; she said she did not hear what the nature of her address to the populace had been, for that, overcome by the noise, and singularity of the scene, she had lost the powers of perception at the moment when Miss Moreton began to speak.

'And I don't wonder at it – I don't wonder at it at all,' said Mrs. Deborah; 'but lucky was it for you, that you were in a fit, for you were saved from hearing your cousin, *my* niece, disgrace herself. – Oh! that I should ever have lived to see this day; – the respectable name and family of the Moreton's to be so scandalized! – My niece is become the public cry, and the public odium; – she is called an incendiary – an enemy to her country, the friend of the French and a secret emissary of Buonaparte. The whole town of Coventry was a scene of riot and confusion last night; and the mob were only dispersed by the military this morning. The ringleaders of these disturbances were taken to prison, where, if the head had been carried along with them, it would have served her right.'

'You affright and astonish me, Madam,' said the trembling Mary; 'surely Miss Moreton could not foresee such dreadful consequences; I do not think she can have been told of these alarming events.' 'She! no; she sleeps securely, like another Helen, or any other of the wretches that she imitates.[27]

'After she had intoxicated all the wretched gang that followed and brought her here, it seems that they re-assembled at midnight, round the houses of the principal manufacturers in Coventry, and declared they would not work unless their wages were raised, and that Miss Moreton would uphold them in their resolution. It was in vain that the respectable manufacturers would have spoke peace; they would neither hear peace or reason; they assailed their houses with stones and brickbats; windows were demolished in a moment; and nothing seemed capable of opposing their licentious and mad-headed folly, till an armed force was called out; and, as I told you before, the ring-leaders were put under confinement.

'And, now, behold the consequences of this wild girls conduct; not a single loom is at work this blessed day, in the whole city of Coventry, and at night when the poor woman shall look round on her supperless babes, and think of her imprisoned husband, it will go hard, but she will *curse* the name of Moreton!'

'My dearest Madam,' said Mary, 'I can say nothing to comfort you, except that, seeing the sad consequences of giving way to such impetuous and romantic feelings, I trust Miss Moreton will, for the future, adopt a different and more retired mode of conduct.'

'Of that I have no hopes,' said Mrs. Deborah, an expression of bitter sorrow overspreading her marked features. 'A young woman, any woman who could voluntarily set out to witness the procession of the naked Lady Godiva, must be lost to decency, as well as to the sense of public opinion!'

'*There* you *must* give me leave to acquit Miss Moreton, Madam,' said Mary eagerly; 'I am *sure* her being in Coventry at such an unfortunate time was purely accidental, as I heard her repeatedly inquire the meaning of the throng, and heard the servant inform her.'

'If there is any circumstance, which can take off from the edge of my feelings upon the present occasion, it is,' said Mrs. Deborah, 'the general detestation in which that French Dobbert is held; I do not think he can show his face again in this neighbourhood, without endangering his safety; and I trust that my niece must be quit of him soon, in order to secure herself. Think what have been my sufferings! but indeed, child, I ought not to say *think*, for I see by your *looks* that you have been a sufferer also; but alas! you cannot form an adequate estimate of my agonies; for I still love my niece, whilst I abhor and detest her faults. I still cling to her as the dear child of my only brother, the last branch of the Moreton family; while she repulses my advice – repulses and disdains me!'

Mrs. Deborah now leant back on her chair (the first time that Mary Cuthbert had ever seen her verge from the perpendicular position since she had known her), and sobbed aloud!

Mary wept with the old lady; for she sincerely sympathised in her affliction. Miss Moreton refused to see her aunt, on a plea of indisposition; but, in reality, she wished not to have the pleasing visions of fancy broken in upon, by obsolete lectures on prudence and propriety; and she was busily engaged with the Chevalier in a re-perusal of the celebrated Corinna's public entry at the Capitol, and making a comparison between it, and her own triumph at Coventry.

The Chevalier determined for her, that she had arrived to the sublime height of her model; and that, in England, it was impossible to have gone further than she had done in the *enthusiasm of genius* and *sentimentality*!

Mrs. Deborah Moreton was much hurt at being refused admittance by her niece; but, telling Mary Cuthbert that she should repeat her visit the next morning, she walked off, alleging as an excuse for not staying the day at the Villa, that she wanted to make a few visits in her immediate vicinity, to try to hear what was said of her niece, and to endeavour to extenuate her conduct, if possible. 'Keep up your spirits, my good girl,' said she to Mary, on taking her cane, and going away; 'I see that you are almost as much overcome as myself; but we must put the best face on the business.' Mary Cuthbert felt that she was indeed overcome; she was weak both in frame and spirits; the remainder of the day was passed in solitary abstraction. For the first time in her life, she found it impossible to employ herself; her heart was sick, and her spirits were in too irritable a state for any sort of application.

Mr. Germ had taken his leave with the dawn of morning, and was gone to London to seek new spectacles, with which he might again astonish the eyes of the vulgar; in fact this great philosopher did not like to be stared at for a *reptile* Frenchman, in a neighbourhood that was so soon in commotion; and probably this was the latent reason of the Chevaliers detaining Miss Moreton in the Boudoir the whole of the morning.

The quiet and inoffensive Copy had taken advantage of Miss Moreton's engagement above stairs, to draw a group at a village ale-house a few miles on his road towards town; and hence the day was passed in uninterrupted solitude by Mary (our Heroine in the Shade!), who sought her pillow very early in the evening, her head throbbing from nervous agitation, and her mental retrospection being of a most unpleasant kind.

She had no friend, in whose breast she could repose her fears and her sorrows. Miss Davenport had left the Cottage for a few weeks; and, an isolated being in the vast world, our youthful and interesting orphan bathed her pillow with the tears which were wrung from her eyes by the bitterness of her feelings! She reverted to that recent period, when, embosomed in domestic privacy and in fond affection, she had never known a care. The sad reverse was too distressing to be contemplated with tranquillity; yet, aware of the weakness and folly of giving way to despondency and unavailing retrospections, Mary tried to tranquillize her spirits, and to put her trust in that Almighty Being who had hitherto preserved her.

For a few moments her fond, her female heart, turned towards Montgomery. What would have been the indignant emotions of his generous breast, had he witnessed the distressing scene of yesterday? Blushes dyed her cheeks at the idea – she hoped he would never hear of it; and yet he alone could enter into the real nature of her distressing feelings!

She longed for the period of Miss Davenports return; that kind, that disinterested friend, would console her by her conversation; would embolden her by her example; and would yield her her advice with regard to her future conduct, with a final reference of every thing that regarded herself, to an all-wise, and an all-seeing Being.

Mary, at length, sunk into a quiet slumber, from whence she was awoke by loud and tumultuous shouts – shrieks of distress were mingled with peals of riotous mirth; the crashing of glass; the pelting of stones; repeated knockings from without, hurried steps from within – 'Pull out the Frenchman,' – 'throw out the spy,' – 'the French spy,' – 'the democrat,' – 'well tear down the house,' were sentences which Mary plainly distinguished. The assailants levelled their attacks at her windows; and, at the moment she was getting out of bed, a fragment of glass, impelled by a large stone, sprung to her face, and stuck into her temple. Terribly frightened, not daring to stay in the room, and afraid to leave it, the situation of Mary was truly pitiable.

In the hurry of the moment she hastily put on her clothes; and then, assuming desperate resolution, she ran wildly round the corridor gallery to the chamber of Miss Moreton. The door of it was open, but Miss Moreton was not there. The noise and tumult increased; and poor Mary, almost sinking with apprehension, and trembling all over, sat down on a chair.

She heard the hasty pacing of the domestics in the passages, who seemed to be in as great consternation as herself. At length the house-maid appeared, 'Oh! laws mercy me! Miss Cuthbert, be you here? I've been in your room a calling, and a calling, and nobody spoke, and I thought as how you must be quite gone dead, with fright, and I was fear'd to carry a candle for fear the rioters should see me pass along.' 'Where is your mistress?' asked Mary, 'where is Miss Moreton?' 'Oh! she is got out on top of the balcony to preach to 'em again, as she did tother day in Coventry, and to try to send 'em off.' 'What is it all about?' 'Oh! they wants the *Civilear*, Mr. Dobbert; they say as how he be a French spy, and a *send here he*. And I believe for the matter of that, he's no better than he should be; but he's off far enough from 'em all by this time; he sat off last night by dusk of evening, and Miss Moreton put en upon the very best horse she had in the stable. But Miss Moreton cant make the people believe it for the life of her, though she preaches ever so; and I *do* think, if they still believe that he be really here, they will set fire to the house, and burn us all in it!'

Mary shuddered; at this moment the uproar increased with redoubled violence; the great doors of the corridor were undrawn by Miss Moreton's orders; she gave the rioters leave to search the house for the fugitive; this was their ostensible motive, but pillage, wild riot, and devastation ensued. Miss Moreton could not precede or follow twenty furious men eager for plunder, and already in a state of frenzical intoxication. Her elegant apartments were rudely searched; her costly furniture torn and disfigured; an eager booty made of the most portable and valuable articles, and her ears assailed on all sides by wanton and indecent exclamations!

Poor Mary shrieked with affright, when she saw three of the licentious rioters enter the chamber where she had taken refuge. They held a candle to her face; the picture of affright which was there displayed to the view, seemed to have some effect, even on their brutish and besotted faculties; they presently quitted the apartment, and left the unhappy girl in a state of insensibility, extended on the floor!

It was not till day-break that the rioters were dispersed, and Miss Moreton's money had been plentifully distributed amongst them, ere she could succeed in dismissing her self-invited guests! The adventures of this night had not been quite in unison with the picturesque visions of her imagination.

In order to ensure the safety of her Platonic and sentimental friend, she had advanced him a large sum of money to provide for his flight, but she could have formed no idea of the succeeding events. She had read nothing *like* them in *Corinna*! – but the vanity of Miss Moreton's heart yet reigned triumphant, and could not easily be shaken from its throne. She was yet a greater heroine than Madam de Stael's. Her haranguing, and finally dispersing the assembled mob, without yielding up the object of their fury, was surely a matchless piece of heroism! Yes, Montgomery must hear it! Her magnanimous conduct would reach his ears, and how would his whole soul dissolve in rapturous admiration!

CHAPTER XVIII

'E'en so we glad forsook these sinful bowers.'[28]

THOMSON.

The sun shone in upon Miss Moreton's bed, whilst indulging in these delusive and visionary reflections; and it required that she should be fully persuaded of them, to make her amends for the devastating wreck which surrounded her. The mischief done to the Villa and to its internal decorations was very serious; but the *noble soul* of *Corinna* soared above common evils, and she gave orders for cleaning, mending, and *replacing*, with the greatest *apparent* unconcern. But she was sensible of a sad vacuum at her heart. She was now alone, deserted by all her flatterers, and obliged to relinquish that society, which, next to Montgomery's, was the most delightful to her. Miss Moreton was sensible that this relinquishment had been absolutely nec-essary to ensure her safety, as well as that of her friend; but she deeply lamented the dullness, and mistaken and low notions of the people of Coventry, whom she had vainly endeavoured to enlighten by a ray of her own Divine Genius! In the absence of all beside, Miss Moreton had recourse to her cousin and her ward! She found Mary with her forehead bound (for though the glass had made only a skin-deep wound, yet it was necessary to exclude it from the air), and her cheeks despoiled of their roses. On Miss Moreton's addressing her with more tenderness than she usually evinced towards her, the full heart of the poor girl overflowed at her eyes, and she burst into tears! Miss Moreton appeared to be somewhat moved with her distress. 'These people frightened and hurt you last night, I perceive,' said she; 'it requires a very strong mind, to meet the torrent of public applause with equanim-ity and composure.'

'Surely you do not believe, that your visitors of the last night meant to compli-ment you, Madam?' asked Mary, putting her hand to her sore temple, yet smarting with pain. 'Not exactly that, perhaps: poor creatures! they could not exactly define the nature of their own sentiments, I believe;' said Miss Moreton, 'if we were to ask them for an explanation; but no matter.

'I came to propose a little plan to you, Mary, which I have been agitating this morning on my pillow. My Villa, as you will perceive, wants a little brushing up and gilding, after such a series of rejoicings and festivities; and as all my friends have left me for a time, I think I cannot do better than to change the scene for both of us by a little tour! – What say you?'

'Mary paused; she seldom had spoken her sentiments to Miss Moreton; but her mind yet harassed; her frame yet trembling from those occurrences, which had been derived solely from her imprudent eccentricity; and, fearing a repetition of them, from any new plans which she might have in agitation, she felt that she *could* not be silent; and, timidly interesting as she spoke, she said, 'My dear Miss Moreton, knowing as I do, that I am placed entirely under your guidance, it is an awkward thing for me to give you my sentiments.'

'Oh! not at all,' said Miss Moreton, with something of a confused surprise in her manner; 'pray go on – let me have them by all means.' 'I must go with you wherever you wish,' said Mary; 'and with the utmost pleasure should I accompany you, were I assured, were I certain, that your intended journey had no reference to the Chevalier D'Aubert. But the impropriety of following him; the disrepute attached to his character; and above all, the disrespect into which yours must fall –'

'You have *said* enough,' said Miss Moreton, coolly, 'I perfectly understand you, Miss Cuthbert. You have adopted those narrow notions, which Mrs. Deborah Moreton, and other strait-laced damsels would *impose* on hearts and dispositions like mine! I am not at all alarmed at your *lecture*, believe me, child. Alas! poor D'Aubert is far from my protecting care and sympathising voice. I may never see *him* again; but *mine* is a capacious mind, Miss Cuthbert, and I yesterday heard of a friend, who, ill and at a distance, pants for my society, and lingers for my presence. I feel for the illness of *all*, for whom I profess regard, and, with the balm of comfort I would now visit the poor invalid. *This*, I think, even my aunt Deborah would allow me, – not that I shall consult her. And now I consider that I have entered into a sufficient explanation with my *ward*.'

'I grieve that I have offended you, dear Madam,' said Mary; 'but when you consider the very great difference of my present life to that to which I have been accustomed; when you consider, too, that my good name is almost all that I can call my own, you will perceive that my fears are natural ones. I am very young, Miss Moreton. You likewise are in the season of youth; the conduct of females is narrowly observed; and, if there is no real impropriety discoverable, still a thousand invidious and uncharitable remarks may be made, and innumerable incidents and circumstances may wear the hue of culpability.'

'Conscious virtue has in it something too *profound*, to be swayed by public opinion,' said Miss Moreton, 'even if it was not confident of its general *suffrage*; but it has likewise an *imposing* air of superiority, which fixes universal applause! and admiration will always follow the *destiny* of *her* who soars

"Above the fix'd and common rules
Of vice and virtue in the schools!"[29]

Since Miss Moreton's perusal of Delphine and Corinna, she had adopted those words which are so frequently met with in the works of Madam De Stael, and which seem to carry more meaning in them than 'meets the ear,' or even the understanding. These words, it scarcely need be mentioned, are *'impose,' 'profound,' 'suffrage,'* and *'destiny.'*

Mary Cuthbert perceived that it was a vain attempt to try to reason with her protectress; she had no right to oppose her wishes, and even, should she request to be left at the Attic Villa, whilst Miss Moreton took her excursion, its present disordered state, and the fermentation not yet subsided in Coventry, might subject her to frequent and serious alarms.

Mary wished to mention to Mrs. Deborah Moreton the intention of her niece; but Miss Moreton employed Mary (for the first time since she had been at the Villa) in arranging the books in the Lyceum, which had been sadly soiled and scattered about the preceding night; and, as if to prevent her from making her escape, she took a chair and a book, and remained in the room.

The journey was to take place on the following morning; Miss Moreton mentioned her intention of travelling in a post-chaise, with as little show as possible, and without an Abigail. 'In a visit to the sick, dress is the last idea that could take possession of my mind,' said she; 'and how much more unrestrained and confidential will be my conversation with you, when unimpeded by the presence of a third person.'

Mary ventured now to inquire if Miss Moreton intended taking a long journey? 'To *you,*' said she, 'it may appear long – my friend is in Sussex; but I could say with Imogen,

> "If one of mean affairs may plod it in a week,
> Why may not I glide thither in a day?"[30]

'Is the illness of your friend dangerous?' asked Mary. 'Dangerous, in as much as it is hopeless!' said Miss Moreton, with a deep-drawn sigh. Before Mary retired to rest, she snatched a minute to write a few lines to Mrs. Deborah Moreton, and, through the assistance of the house-maid, she sent it off unknown to her protectress. Her note ran as follows: –

'MY DEAR MADAM.
'Wednesday night.
    'I think it my duty to inform you, that Miss Moreton and myself are to set out on a long journey to-morrow morning. I do not imagine that your niece wished you to be acquainted with her intention; and I can only pray Heaven, that it may turn out such an one as you may approve. Miss Moreton has merely told me that she is going on a visit to a sick friend; but of the sex of that friend I am left in doubt.

'I received her *word*, that the journey has not the *remotest reference* to the Chevalier D'Aubert, which has contributed to embolden me; and I have just learnt that Sussex is the county to which we are to bend our course.

'That I would much rather remain quietly at home, you will believe; but the choice is not left me; I must obey my guardian, and I suspect, though *she* will not acknowledge it, that recent occurrences have had some influence on her present movements, and that Miss Moreton thinks it may be as well to leave the Villa for a short time.

'Wherever I go, I shall carry with me a grateful sense of the kindness which you, my dear Madam, have evinced towards your much obliged,

'And grateful,
'MARY CUTHBERT.'

Just before Mary Cuthbert quitted her apartment the next morning, the house-maid put the following letter into her hands: –

'DEAR MISS CUTHBERT,

'I return you my cordial thanks for your favour, which has given me great satisfaction. The very best and most prudent thing which my niece, Miss Moreton, can do, is to leave this country for a short time. Mrs. Rebecca Nailsbury, cousin german to my late respected mother, resides in Sussex. She has long laboured under an incurable and hopeless disease; and, confined to her bed at upwards of ninety years of age, has long wished to behold her relative and my niece, Miss Clarissa Moreton.

I rejoice at Clarissa's having at length determined to introduce herself to Mrs. Nailsbury, as it is what I have long urged her to do; but she always expressed an utter repugnance to the visit when I suggested it, and, following her usual plan of opposition, will not inform me that she is now acting according to my advice. I sincerely wish you a pleasant and comfortable journey. You will find Mrs. Rebecca Nailsbury a very good and regular behaved woman, and will have nothing to fear, with regard to any improper acquaintances that may be met with at her house; as she is remarkably scrupulous, and choice in her friends. This is the first time in my life that I ever entered into a clandestine correspondence; but the occasion seems to justify me, and I avail myself of the opportunity to conclude myself,

Dear Miss Cuthbert,
Your sincere friend, and well-wisher,
DEBORAH MORETON.'

CHAPTER XIX

'The timorous eye retiring from applause,
And the mild air that fearfully withdraws.'[31]

LANGHORNE.

Nothing but the most decided dread of remaining at the Villa, could, in Mary's opinion, have reconciled Miss Moreton to such a visit as Mrs. Deborah had described. And indeed she feared that the old lady was still in a secret, with regard to the intentions of her niece.

Mary could only hope that she was right; and she was presently called to Miss Moreton who was ready for the journey. After what had been said concerning dress, Mary had put on a close robe of black, and a large bonnet on her head. She found Miss Moreton arrayed for travelling, in a blush-coloured sarsnet, made tight to her body, and very scantily over the lower part of her form; her hair hung in ringlets on her shoulders, and was slightly shaded by a white veil; her stockings and slippers were of the same colour with her dress; a gold chain, to which was suspended an Opera glass, was hung round her shoulders.

Mary was soon seated by her protectress, who *maugre* the *confidential conversation*, which she had spoken of, seemed to be fully employed by her own thoughts, except when she stopped for relays of horses, or to take refreshment; when her inquiries were so odd, and her manner and appearance so extraordinary, that her companion painfully perceived that Miss Moreton was a universal object of attention and curiosity, and that, delighted at perceiving this, she conversed in a louder key, and with still greater energy, in order to increase the number of her observers.

The second morning Miss Moreton said, 'we shall stay this night in London, Mary; and I can amuse you in the early part of the morning, by taking you to see a few of the streets and squares. Perhaps we may return by the same way; but the course of human destiny is *so* uncertain, and so *profound* in mystery are the intricate recesses of the future, that I always like to seize the present moment, whilst it is in my power!'[32]

Mary was not much exhilarated at the idea of being dragged through the streets of the metropolis by a person of Miss Moreton's peculiar air and manner; and she

said, that she hoped Miss Moreton would not retard her journey or inconven-
ience herself on her account. 'An invalid,' said she, 'must of course be regular,
with regard to hours. You will be anxiously expected, and –.'

'I am not expected,' said Miss Moreton; 'my friend does not know of my
intention – No! I have imposed a painful silence on myself, in order to impart
a more *profound* sentiment of pleasure when I shall unexpectedly appear. My
friend is at that period of life, when hours make no difference with regard to the
distribution of time!'

From this ambiguous speech Mary gathered, that Miss Moreton thought
Mrs. Nailsburys confinement to her bed made day and night the same to her;
and, though she was still of opinion that propriety and regularity should be particularly observed in an approach to a house of sickness, yet she saw that it would
be in vain to urge any thing more on the subject.

Our travellers reached London late at night, and much fatigued with the
journey. On arriving at an Hotel in the Strand, Mary Cuthbert was glad to go
to bed.

The next morning she was taken by her protectress from street to street, and
square to square, jostled by some people, spoken to by others, stared at by all; for
the extraordinary figure of Miss Moreton, and the '*mauvaise honte*' and beauty
of her companion formed a general subject of curiosity. Remarks were made,
which frequently reached the ear of Miss Moreton and of Mary. – The latter
'blushed carnation deep;' the former returned, what she would have termed, 'a
profound and silencing stare!'

Mary Cuthbert wondered that Miss Moreton should prefer walking the
streets unprotected, to going in a carriage; but *she* had not read *Corinna*, else she
would have known that, in strict obedience to her *model*, Miss Moreton took this
pedestrian excursion. – Corinna had walked over *Rome* with Lord Nelville![33]

'Time will not allow of our *now* visiting that noble pile of building, the
mausoleum of the mighty dead,' cried Miss Moreton, pointing to Westminster
Abbey: 'Ah! it is amongst the tombs of heroes only, that the soul is imbued with
that *profound* and peculiar sentiment which may be said to give it *double life*!'[34]

It was in the afternoon, when our two ladies departed from London. Mary
Cuthbert had so frequently heard of the highwaymen who infested the environs
of the metropolis, that her young and timid heart began to sink.

'How far is it to the place of our destination, Madam?' asked she, (for the
name of it had never yet been mentioned by Miss Moreton.) 'Only six-and-thirty
miles from town,' said Miss Moreton; 'we shall soon be there. – You see I have
had four horses put to the chaise; and shall have them at the next stage likewise,
in order to expedite our journey.'

Mary kept her fears within her own breast; – Miss Moreton seemed lost in
reflection; and they reached a down about ten o'clock, which Miss Moreton

said was near the end of their journey; the postillions had previously received orders from her, and they drove through it with much velocity. It was a cold and chill night; the clouds looked murky, and seemed to portend rain; – an indefinable sensation of dread seized on the mind of Mary Cuthbert, as she felt herself bowled over a wide down, where no friendly star afforded glimmering light.

The silence of Miss Moreton – the mysterious manner in which she had spoken of her friend, and of her friends residence, filled her with alarm; yet she knew not what to fear; for such was the strange inconsistency of Miss Moreton's character, that it was impossible to fathom any of her projects.

At length they entered a long and gloomy avenue. – Mary could perceive, by the lights which issued from it, that they were approaching a large and massive pile of building; it appeared to wear the air of grand and feudal gloom; and the partial illumination of the building, at the termination of the vista, added to the solemn and sombre look of the avenue.

With an instinctive emotion of apprehension, Mary seized the arm of Miss Moreton, and said, 'Is this large place the house of your friend, Madam?'

'My friend resides here at *present*,' said Miss Moreton; 'his continuance here is amongst the profound mysteries of *human destiny*!'

Mary Cuthbert now saw several sentinels, clad in military array, pacing before a structure, which she perceived was not a private habitation; the momentary idea which it gave birth to, was that of its being the county prison.

Miss Moreton then had come to visit a friend under confinement; and, whether for debt or for some unexpiated offence, was doubtful, in as much as in her selection of intimates she used no discrimination!

The step of the chaise was let down; a sentinel advanced, and asked Miss Moreton her business, telling her, at the same time, it was past the hour of admittance. 'I come to speak to Captain Walwyn, friend,' said Miss Moreton.

Mary's heart sank within her; she flung herself back in the chaise with a despairing and impetuous emotion. Miss Moreton perceived her not; the soldier answered, 'What, Captain Frederic Walwyn of the — regiment? please to come in, Ma'am; he – is just –' 'Is he dead?' said Miss Moreton. 'Speak! I charge you speak; but say not he is dead!' 'Dead – oh! no, no, Miss, he's all alive and kicking – he's the captain on guard in the mess room; and if you'll follow that man – here Walter, Walter, show Miss to the mess room.' 'Where are we, then? For Gods sake tell me, where are we?' cried Mary Cuthbert, retreating with an impulsive movement of horror. 'Oh, you are in H— barracks, young lady,' said the soldier, tipping the wink to the man, and whistling as he walked off.

It may now be necessary to account (as *far as we are able*,) for Miss Moreton's having undertaken the journey to H—. Walwyn had been very loth to leave the Villa, and such a formidable enemy as the Chevalier D'Aubert. He saw that this gentleman seemed to get on better by sighs, and interjections, and languishments, than he had done by ranting and poetic fervour; but he determined that, to guard against the mischief which might be done in his absence, he would also change *his* mode of attack; and, therefore, he indited a letter to the full as tender, and as pathetic, and as thick of notes of admiration, as the Chevalier could have done.

He bewailed his hard fate in being torn from the society of *her*, who only could sooth his soul; and he talked of the *racking pangs of absence*, and of his *wasting form*, and *broken spirits*, in a strain which he thought *must reach the heart* of his fair Dulcinea.[35] He wrote the letter on the *pillow of sickness*, and he besought his *idolized* Miss Moreton, the *phoenix of her sex*, the *embodied image of genius and perfection*, to raise him from the *grave*, by a few lines from her own *dear hand!*[36]

In some parts of this epistle Captain Walwyn had certainly been too verbose and overstrained; but, with regard to the *pillow of sickness*, he had not been guilty of any exaggeration. – The last nights intemperance had been succeeded by the usual nausea of the stomach, – an aching head, a heavy eye lid; and, not wishing another post to escape him, he had raised himself on his bed, at noon-day, to dispel the misty vapours of his brain, by composing an epistle to his mistress.

Miss Moreton received it in an auspicious moment. – She had just separated, perhaps for ever, from her beloved friend, the Chevalier; and had accommodated him with a thousand pounds, to insure a flight from his unjust and savage enemies. – She saw the Attic Villa, that elegant mansion which had been ornamented and decorated by her orders, and according to her taste, 'by the coarse hands of village ruffians,' cruelly despoiled of half its beauty; all her friends had quitted her, and her sick and jaundiced mind, recurring on self, would probably have been visited by some compunctious emotions, if this letter had not given a new stimulus to her ideas.

'Walwyn was ill, and at a distance! She had never before received a letter from him, so tender, or so touching. – True, her heart was Montgomery's alone; yet *he* would rejoice to hear that she had visited *his* friend whilst he lay extended on the bed of sickness; – the *world* might blame – Montgomery *must* applaud! Had not Corinna gone immediately to Lord Nelville on hearing of his illness? And did she quit him while his recovery was doubtful?[37] Besides, *should* the illness of Walwyn increase, (and that *of course* it would,) it surely was the most natural circumstance for him to send for his friend Montgomery, the beloved confidante of his soul! *Then*! – oh! what an ecstatic scene would ensue! Montgomery would behold the woman he *adored* make her appearance on such an amiable, such a benevolent errand! How would his noble heart dilate with rapture at beholding such a proof of generous, of exalted friendship in a female! For he then would learn, – yes, surely he *must* learn, that the most pure, the most disinterested emotions, had alone impelled her in this visit to his friend; and that Montgomery – Montgomery alone was the master of her *destiny*!'

Eager to execute this scheme of sentimentality, we have seen how adroitly Miss Moreton managed to make Mary Cuthbert a participator in it. The Corinna of Italy, indeed, had never chosen a female companion; but, had she been left the guardian of an orphan cousin, Miss Moreton was confident she would not have left her behind; and her own tall and majestic form looked so graceful, when gently bending on Mary; it formed, besides, another so pleasing a trait in her character, to have it said, 'She was always accompanied by her ward;' – it looked so affectionate, so benevolent, that, on no account, could she let her remain at the Villa.[38]

Besides, Mrs. Deborah Moreton would take advantage of her absence, to impress her formal and ridiculous dogmas on the ductile mind of Mary; and Miss Davenport might make her as puritanical as herself; therefore, if only in *common justice* to the girl, she must take her with her.

But the retired and obsolete notions of Mary might render her averse to enter the habitation of soldiers, (even on an errand of mercy,) if she were to apprize her of her intention; and the surprise of Mary on her arrival at H—, would give additional interest to the whole scene.

Mrs. Deborah Moreton might interpose with starched advice and curious queries, as to where, and to what place, she was about to bend her course; it should, therefore, be her business to elude her aunt, and detain Mary at the Villa till the hour of their departure.

We have marked how Miss Moreton's plan succeeded, and if our readers have curiosity sufficient to take another peep at H— barracks, they must follow us to the next chapter.

CHAPTER XX

'Let us go, and let us fly!'[39]

GRAY.

Undauntedly Miss Moreton followed the servant who was her conductor through a long passage, lighted occasionally by a lamp, and from opening doors as they passed, from whence soldiers were seen issuing, or were discovered cleaning their arms, and brushing their uniforms. The laugh, the song, the oath was heard; and while Mary, with hesitating step and down-cast eye, walked on in trembling agitation, *Corinna* seemed to have acquired a firm and martial tread, on breathing a military atmosphere; and as the folding doors of the guard room were thrown open, she expanded her arms, and hastily looking round the large apartment, and seeing numerous faces, she no sooner caught a glance of Walwyn's, then, rushing towards him, she cried out, 'He lives, he lives!' and sunk at his feet.

Surprise and consternation for a moment intimidated the whole party; even Walwyn was struck dumb, and could hardly believe his eye-sight had not deceived him, and that he *really* beheld Miss Moreton at his feet in the guard room of H— barracks; but he had taken his usual quantity of wine, and, soon recovering himself, was able to raise the prostrate fair, and to express his wonder, his surprise, and pleasure!

The terror-struck Mary, seeing the doors opened, and beholding the numerous lights, and the large party of red coats, who were promiscuously dispersed over the room, some engaged in drinking, play, negligently lounging, or parading to and fro in the apartment, made a sudden retreat; but, not knowing where to fly for protection or shelter, she ran into the corner of the room, turning her back to the whole of the company.

No sooner was her situation perceived, than it added to their entertainment, (which was become very general,) at witnessing the behaviour of Miss Moreton towards Walwyn, and the surprise attendant on his first reception of her.

'To what cause am I indebted for this unexpected honour from Miss Moreton?' asked Walwyn, reassuming his self-possession, and hoping to impress his brother officers with respect, from announcing the name of his visitor, of whose fortune and consequence they had been frequently apprized by his conversation.

'Your letter – your own letter, my dear friend,' said Miss Moreton; 'Alas! I scarcely thought to find you alive, so forcibly did it describe your illness.'

Walwyn seemed a little confused; – two or three of his comrades broke out into a horse laugh. – 'Fairly bit, by G—d, Walwyn,' cried one; – 'Well done, noble captain!' said another; 'And which is YOUR *chere amie* of this good company, my pretty incognita?' asked a young man, very much intoxicated, reeling to the part of the room where Mary was yet hiding her face, and rudely putting his arm round her waist, he turned her towards the candle, saying, 'Come, come, my little Q in a corner, you need not hide your blushes, they will bear the light of day; come, choose a *chere amie*.' 'And pray let that happy lot be mine,' said a mincing Jemmy Jessamy red coat, tripping up in a most effeminate manner, and leisurely biting his nails to show his white hand, and cocking his opera-glass to his eye as he spoke.

Mary Cuthbert broke from the retaining grasp of the first gentleman, and springing towards Miss Moreton, she said, 'Pray, Ma'am, leave this room – leave this house instantly! Miss Moreton, consider; I conjure you consider the imprudence of your conduct. – Captain Walwyn, I beseech you lead Miss Moreton to the carriage!'

'Do not alarm yourself, child!' said Miss Moreton, rising and leaning on the arm of Walwyn, and looking round with the utmost *non chalance* on the company as she spoke. – 'So happy, so blest am I to find my beloved friend in a state of convalescence, that I have no room for the entrance of any other sentiment!'

'Do not alarm yourself, Miss Cuthbert,' said Walwyn, offering Mary his disengaged hand, which she snatched instinctively, and, whispering in his ear, said, 'Pray, Sir, let us go.'

Her ingenuous manner redoubled the mirth of the spectators, and, – 'Two at a time! – Two strings to your bow! – How happy could I be with either!' and various other witticisms were heard on all sides.

'I will call on you early in the morning at H—,' said Walwyn, pressing the hand of Miss Moreton, 'and would fain escort you there myself to-night, but that, being the commanding officer on duty, I must not desert my post.' 'Alas! how unfortunate!' said Miss Moreton.

'*She* sighed for love, and *he* for glory!'[40] sung out an officer, with no bad voice or expression.

When they had reached the passage, Walwyn called his servant,' – Light us to the carriage.' 'Sir?' said the man, and he looked all consternation. – 'Do you hear my orders?' 'The chaise *as* brought the ladies, Sir, drove off again as soon as it had set *they* down!' 'Good Heavens!' cried Mary Cuthbert, stamping her foot in agony. A horse-laugh saluted her from behind, and she perceived that all the officers were crowding after them.

'What is the reason of this, Ma'am?' asked Mary. 'What shall we – what can we do?' – and the distressed tone in which she spoke might have moved a stoic.

'My anxious fears on *your* account, my friend,' said Miss Moreton, turning to Walwyn, 'were uncontrollable, and imagining you at the very point of death, I thought of nothing save the receiving your last sigh in my arms, and watching your livid corpse through the long and solitary night. I neglected to tell the postillions to await my further pleasure; and, having paid them at the foregoing stage, in order to save time, they doubtless thought I had no further business for them here.'

'Good morning to my night-cap!' sang out a gentleman from behind. 'What is now to be done, Madam?' asked Mary Cuthbert, in an impatient tone. 'Cannot you accommodate us for the night?' asked Miss Moreton; 'you know that I mind no hardships in the cause of friendship, and that with a kindred mind, all situations are alike to me!'

'My sitting-room is so very small,' said Walwyn, 'that I can scarcely ask you to go into that. It is very unfortunate – but these *cursed* barracks are so very inconvenient. Suppose you return again to the guard-room, well make it as comfortable as we can for you; and I am confident that my brother officers will pay you every attention.'

'Any where,' said Miss Moreton. 'Oh! no, by no means, by no means,' cried Mary Cuthbert. 'Pray let us go into a private room, no matter where; and send instantly to H— for a chaise. I beg of you, Captain Walwyn, do not delay another minute!'

'That will be the better way, I believe,' said Walwyn; who, feeling assured that Miss Moreton meant to bestow her hand and fortune upon him (and that anxiety for his health had been the real, as it was the ostensible, cause of her taking this journey,) though very free in his notions with regard to the female character, was yet inclined to be careful of the reputation of her, whom he was hereafter to call his wife, and consequently he did not like the idea of her remaining all night in the H— barracks.

A door in the passage at this moment opened; it was the entrance to a small and desolate apartment with a stone floor; and a broken drum, on which was rested a lighted candle, was all its furniture. The officers in the passage crowded on the ladies; and Mary could not retreat or advance; she felt as if she could not breathe.

The soldiers, as they passed, looked with unlicensed freedom at her; and, rushing into the narrow room, the door of which was left open by the soldier who had quitted it, she ran in there as to a place of refuge, crying 'here, here, Miss Moreton, come here, till the chaise arrives!'

Miss Moreton, it was evident, would have preferred the guard-room; but Walwyn following Mary Cuthbert's motion, she suffered herself to be led in by him, and, while chairs were procuring for their accommodation, Mary shut the door, to prevent the intrusion of the gentlemen, who were still jostling, laughing, and quizzing, in the passage.

'This place feels like a grave!' said Miss Moreton. Mary Cuthbert felt an internal shiver, and her teeth chattered in her head; but she attributed this to the agitation of her mind, and waited in a state of most dreadful and perturbed anxiety, for the return of Captain Walwyn's servant, with the chaise, to convey them to the town.

This was no time to expostulate, or to reason with Miss Moreton, on the impropriety of her conduct, had she been at leisure to hear it; but she was listening to the flaming professions which Walwyn was pouring into her ear, when the door suddenly opened, and a gentleman of graceful mien, and elegant person, entered. Seizing Mary Cuthbert's hand, he cried out, 'Good God! Walwyn, what are you doing? lead out these ladies instantly; do you not know that contagion is in this room; that they are even now breathing the pestilential air of fever?' And he forced Mary Cuthbert along the passage, and back again into the guard-room.

No fear of infection, no dread of fever, could have induced Mary Cuthbert to re-enter this room, had she not been forced into it; but Miss Moreton, who, spite of modern philosophy, had most *feminine* fears with regard to contagious disorders, absolutely screamed from affright, as she heard the gentleman speak; and, outstripping Walwyn in speed, she ran like a frantic woman into the guard-room; and when Captain Walwyn approached both the ladies with wine, Miss Moreton could scarcely be prevented from casting a reproachful look at him, for exposing her to such imminent danger; but she recollected herself in time, and was silent, for it was not certainly by *his invitation* that she had come to the H— barracks.

Interested by the beautiful countenance of Mary, and seeing her agitation and distress, the gentleman who had snatched her from lurking and unsuspecting danger, did not quit her, on having brought her to a place, which he readily perceived it was very repugnant to her wishes to be seen in.

In a manner, at once humane and respectful, a manner calculated to inspire confidence, and to conciliate esteem, he addressed her; he seemed to have placed a magic circle round him, to defend her from the rude attacks of all invaders.

The other officers remained at a decent distance; and, while they contemplated her beauty, and entertained themselves with the distress of Miss Moreton, they dared not advance within the distance prescribed them by *the looks* of Miss Cuthbert's protector.

At length Captain Walwyn's servant announced the chaise. Miss Moreton was now as eager as Mary Cuthbert to leave a place, in which she had learnt with feelings little short of horror, that a pestilential fever had appeared within the last week amongst the soldiers.

Walwyn attended the ladies to the chaise, apologising for not accompanying them himself to H—; but as his leaving the barracks that night was impossible, he accepted the offer of Captain Walsingham's escort, who, jumping after them into the chaise, promised to conduct them in safety to the town.

Miss Moreton squeezed the hand of her 'beloved Walwyn,' and besought him to come to her in the morning, as she should sadly want his enlivening converse to detach her mind from the gloomy pre-sentiments of death and fever, which had taken possession of it; and had filled it with such *profound* ideas, that it seemed as if her *destiny* was fixed.

Walwyn assured her that he would not fail to attend her. He besought her to be composed and tranquil, as he was convinced no ill consequences could accrue to her from the transient visit that she had made him.

The chaise drove off; and, in silence, the travellers reached the place of their destination. Miss Moreton was really apprehensive of a dangerous illness, and imaging a final and untimely end of her bright career. Mary Cuthbert was retracing the scenes of the past evening with the most torturing feelings of wounded delicacy and mortification.

She was determined to enter into an explanation of her sentiments with Miss Moreton; and to inform her, that it was impossible she could continue with her, unless she adapted her conduct to the rules of propriety, and was more careful of the character and reputation of her ward. Mary even thought that she could obtain legal redress, were she to apply for it; and that in decent privacy, she might be placed where the interest of her little property would keep her from absolute want. But she would on no account have recourse to coercive measures, unless Miss Moreton refused to hear reason.

Yet, much as Mary Cuthbert respected the memory of her father, and unwilling as she must ever feel to depart from his last instructions; her fame and her peace of mind were at stake, in continuing with Miss Moreton, unless some very essential alteration took place.

Mary Cuthbert's disposition was generous and humane. She had not the slightest desire of trampling on the fallen; and, though some tempers, and those too in general reckoned amiable, might have enjoyed the sight of Miss Moreton's present distress, in which her own romantic and extraordinary conduct had alone involved her, yet Mary was full of pity, when she witnessed her fears and her evident distress, at the idea of having caught the fever; and determined, on no account, either by word or look, to give her a hint of what was passing in her mind that night.

Captain Walsingham saw the ladies to the inn; and Miss Moreton declaring her intention of going immediately to bed, he left them, having politely desired permission to inquire after their health in the morning; a permission which was readily granted him by Miss Moreton.

Really fatigued, and extremely frightened, Miss Moreton immediately went to bed. Mary Cuthbert attended her to her apartment; she tried to pacify her fears; and, by those gentle and spontaneous attentions, which spring from real humanity, to lull her to repose, and to divert her from dwelling on the cause of them.

Peevish and querulous, Miss Moreton was well inclined to be out of humour with every thing about her, and most of all with the undeviating sweetness of her companion, she at length hit on something to keep her ill humour alive; and blaming the weakness and the imbecility of Mary, who could not bear to meet the faces of two or three strange men, she said, 'that if she died, her death must always lay at her door, for being so foolish as to run away where none pursued, and take possession of a pest-room! This comes of the overstrained affectation of you uninformed girls,' said Miss Moreton, as Mary was quietly smoothing her pillow, and arranging the bed-clothes. 'You read romances till your brains are turned, and then you fancy every man you meet with is to turn ravisher; and thus probably is my *destiny* completed, just as I was attaining the very climax of fame; and about to receive the *suffrage* of the whole world!'[41]

Mary Cuthbert knew the cruelty and injustice of Miss Moretons upbraidings; and, secure in conscious innocence, she disregarded them; though, when she had at length escaped to the apartment allotted for her, she gave way to those natural bursts of sorrow, into which her whole soul was swelling, and which were only quelled when raising her hands and her heart towards Heaven, she besought its protection and support.

CHAPTER XXI

'Come, gentle Venus, and assuage —'[42]

THOMSON.

The following morning, Miss Moreton, finding herself languid and enervated, as might naturally be expected after a long journey and the exertions of her *mental powers*, *determined* on having taken the infection the preceding evening, and was sickening of the fever. Medical assistance was immediately applied to, and Mary Cuthbert was stationary at the side of the bed. She was delighted to hear the physician give it as his decided opinion, that Miss Moreton had not the least symptom of approaching fever; that her pulse was regular; that her skin was moist; and that her whole frame wore the appearance of health.

Mary had no idea that the powers of imagination could be carried to so great an extent, and really supposed Miss Moreton to have been as ill as she had described. But when the physician, who was a sensible, rational man, assured her that her friend was the victim of fancy, and bade her keep up her spirits, for that there was nothing to be apprehended on her account, she felt reassured; and, though she continued her gentle attentions to Miss Moreton, yet they were unaccompanied by the anxiety which she had previously felt.

The two Captains, Walwyn and Walsingham, were soon announced. Mary was sitting at the bed-side of Miss Moreton. 'Show Walwyn up, and do you go and entertain Captain Walsingham, for he seemed *exclusively* your beau last night,' said Miss Moreton, in a tone of pique, and in a louder key than was quite consistent with the *sickening* stage of the fever.

'Surely not,' said Mary Cuthbert. 'Surely, Miss Moreton, you cannot mean to admit Captain Walwyn into your bed-room; and it would be almost as improper for me to entertain Captain Walsingham alone. Your illness, and consequent confinement to your bed, will be a sufficient apology to the gentlemen; and I am confident, when they shall be thus informed, they will not expect admittance.'

'You seem *confident*, indeed, Miss,' said Miss Moreton, in a sarcastic tone; and, raising herself in the bed, 'What! shall I be refused to see my dearest friends? When lying on the bed of sickness, I am isolated from all who love me, from all who care for me.

> "'On some fond breast the parting soul relies,
> Some kindred drops the pious eye requires.'"[43]

'And shall I not see Walwyn? Miss Cuthbert, what right have you to keep him from me?'

'I have no right, certainly, Madam,' answered Mary; 'but my sense of propriety, and the delicacy of the female character, both impel me on this occasion to desire you, my dear Miss Moreton, to reflect on the injury which such a visit will do your reputation. Of course it is known in this house, that you were last night at the barracks; this, of itself, is an unpleasant circumstance; and think how many disagreeable reports may be added to it, if you were known to receive Captain Walwyn in bed the next morning?'

'If I could have foreseen what Mr. Cuthbert had *imposed* upon me, *worlds* should not have tempted me to have undertaken the charge of a person, who, like a baneful planet, interposes to shroud my destiny with malign influence! Miss Cuthbert, I *will* see my friend. What! are all our hours of confidence as nothing? Are the sweet interchanges of sentiment to be forgotten? And shall I discard a rooted and cemented friendship, like ours, to please a prudish girl, who has taken her cue from Mrs. Deborah Moreton's code of formality, and sticks, chapter and verse, to her author. Miss Cuthbert, I *will* have Walwyn admitted; I have *much* to say to him; and while the pestilential disease is gradually stealing over my frame; while sense and reflection are yet mine, and ere my irrevocable destiny be fixed, I would embosom my full soul to a friend, able to advise and to assist me!'[44]

Mary Cuthbert saw that Miss Moreton was determined. The bell was rang, and Captain Walwyn was admitted. Mary remained in the room till Miss Moreton commanded her to leave it. She did so very reluctantly; but, instead of going to Captain Walsingham, as she had been ordered, she retired to her own room, sending a verbal apology to that gentleman on the score of Miss Moreton's illness.

Miss Moreton had really felt great part of the alarm which she had expressed, till the physician had visited her, when her symptoms gradually yielded to his cheerful countenance; but she had *assumed* an illness, and she could not acknowledge that her fears had led her so far, without discovering great weakness of character; she therefore resolved, that she would have the disorder slightly, and remain in bed for a *few days*, which would make her highly interesting in the eyes of Walwyn, and moreover have a wonderful effect on Montgomery when his friend should *describe* it to him.

Miss Moreton really panted to behold Montgomery once more. In her latent hope of meeting him at the — barracks she had been foiled; his friends convalescence precluding the necessity of his attendance. Neither did she understand that Walwyn had lately heard from him. But the passion of Miss Moreton was now grown to such a height, that it could not brook unnecessary delays, under the pretext of her illness she once thought of sending an express for the 'dear possessor of her heart;' but her affection ought to appear disinterested in his eyes, and to expose him to the hazard of taking the infection would clash with this sentiment.

Assured of the affection of Miss Moreton, of which no greater proof could have been given, than her having taken this long journey on his slight mention of indisposition, Walwyn felt grateful for it; and his affairs being just now in a deranged state, it behoved him to make the most of the present opportunity.

Marriage was a bitter pill; and Walwyn had frequently recoiled at the idea. He felt no regard for Miss Moreton; he had ridiculed her follies in all companies, before he had thought of making her his wife; and now he felt ashamed of them. But he was determined that, the connubial knot once tied, the conduct of Mrs. Walwyn should be under his sole direction; and as he had some regard for his own honourable name, he thought it would be better to conclude on the marriage, while the lady was still at H—, as this event would be some apology to the world, for her otherwise most extravagant behaviour.

In the most fervid, bombastic, and poetical strains, had Captain Walwyn often breathed his amorous tale into the ear of Miss Moreton. She had answered him with the melting pathos of a Monimia and Calista. But the question of marriage between Clarissa Moreton and Charles Walwyn had never been brought to an issue; nor was there one which was more remote from the idea of Miss Moreton.[45]

Tender and assiduous as was Walwyn, he yet let the first and the second visit escape him, without having declared his wishes and his expectations to the fair invalid; but the third was to be the critical one, and, 'nothing doubting,' he entered the sick chamber of Miss Moreton, the attentive Mary Cuthbert was dismissed, and raising herself in the bed, in an interesting attitude, holding out her hand in answer to Walwyn's tender inquiries, the fair invalid pointed to the chair which Mary had vacated, saying, 'sit here, for I have much to say to you.'

Walwyn was pleased at this beginning; for there was a feminine consciousness in her manner, which assured him that his premeditated declaration would now be spared him, and that the lady (acting, as usual, in opposition to the strict observances prescribed to others) was about to make an avowal of her sentiments in his favour. The address of Miss Moreton corroborated this idea.

'My dearest Walwyn, – I am about to enter into an explanation of feelings, with which my heart is fraught – I know that, in discovering them to you, I am diverging from the general line of dissimulation practised by my sex; but you, who know my character, must know that *I pride* myself in opposing the foolish laws which enslave the female mind. Yet such is the contrariety of my feelings, and my sentiments, that while I am acting in concordance with the latter, I feel as if I was trampling on the former, and my blushes, and my palpitating heart betray my confusion.'

'They give you the most interesting air imaginable; you are at once the most bewitching and the most exalted of women!' said Walwyn, who took advantage of this pause to say something expressive of his passionate adoration.

'This heart was formed for the indulgence of tender sentiment,' said Miss Moreton, laying her hand on it. 'I confess to you it was long ere I found an object on whom it could bestow itself; the foolish distinctions of the world were always trifles in my estimation. I looked for a kindred soul! my fortune is ample; of what consequence can it be to me, that he, whom I love, is without one, any more than that I shall have the *divine* pleasure of imparting to him, with no sparing hand, the benefits which I enjoy?'

'Charming, exalted creature!' said Walwyn, sinking on one knee, and rapturously kissing the white hand, which had been extended in order to give grace to utterance!

'I have an independent mind,' continued Miss Moreton, 'and, my notions were always at variance with the marriage vow, and the *slavish obedience* which it *imposes* on women; I never thought that I could become its advocate. But now – *now*, when every aspiration of my heart is directed towards the object of my affections; when I would make him mine by the most endearing, and the closest ties – the sound of *husband* carries something sweet to my ears, which never reached them before; and, in bestowing myself and my fortune on the selected object of my affections, now in the bloom of my fame, when my name has attained so high and so just a celebrity; I am confident that I shall give him no mean proof of affection!'[46]

'Mean,' exclaimed Walwyn, passionately clasping his hands; – 'No! it is the most glorious, the most exalted proof of love, which ever was bestowed on mortal – Oh Clarissa! Clarissa! my senses ache in contemplating such transcendent loveliness and virtue!'

'That the object on whom I have bestowed my heart feels a reciprocity of sentiment, I am well assured,' said Miss Moreton. 'His feelings have betrayed him to me; and the generous conflict, by which he essays to evade a declaration of passion, imagining that there exists some disparity in our situations!'

'Who that sees, – who that hears you, – but must feel their own inferiority,' said Walwyn, affecting to be overwhelmed with confusion and gratitude.

'Having now explained my meaning,' said Miss Moreton, 'I hesitate not to say, that I have made up my mind to reward the affection of my lover, and to resign my happiness to his keeping.'

'Charming! – incomparable Miss Moreton! How can he sufficiently evince his gratitude?' cried Walwyn. 'It was not till the period of your last visit at the Attic Villa,' said Miss Moreton, 'that I yielded up my heart to the influence of the tender passion. My destiny seemed, then, to have taken a new turn; and my heart, hitherto actuated solely by the emotions of benevolence and universal philanthropy, involuntarily resigned itself to the imposing sentiment, which had taken possession of it. Walwyn, pity and respect my feelings; you must have guessed the object on whom my heart is bestowed; I need not name him to you; I shall write to him, in order to explain myself more particularly.!'

'Why write? lovely and beloved Clarissa!' asked Walwyn; 'why not repeat to his entranced ear, in music all thine own, in all the polished harmony of numbers, those thrilling sounds which now have reached my heart!'

'The awkwardness of our respective situations, the distance –'

'But all futile distinctions you justly condemn,' said Walwyn; 'and I glory in the liberality which you have displayed; I justly count it as your *first* distinction. Then why, oh! lovely and beloved Clarissa! why have recourse to further explanations? Have courage to contemn all the forms and the foolish punctilios of the world. You have not hesitated to avow your preference; be generous, and reward your happy lover! Kill me not at the moment you have raised such delightful hopes; but say that you will be mine immediately, and our union shall be as private as your modesty can wish; only say that you consent, and my whole life shall be spent in showing my gratitude for your goodness!'

'Mr. Walwyn!' said Miss Moreton, 'I scarcely understand the nature of your address! Is it possible that you can have made a *mistake*, as to the object on whom I have placed my affections? or is your friendship for *him* of so sanguine a nature, as to make you appear as if you were pleading your own passion rather than his?'[47]

Walwyn hastily arose from his beseeching posture; his cheek was crimsoned, as he stood rather awkwardly, awaiting the explanation of the fair recumbent. 'Montgomery!' cried Miss Moreton. 'Tell me, Sir, where is he? That I may on paper pour out my whole heart to the beloved of my soul!

"'Heaven sure sent letters for some wretch's aid,
Some captive lover, or some banish'd maid!"[48]

'Where is your friend, Mr. Walwyn? Where is my Montgomery? In what sad solitary spot does he wear away the tedious hours of absence?'

'Madam, I do not know;' said Walwyn; 'but surely it is ungenerous thus to trifle with my feelings; it is inhuman, Miss Moreton, thus to sport with your victim. Oh! Clarissa, dearest, sweetest, Clarissa! be merciful as you are lovely!' and he snatched her hand, and pressed it to his lips.

'Mr. Walwyn! what part of my behaviour has led you to suppose I had the *smallest* partiality in *your* favour, except what friendship might lay claim to?' And the Corinna withdrew her hand, and fixed her eyes on his truly mortified countenance. '*What* part? *Every* part!' cried Walwyn, with indignant sullenness.

'What brought you here, Madam, if you did not mean to make me believe that you loved me?'

'As a *friend*; as a lively companion, to amuse my comic hours; and as one who could cull the tragic page for more sublime relaxations, I countenanced and received you; but for my heart of hearts companion, Oh! Montgomery! Montgomery! I could never turn traitor to thee!'

'Good God!' said Walwyn, 'you really amaze me, Miss Moreton; the lengths you have gone in pursuing me; your introducing yourself uncalled, unlooked for, at my barracks, was a step without precedent; and nothing but the excess of affection, and our speedy union can justify you to the world, or save your character from *public degradation*.'

'Oh! Man! Man! this is thy gratitude!' apostrophized Miss Moreton. 'Hear him, ye powers of benevolence, he *reproaches* me for my kindness to himself! Mr. Walwyn, I know not which to admire the most, your consummate vanity, or matchless ingratitude; but fare you well, Sir! from this moment I disdain to hold any further intercourse with you. To avoid your presence I would fly to the Antipodes! Go, Sir! leave the room, I charge you, and send Miss Cuthbert to me. This neighbourhood no longer retains us both. And as you, a *gallant warrior*, cannot absent yourself from the post of honour, which your country has (ignorant of your coward qualities) bestowed on you, I leave the place.'

'And is it possible that you can be serious, Miss Moreton? Hear me, for your *own* sake, hear me!' but Miss Moreton, rang the bell violently, and then wrapped her face in the bed-clothes.

Walwyn found it useless to try to appease her wrath; and he left the room, muttering a string of curses, 'not loud but deep,' as he went down stairs.[49]

CHAPTER XXII

'Heard you that agonizing throe?
Sure this is not romantic woe!'[50]

LANGHORNE.

Miss Moreton had sent for Mary Cuthbert, but no Mary Cuthbert appeared. Rather angry at this inattention, the impetuous heroine re-essayed her bell with additional violence. Alas! poor Mary heard it not; for, on leaving Miss Moreton's apartment, a faint sickness had overcome her, and she was found extended on the floor in her chamber, bereft of sense and motion.

Medical assistance was sent for; and the physician, who had attended Miss Moreton, was soon at the side of Mary. With looks of undissembled concern, he felt her pulse and observed her symptoms; and, asking to be shown to Miss Moreton's room, he instantly gave it, as his unequivocal opinion, that Miss Cuthbert was really seized with an alarming and dangerous fever, and that in all probability she had taken it at the barracks.

On hearing this intelligence, unmindful of Doctor Saville's presence, Miss Moreton began to look about her for her cloths, in order to array herself. He respected the enthusiasm of her feelings, which made her forget appearances in the contemplation of her young friends illness; but his own were speedily experiencing something not very remote from horror, when he heard Miss Moreton order a chaise, that she might immediately leave the house. – 'I cannot answer for myself, if I witness the illness of my poor *Eleve*,' said she to the Doctor; 'on *your* care, Sir, I shall confidently rely; you have already rescued me from the jaws of the grave, to which the same cruel disorder had hurried me; my constitution could not brook a relapse, in the midst of the tumult which would oppress my anxious soul; and since 'tis "hard to combat," I must "learn to fly."[51]

'Here, Sir, is a *small* return for your attention to me; and assure yourself that, if you save the life of my friend, you shall not go unrewarded!'

Dr. Saville took five guineas of the twenty which Miss Moreton offered him. – 'This, Madam, amply repays me for my attendance on you; and assure yourself, that every exertion shall be used on my part to save your interesting companion. – I know not that I have ever seen a young creature for whom I have taken such a sudden prepossession as I have towards her; there is such gentle modesty in her manner – such –'

'Had you not better send off your prescription, Sir,' coolly asked Miss Moreton, 'than thus to indulge in the *sanguine* description of feelings, which do not well accord with your age or appearance?'

'I have done that already, Madam,' said Dr. Saville, with great easiness of manner; 'I have not lost my memory, or my reflection; and though I will do every thing for Miss Cuthbert which lies in my power, yet I must hint that, lying as she now does at an inn, she requires an experienced and an attentive nurse; a great deal – all, indeed, depends on attention, and the regularly administering of the medicines I shall prescribe.'

'Leave that to me, Sir, leave that to me,' said Miss Moreton, 'I shall provide every thing necessary previous to my quitting H—.'

Dr. Saville quitted the room not much better pleased than was Captain Walwyn, when he had received his dismissal; but the good Doctor whistled off his spleen, and told Mrs. Saville when he went home to dinner, on no account to teach his girls the words *sentiment* or *feeling*.

Miss Moreton, immediately on the departure of the sensible physician, wrote the following note, and dispatched a messenger with it to H— barracks, and then discharging her bill at the inn, she got into a post chaise, and set off no one knew whither, without once looking in on the still insensible Mary. –

'*To Lesley Walsingham, Esq.
H— barracks.*

'DEAR SIR,

'The baseness and ingratitude of him, whom I once called friend, forces me to apply to you on the present imperious occasion. – My poor *protegée* and *elève*, Mary Cuthbert, has taken the virulent infection of your frightful barrack-fever, from nursing me in the disorder, and now is extended on a sick bed – a stranger in a strange place. – I call upon *you* to afford her every assistance which *her* situation demands from a man of honour and of sentiment! *mine* imposes on me far different claims; and it is required of me to lengthen the period of my destiny, by flying immediately from this pestilential atmosphere! On Dr. Saville as a medical attendant I confidently rely. – For a *nurse*, and a *compassionate companion*, I look to Captain Walsingham; and my skill in physiognomy tells me I shall not look in vain. I enclose a bill of fifty pounds to defray all incidental expenses; and, as a proof of my confidence and of my friendship, I need say no more, than that I depute Captain Walsingham to the guardianship of Mary Cuthbert!

CORINNA MORETON.'

'P.S. Expect to hear from me again when the tumultuous emotions of my soul are a little subsided, and I have acquired resolution to sit down and collect my thoughts!'

Words cannot express the surprise of Lesly Walsingham on receiving this note; but his surprise was not unmixed with concern. He had been much interested for the youthful and lovely Mary; it was he who had forced her from the infectious room, the moment he had found that she had sought shelter in it; but he had been too late, for she was visited by the disease. Unaccountable as was the general conduct and deportment of Miss Moreton, there was something so very inconsistent in her throwing the care of Miss Cuthbert on him, that he could scarcely believe the evidence of his senses, and in some trepidation he sought Walwyn, to see if *he* could give any probable reason for so extraordinary a proceeding.

Walwyn was too much disconcerted at the unexpected rebuff he had received, to have a good word to say of Miss Moreton; and yet he did not like to acquaint Captain Walsingham with all that had passed between them.

Affecting a laugh, he said, 'My friend, I give you joy; *you* are enlisted in the service, but hang me if it be not worse than an Egyptian one. I have washed my hands of her, and will never pay her any attention again; for the slightest civility she construes into a mark of particular attachment, and absolutely *persecutes* every man with her addresses on whom she casts an eye. – You are now in for it,' shaking Walsingham by the hand; 'I wish you well out of it again. But the poor girl, who is lying ill, she *really* deserves your attention; and, as you are a man of known benevolence, I think seriously now, I think, Walsingham, Miss Moreton could not have deputed a more suitable man to perform the nurses office!'

'Her application to me is most singular,' said Walsingham; 'and though it be in some measure accounted for by her having broken with *you* –' 'By *my* having broken with *her*, if you please, good Sir,' interrupted Walwyn. 'Well, though it may be partly accounted for in this way, yet, surely, a female would have been far more proper to have selected for such a charge.'

'You do not like to be considered as an old woman,' said Walwyn, jestingly. 'I feel myself awkwardly situated,' said Walsingham, 'and by no means in a humour for jesting. With regard to catching the disorder, I have not the smallest fear; but for me to enter the sick room of Miss Cuthbert, is wholly improper; and I have already seen enough of her to know, that I should offend her modesty by so doing. – And yet, how shall I execute the charge which is designated to me, if I stay away? How shall I be assured that she receives every attention and care which her situation demands?'

'On Dr. Saville you may confidently rely,' said Walwyn; 'he is a clever and an experienced man, and if the life of Miss Cuthbert can be saved, he will leave no means unessayed.'

'*If*,' repeated Walsingham, and he heaved a deep sigh as he turned away from Walwyn, and left the apartment to proceed to —.

Our readers probably recollect Lesly Walsingham for the lover of Clara Davenport. He had not forgotten the amiable Clara; and though time had in some measure weakened the influence of her charms, it had not rendered Walsingham an happier man. He had plunged into dissipation to drive away the image of Miss Davenport; but it pursued him in his most retired moments, and painted the 'compunctious visiting of conscience!'[52] From the midnight revel and the unhallowed pursuit, he had frequently looked back on the peaceful cottage at Heathfield, and the pure spirit which presided there; and he had wished himself a convert to those precepts and that actuating principle which formed the rule of her conduct, and was the guiding star of her life. – But the *wish* only of being a convert to her opinions had yet been his; and this inefficient movement of the soul, though sincere at a moment when the disappointments of the world, the futility of his pursuits, or the emptiness of his enjoyments pressed on his imagination, was soon stilled in the intercourse of society; and, immersed in new pleasures, he forgot his former longings after immortality.

With regard to the general tenor of his actions, Lesly Walsingham was considered a man of strict honour and probity. – He was generally respected; his acquaintance was courted; and the charms of his conversation, and the graces of his manner, obtained him universal suffrage. He had never thought of marriage since he had been refused by Miss Davenport; and he had not again felt himself particularly interested, till his eyes had fallen on Mary Cuthbert – an orphan, dependent entirely on Miss Moreton, as he understood her to be, and now thrown in so unheard of a manner on his protection; an entire stranger. – His heart beat tumultuously. – It might now be in his power, by a series of the most delicate, the most undeviating attentions, to make an interest for himself in her gentle breast – to win the heart of this attractive and ingenuous maiden.

To win it, – and what then? – Could he marry a girl devoid of fortune, so closely allied to the strange Miss Moreton! – So – would not the whole world laugh at him? And was not the institution of marriage merely a piece of worldly policy, which would be 'more honoured in the breach than the observance?'[53] Could he then injure Mary Cuthbert, by inducing her to forego such illiberal and superstitious *observances*? Such was the sophistical reveries of this modern philosopher, while he bent his way to Dr. Saville's.[54]

The good Doctor was just stepping out on his fourth visit to Miss Cuthbert. – In a few words Walsingham unfolded his business.

'Ah!' said the Doctor, shaking his head, 'I fear this poor girl will soon be released from all human ties. – *Her* guardian is there,' looking upwards, 'to Him she will soon go, and dwell with Him for ever!'

He took Walsingham's arm, and they walked towards the inn together. – 'I declare I can scarcely grieve as I should do for this young creature,' said Dr. Saville; 'for, seeing her extreme youth and ingenuous loveliness, and the caprice, folly – I may almost say *madness* of her protectress, it appears to me, that if she is taken, it will be from the evil to come; for, surely, *she* must require a more than common share of prudence and resolution, who can accompany this wild and fantastic Miss Moreton in all her extravagant flights, and escape uninjured!'

'But, *dear* Doctor, may it not be *yet* possible to recover her?' said Walsingham, grasping his arm. – 'All that I can do I will,' said Dr. Saville; 'I am now going to have her removed to a neat and tranquil lodging in the environs of the town; and I have engaged a steady and humane nurse to attend her. The people at the inn were naturally enough alarmed at having her with them; and the noise of such a house is quite inimical to my hopes of a recovery. – Come with me, if you are not afraid of infection, and see her removed. I have had a sedan chair taken to the inn, and believe the poor girl will be wholly imperceptible of any thing that is going on.'

'No, I am not at all afraid of infection,' said Walsingham, 'I received the last words of my poor corporal; he died in a few minutes after I quitted his room.'

The nurse engaged by Dr. Saville had dressed Mary Cuthbert, and she lay extended on the bed, bereft of sense, and apparently motionless. – Her rayless eyes were fixed on vacancy; her cheeks were flushed by fever; her lips frequently severed; and she muttered from time to time short sentences, in a monotonous and almost death-like tone.

'No, no, Miss Moreton, do not take me there. – My papa sees you – he sees you from Heaven. – Look! he will not love you, if you carry his child to the soldiers. Poor Mary! nobody cares for her now; all the world will despise her; but she will go home soon; she will go home to her fathers house – there are many mansions there – her Saviour has told her so! – Fie, fie, Miss Moreton, don't YOU believe in *Him*? What would poor Mary do, if she had not got this comfort?' Then she stopped; – heart-piercing sighs issued from her bosom. 'No, no, no, I never *will* enter the hateful barracks again. – Pray, pray Miss Moreton return home; look, look, they are coming; they will fetch us back – the soldiers will keep us there!' and, with a strong convulsive motion, she turned and grasped her pillow with violence.

The marks of strong sympathy were visible on the countenance of Dr. Saville, while Walsingham turned to the window to conceal his emotion and his bitter feelings!

Yes! extended on the bed, the victim of fever, and in a state of mental delirium, yet Mary Cuthbert had spoken to the heart of Lesly Walsingham! – *She* had talked of that Heaven which he had abjured; she had talked of the comforts of a *Saviour*, whom he had never known. – But was there not something unintelligible, mysterious, in his feelings and his emotions? Did not his heart smite him for remaining deaf to the calls of conscience, to the voice of Heaven itself, speaking as it did now by one of its *own angels*!

With the utmost care, Mary Cuthbert was at length placed in the chair which had been provided for her; the nurse went before to the lodgings, and the two gentlemen walked at her side.

Although she continued in a state of insensibility, yet her weakened frame experienced the effects of this exertion; and when the nurse had got her into bed, she almost immediately fell into a sound sleep, which, when the attentive Saville was informed of, appeared to give him the greatest satisfaction; and, clapping the shoulder of Walsingham in an ecstasy, he declared that he augured every thing from this repose.

Several days passed, during which the disorder of the youthful invalid scarcely appeared to abate; her two friends were unremitting in their attention; and the skill and exertion of Saville kept pace with the good wishes of Walsingham, who ransacked the neighbourhood for any thing and every thing, which had a shadow of benefiting Mary Cuthbert.

CHAPTER XXIII

'Heaven first taught letters for some wretch's aid,
Some banish'd lover, or some captive *maid*.'[55]

POPE

Miss Moreton had retired only a few miles from — , left entirely to her own profound reveries, without flatterers or admirers; when it occurred to her that it might look unfeeling to enter the world, whilst her charge remained at the point of death; and this period was not uninterestingly filled up, by writing to Montgomery, and in anxiously awaiting his answer. – *The Corinna's* letter ran thus: –

'In what words shall I address the worthiest of his sex, on a subject so near to both our hearts. I have seen, I have witnessed that fervent passion of yours, which breathed in every look and action, whilst in the presence of the object of it. I saw also the struggles of your noble mind, which refused to ratify the wishes of your heart, when deeming them inimical to the interests of the object of your love. Such love *must* be rewarded. I *have* the power, Montgomery; I have also the will. Fortune has not been unworthily placed in my hands; sufficient is it for me to say, that your passion is approved by me! nay more, that it is *returned*; and in cementing and ratifying the union of two affectionate hearts, I feel that I am rising to the very acmé of my existence! Write me by the return of the post. My heart aches to see you; and I shall remain at the place from whence I date this letter, till I hear when I may expect it.[56]

'CORINNA MORETON.'

Montgomery's sensations of regret on quitting the Attic Villa had accompanied him to Oxford; and the image of the beautiful Mary Cuthbert, exposed to all the follies and insults of Miss Moreton's companions, was ever rising to his imagination. His heart had taken a more than common interest in her fate; and he was unusually curious in making inquiries of those of his acquaintance, who lived in the neighbourhood of Coventry, for information and anecdotes of Miss Moreton. The knowledge, thus acquired, was not calculated to set his heart at ease with regard to the youthful orphan. All agreed in ridiculing Miss Moreton, and in contemning her manners and her conduct. It happened one morning that Montgomery carelessly took up a news paper, and read the following paragraph: –

'NOTORIETY.

'The celebrated Corinna, mistress of a certain Villa, not a hundred miles from C—y, has lately displayed great novelty of conduct. Attended by several of her train, and a nymph to whom she is guardian, she proceeded to that city on the first day of the fair, in a sort of triumphal car; and, crowned with bay, harangued the *mobility* in a manner which caused no little ferment in the public mind. Lady Godiva was deserted for this priestess of the new school; and the business ended with all that noise and tumult, which usually attends a popular commotion. The horses of the carriage were taken out, and the heroine was drawn home, by an infatuated mob, who returned at night to pillage the mansion of their new teacher. We have heard of several accidents which occurred in this temple of disorder and wild liberty. Most of the females, resident under the roof, experienced insults of the most degrading kind; and one or two *enlightened Parisians* were forced to save their *heads*, by an instantaneous use of their *heels*. The fair lady of the mansion seems perfectly pleased at becoming the object of general animadversion, and, like another Helen, enjoys the confusion she has caused.

'*O Tempora! O Mores!*[57]

Such was the paragraph which Montgomery read with horror. 'Good God! had Mary Cuthbert, the gentle Mary Cuthbert, been in a scene like this? Had the modest, the lovely Mary, been exposed to the rude insults of a brutish rabble?' He smote his forehead; he stamped his foot in agony on the floor; he wished – yes, he wished her in *Heaven*, rather than at the Attic Villa. 'The temple of disorder, say, rather the temple of immorality and licentiousness,' cried he, 'would that it were razed from the ground!'

Many hours elapsed ere Montgomery could recover, from the agitation which the perusal of this paragraph had caused in his bosom; but at length he resumed his studies, and tried to compose his mind; though this hardly acquired composure was completely overset, by a letter which he received from home, acquainting him with the dangerous illness of his beloved father. The filial heart of Montgomery bled at this intelligence; his father, his beloved, his honoured parent! could it be possible? and should he indeed lose him for ever? Must he be snatched from the fond arms of his faithful wife? Must he be taken from his helpless children? Helpless indeed! for on him had been the sole dependence of his family.'

Montgomery lost not a moment in leaving Oxford. The letter of Miss Moreton followed him home, and his answer to it will best describe the hurried state of his mind at this period.

'DEAR MADAM.

'Elmsly – Tuesday.

'Your kind favour followed me to this place; and, grateful as I must ever be to you for its contents, and an explanation of your generous intentions in my favour, yet I must at this moment recoil even from a *perspective* of happiness! for, alas! I am surrounded by distress of the most afflicting nature! The grave receives my beloved father into its peaceful bosom. It has been my hard duty to see him close his eye, an eye which beamed with goodness and virtue on all around him. You, my dear Madam, will picture the distress of every individual under this roof. The gentle being who honours Montgomery by her good opinion, will afford him her sympathy on this most trying and conflicting period of his life. When my mind is a little more at ease, I will resume my pen to express all with which this heart is fraught, to the object of my fondest affection and respect; the gratitude which he must ever feel towards you, my dear Madam, who signs himself, Your obliged and devoted

FREDERIC MONTGOMERY.'

CHAPTER XXIV

'Fallacious hope deludes her hapless train!'[58]

LANGHORNE.

Overwhelmed by distress, Montgomery had read the letter of Miss Moreton with trembling agitation. The sorrow of his mother, the affliction of his sisters, had almost bereft him of his self-possession, and he had been fearfully conjuring up the thousand evils which would await them.

His own prospects, if not blighted, were wholly obscured. Instead of pushing his way in the bustling and crowded walks of life, in order to further his advancement; his narrow path now lay before him. The small living which his father had held would remain in the family. He must immediately take orders; and, residing with his mother and sisters, try to contract his wishes, and to repress his hopes; and be to them the husband, the father they had lost.

Montgomery had never been ambitious; but independent in principles, and liberal in his disposition, his warm heart panted to be the protector of all around; and his sanguine fancy had often portrayed, in the gayest tints, that picture of domestic felicity, which could not be completed, unless a gentle being, like Mary Cuthbert, had formed the prominent figure of the piece. Alas! this picture was now obscured for ever.

While such had been the gloomy images of Montgomery's mind, the letter of Miss Moreton had been put into his hand. He read it with the eagerness of a drowning wretch, who catches at a twig to preserve him from the overwhelming wave. He saw in it only a description of his affection for Mary Cuthbert, he saw (transporting sight!) that the dear maid returned his love! That Miss Moreton, her protectress, favoured it, and meant to reward it! Who can wonder at this misconstruction of the letter of Miss Moreton? Who can wonder that it was some days ere Montgomery became convinced of his mistake?

The interment of Mr. Montgomery had been succeeded by that calm which casts so chilling a feel on those who have recently witnessed the spectacle of human annihilation, and who mourn the loss of a beloved friend. Although autumn had scarcely began to tint the foliage with its varied hues of brown and orange; yet the forlorn group at Elmsly had drawn round a fire towards the evening; and whilst the tears were silently coursing down the cheeks of Mrs. Montgomery, her two elder girls were trying to repress their own feelings, and to engage their younger sister and brother, by artless prattle, to cheat their mother of her cares.

Frederic had strolled out; and the tempestuous appearance of the evening, as viewed from the high and tremendous cliffs which overlooked the sea; the rolling of the mountainous surge, and the roaring of the winds, had been more congenial to the present tenor of his mind, than that stagnant calm which reigned throughout his late happy home. A post-chaise drove up to parsonage gate; the bell rang violently; a servant entered the parlour; 'A lady, Ma'am, wishes to see you,' said the maid. 'I can see no visitors,' said Mrs. Montgomery, in a desponding tone – 'But she is here, Madam,' replied the maid. 'I am not a common visitor, the usual forms of the world and the ceremonials observed in what is called society, are wholly disregarded by me,' said the lady, advancing towards Mrs. Montgomery, seizing her hand, and pressing it energetically to her lips, to her heart, and to her forehead.

'I come to visit the afflicted!' said she, in a tone monotonous and sepulchral enough to give just expression to the words which she uttered – 'I come to mourn with the fatherless and the widow!'

The little children crept nearer to the door, as the lady raised her voice, and extended her arms; and Arabella and Lucy instinctively advanced towards their mother, as if to guard her from her strange guest. But, composed under every thing which could now assail her, Mrs. Montgomery merely said, 'May I ask the name of the lady who favours me with this visit?'

'And has not my Frederic talked of his Corinna?' said Miss Moreton, (for so will our readers have discovered the visitor to have been). Ah! tell me, tell me, where he is? Where is the dear, the pious youth? Oh! let me strain him to my breast, and receive the fond sigh of affection; let me speak comfort, happiness, and love to his sad soul!' Lucy Montgomery now led the children out of the room, while Arabella, believing that the stranger was out of her senses, looked out of the window, vainly trying to discover Frederic.

'Say, Madam,' asked Miss Moreton, taking the hand of Mrs. Montgomery, 'has not my Frederic revealed to you our mutual love? our fond regard?' 'Never, Ma'am,' said the surprised Mrs. Montgomery – 'Alas! my son has had duties to perform, which have exclusively and painfully engrossed his whole thoughts, and his whole time, since his return to us!' – 'I know, I know it all; my Frederic wrote me the sad tale, and, eager to participate in his sufferings, and to comfort every individual of his family, I flew to this place, immediately as I received the heart-afflicting recital.

'But where is my Frederic? where is the partner of my heart, the beloved of my soul!' Arabella's face was suffused by the deepest crimson, at hearing these warm expressions issue from the mouth of a female; even, though the object of them was a much beloved brother!

She had heard of the unblushing profligacy of women who made a barter of their persons, and she should have suspected Miss Moreton to have been one of these, could she for a moment have imagined, that her brother had been the associate of such a character. But the strict morality of his conduct, and the rectitude of his principles, forbade her entertaining a shadow of suspicion against him.

'My son has strolled out, Madam,' said Mrs. Montgomery, with some formality of manner; 'he did not expect a visitor, I believe; and, though his meditations are much of a piece with ours, yet he would rather indulge them alone; for it is not in his power to comfort and relieve, and my Frederic cannot bear to augment our distress.'

'Oh! he is all that is good and tender; my heart has found him so; and I glory in my choice,' cried Miss Moreton. Then, hastily falling on one knee before Mrs. Montgomery, she said, 'Oh! crown our union with your blessing; what have we more to ask of Heaven?' Mrs. Montgomery looked with fearful apprehension in the countenance of Miss Moreton, and said, 'Are you, then, the wife of my son, Madam?' 'Not absolutely his wife,' said Miss Moreton; 'but the monotonous repetition of the dull and lifeless words of that ceremonious observance, cannot more closely cement a union like ours. – Ours, Madam, is the sweet reciprocity of kindred souls!'

'I doubt I do not perfectly understand you, Madam,' said Mrs. Montgomery; now looking at Miss Moreton with an expression of painful curiosity and embarrassment depicted on her countenance.

'Perhaps not,' said the lady, 'it has frequently been my destiny to be misunderstood; the lofty feelings of my soul impose themselves on my expressions; and I cannot easily reduce them to an ordinary level!'[59]

Montgomery had, during his lonely walk, been taking a retrospect of his situation; and, though it was highly pleasing to the young lover, to dwell on the letter of Miss Moreton, and on the image of the charming Mary Cuthbert, (an image rendered still more dear to his heart and his imagination, by that attractive softness which her protectress had described), yet he tore himself from the contemplation; how could he avail himself of the generosity of Miss Moreton? how could he bear to receive obligations at her hands? and could it be any thing but the most selfish passion, which should urge him to take advantage of the prepossession which Mary Cuthbert had acknowledged for him. Alas! he could not be so ungenerous as to wish it; he could not be base enough to desire it.

A large, a distressed family, looking towards himself alone for comfort and support! He must *live* for them alone; he must *think* only of *them*; he must drive the image of Mary Cuthbert from his heart. He wished Miss Moreton had not betrayed the secret of her charge; a secret which had, perhaps, originated in her fertile and chimerical brain, and that had no other foundation than that universal benevolence and sweetness, which the interesting Mary evinced towards all the world.

In the midst of his most tender soliloquies, Montgomery had perceived the impropriety of Miss Moreton's revealing her secret. He was sure the delicacy of Mary could never have authorised it; and he felt jealous of that purity, which had been invaded by the disclosure.

'But,' sighed Montgomery, 'Miss Moreton has no judgment, no discretion, no feeling. Oh! Mary, Mary! what a fate is thine, to live with such a woman! Oh! that I could but rescue thee! insure thy safety, and my own honour!'

After such a soliloquy, what were the feelings of Montgomery, when he opened the parlour door, and beheld the figure of Miss Moreton! He retreated a few paces, at the first moment of astonishment; but Miss Moreton hastily advanced, and, stretching out her arms, in an attitude of recitation, she said, 'Oh! Montgomery, thinkest thou that in the hour of thy distress, thou couldest be forsaken by thy friend? When the tomb has closed over the parent of thine infancy, it is the part of true regard to meliorate thy sufferings, to soothe thy grieves! Thy voice called me from afar, and I hesitated not to obey the summons. It is in scenes like this, that a mind like mine is wont to unfold its inmost recesses, and to show the strong workings of celestial sympathy!'

A deep vermillion covered the face of Montgomery, as he stood, in awkward confusion, to hear this rhapsodic address. He had always felt an unconquerable aversion towards Miss Moreton; he disliked her opinions and her sentiments; but her manners were disgusting in the extreme, and, at this moment, he saw them through a most distorted vision. She had, in reality, never before been so strangely eccentric in his presence; and his breast, aching with the contrariety of feelings, which had followed his recent ruminations – Seeing in her the guardian of his Mary, the *would-be* benefactress of himself; burning to gain some tidings of the gentle girl; and fearing the construction which his mother (regular in her behaviour, and reserved in her expressions) would put on the strange visit, and yet stranger address of Miss Moreton; reading in the modest confusion of his sisters, that her manners were at once incomprehensible and distressing to them, he stood, statue-like; words were for some minutes denied him, though the pause of Miss Moreton, her extended arm, and her attentive countenance, plainly evinced that she awaited his reply. He at length said, 'To what lucky chance am I indebted for the honour of Miss Moreton's visit?'

'Chance!' repeated she, 'You *do* not, *cannot* misunderstand me, Montgomery! know you not that I came purposely to see you?'

'I – I am very much obliged to you, Madam!' said Montgomery, twirling a chair, and forcibly evincing to all but the lady in question, that it was the most painful obligation he had ever received.

'Talk not of obligation,' said Miss Moreton; 'an intimacy like ours, Montgomery, expunges that word from the vocabulary of friendship!'

A great deal more, in the same strain, was expressed by Miss Moreton before her wondering hearers, and her *astonished friend*.

Hurt and disgusted at her behaviour, Montgomery knew not what to do. He felt the impropriety of her visit; he saw, by the countenance of his mother, that her heart ached in the presence of her guest; that she wished to withdraw from the scene of mock sentiment, and mock affection, to pour out her sorrows in private; and that she put a restraint on her inclinations, in continuing one moment longer in the room; but that she thought her stay was a necessary compliment to her sons visitor; and, in fact, the only sanction which that visit could receive. His sisters, too, ingenuous, open-hearted girls! plainly expressed by their countenances, both astonishment and disgust.

Vexatious impatience filled his heart. He longed to undeceive his mistaken mother and sisters – He longed to tell them, that Miss Moreton was more the object of his aversion than of theirs. – He longed to tell them, that a sense of obligation could alone keep him within the bounds of common civility – He longed to draw the contrast in the picture of her whose image was impressed on his faithful memory – He longed to inquire after that gentle maid; but timidity, an unaccountable repugnance, prevented him.

In vain did Montgomery try to rally his feelings; his presence of mind had forsaken him; and he knew not how to start a subject, and scarcely to give an answer to a question.

Mrs. Montgomery had heard of her sons accompanying Captain Walwyn on a visit to the Attic Villa; the succeeding melancholy event in her family had prevented her hearing any particulars concerning it; and, finding the conversation flag, notwithstanding the florid display of Miss Moreton, she, turning towards her, said, 'If I am not mistaken, Madam, it was Captain Walwyn who introduced my son to your acquaintance?'

Miss Moreton started. 'That name is *hateful* to my ears!' cried she, shivering with affected emotion. 'How is this?' said Montgomery. 'What can my friend Walwyn have done to lose the favour of Miss Moreton?'

'He is, at once, the most *treacherous*, and the most *presumptuous* of mortals! Montgomery, he would have supplanted thee in the object of thy love!'

Montgomery was all attention; his agitation was apparent. 'Ah!' thought he, 'who would not wish to gain an interest in that gentle breast? Presumptuous! No! the fortune, the connections of Walwyn are far, far superior to my own. No! I cannot call him so!' and he looked at Miss Moreton with an expression of interest and curiosity, which was highly gratifying to her, and which his countenance had never before displayed. It confirmed the painful suspicions of his mother and sisters; and the interchange of their looks seemed to express their mutual opinion on a lost case.

'I see thy doubts – I mark thy trembling fears,' said the undaunted heroine. 'Be calm, be composed, Montgomery; his unheard of temerity was punished by the loss of my friendship!'

A doubt of he knew not what, now pervaded the breast of Montgomery. He had seen enough of Miss Moreton, to know that she eagerly prosecuted any eccentricity which occurred to her imagination; but he had also seen during his stay at the Villa, that there existed nothing more in her intercourse with Mary Cuthbert than a general politeness. Was it, then, likely that she should thus warmly espouse her cause? that she should go such lengths to facilitate the wishes of a girl, for whom she had neither professed or displayed regard? and would not the delicate soul of Mary Cuthbert have revolted from her cousins strange visit, and yet stranger avowal?

'Did you take this journey alone, Madam,' asked Mrs. Montgomery, willing once more to try to relieve her son.

'I wanted not a companion,' replied Miss Moreton; 'my own thoughts supplied me with subjects of meditation, at once profound and sublime!'

For such sublime flights, neither the taste or the experience of Mrs. Montgomery had prepared her; but she found that her guest could not descend to the common and ordinary topics of conversation.

Montgomery could bear the warring feelings of his bosom no longer; and, in a sort of wild eagerness, and averting his eye from Miss Moreton, as if to know his doom at once, he said, 'Is Miss Cuthbert at the Villa?'

'No,' said Miss Moreton, advancing towards him, and, as if to give greater force to her words, altering her voice, 'I left poor Mary at H—; she is stretched on the bed of sickness.'

'Sickness!' said Montgomery, now seizing, grasping the hand of Miss Moreton. 'Sickness! Good God, Miss Moreton! Sickness! say you? and did you, could you leave her?'

'I did, I could, Montgomery, for I came to *you!*'

The expression of Miss Moreton's look; the emphasis on her words, could no longer be misconstrued.

Montgomery experienced a total revulsion of his frame; the blood seemed to chill at his heart; too late he discovered his error; an error into which his passion for Mary Cuthbert, and a fatal infatuation, had precipitated him.

But Mary was ill, was stretched on the bed of sickness! and while, at one moment, he released Miss Moreton's passive hand, and started back as from a venomous reptile, he, the next, more precipitately approached towards her, as he said, 'Is her disorder considered dangerous?'

'I fear it is,' replied Miss Moreton, 'and if she dies, Walwyn, that treacherous ingrate, will have much to answer for. In accompanying me to visit him at H— barracks, I took the fever which is now so prevalent there. I recovered, and was anxious to follow the leading star of my destiny, which pointed my steps hither. My wards fate was doubtful when I quitted her, but –' 'Madam,' interrupted Montgomery, 'there exists not a word which language can utter, to convey a palliation for such unheard of barbarity. What! leave her to the mercy of strangers! leave her when visited by a pestilential disease, to breathe her last sigh unseen, unheard, unpitied! Miss Moreton, your romantic eccentricities have borne away the common feelings of humanity, and of your sex!' 'Montgomery, Montgomery! surely I do not understand you.' said Miss Moreton, while Mrs. Montgomery looked at her son with surprise, though it was unmixed by displeasure; and the two girls held back still further from the *strange lady*.

'I believe, Madam, that you do *not*,' said Montgomery; 'seldom does plain truth reach the ear of *her*, who, inflated by vanity and conceit, is wholly swallowed up in self! – Miss Moreton, ere it be too late, take the advice of a friend: Return to your own residence – desist from those capricious and culpable vagaries which you have indulged at the expense of your character and your fame – return to the paths prescribed to your sex; and show, ere you are lost for ever, that you have some feeling of shame in your nature!'

'And this from *you*; – *this* from Montgomery, the *obliged, the devoted Montgomery*?' asked Miss Moreton, stamping her foot furiously on the floor. 'To what cause may I impute this alteration, Sir? – Where is the perspective of happiness which you talked of in your letter to me?' 'Where, indeed!' said Montgomery, hiding his face with both his hands, and retiring in confusion to another part of the room.

'Look, Madam,' said Miss Moreton, hastily searching her bosom, and producing the letter she had received from Montgomery, 'Read here, and account to me, if you can, for his frantic conduct of this moment!'

'Oh! rather say my frantic conduct at *that* moment!' said Montgomery, snatching the letter from his mother. – 'This letter, this hateful letter was written when my senses were infatuated, entranced! It owed its origin to an error as gross, as it was unpardonable, and I am now justly suffering for my almost unparalleled stupidity! Suffice it to say, Miss Moreton, that I am extremely sorry for the mistake into which it has led you; and I hope that you will forget that you ever received it!' and he hastily threw it into the fire.

'Forget it? oh! never, never, never!' cried Miss Moreton; 'Cruel, barbarous Montgomery! Have I not learnt every word of it? – Have I not lived on every syllable? – Did you not write this never-to-be-forgotten sentence – "When my mind is a little more at ease, I will resume my pen to express all with which this heart is fraught, to the object of my fondest affection and gratitude –"'

'Oh! no more, no more! it is insupportable, it is *madness*!' said Montgomery.

'My dear Frederic, what is, what can be the meaning of all this?' asked his mother. '*If* you have deceived this lady by false professions; if –'

'I never *did*, Ma'am,' answered Montgomery; 'A most unhappy, a most unfortunate mistake involved my mind at the moment when I wrote to Miss Moreton; but I call Heaven to witness (except what originated from this error, and which was wholly a misapprehension) that I never professed by look, word, or action, an atom, a shadow of regard for this lady; nay more, that while her guest at the Attic Villa, I might frequently have been accused of failing in common politeness towards her.'

'Oh! hear, earth and heaven,' cried Miss Moreton; '*thus, thus* it is – even the tenderness, the softness of my nature betrays me; and I, like my *prototype*, Corinna, am doomed to bear distress in every shape, ere I reach the climax of my *destiny*! but this from thee! from thee, much-favoured youth! – Oh! 'tis hard, *too* hard to bear!' – and, sinking on the ground, Miss Moreton fell into strong hysterics.[60] – Mrs. Montgomery and her daughters essayed their skill to restore her to composure, while Montgomery quitted the room.

CHAPTER XXV

'Ah! still propitious mayst thou deign
To soothe an anxious lover's pain.'[61]

LANGHORNE.

Montgomery rushed out of doors to give way to all the tumultuous agony of his mind, unheard, unseen! – The mad folly of Miss Moreton had disordered his temper; but the intelligence of Mary Cuthbert's illness had sunk deep into his heart. – From reveries of the most flattering kind, he had been awakened to hear that this tenderly beloved girl was, in all probability, breathing her last, the victim of a contagious disorder; that she was unattended, unknown, placed amongst strangers.

And what had preceded the direful malady? – A visit to H— barracks. Heaven and earth! the lovely, the modest Mary taken to be gazed at by soldiers – to be exposed to their unlicensed stare, their rude and brutal insults; perhaps her fame, her reputation gone!

'Oh! can I ever forget the day, when, beaming with modesty and native loveliness, she entered the Attic Villa!' cried he, clasping his hands together; – 'Can I ever forget the thousand nameless fears which glowed on her cheek when she found that the remarks of Walwyn applied to her cousin! Oh! Mary, Mary, and art thou gone for ever!'

This last exclamation seemed to bring reason to the aid of Montgomery. – He returned to the house with more haste than he had quitted it; and, without inquiring about the *heroine* in *hysterics*, he took a candle into the little study, which had lately been his fathers, and there he immediately addressed a few lines to Mrs. Deborah Moreton.

Apologizing in as methodical a way as his agitation would permit, he informed her of the sudden arrival of her niece at Elmsly, and the intelligence which she had communicated concerning Miss Cuthbert, and, with no common energy, he besought Mrs. Moreton to take some immediate steps for her comfort and safety.

Having finished the letter, he instantly dispatched a servant with it to the next town, in order to save the mail of that night; and, feeling his mind a little relieved from a knowledge of its being on the way, and having offered up earnest prayers for the recovery of Mary Cuthbert, he sat down to a calmer retrospect of recent occurrences, than he had hitherto been able to give them.

Through the misunderstanding of himself and Miss Moreton, it plainly appeared that Mary Cuthbert remained wholly in ignorance of his regard for her; and it was probable that she entertained no warmer wishes towards him than a common acquaintance would receive. *If* he felt some mortification at the last supposition, it yet brought with it a proportionable share of consolation. There had been something repugnant to his feelings, and derogatory to the opinion he had previously formed of Miss Cuthbert's character, in the idea of her having confided her attachment to Miss Moreton, and in her having been privy to the letter she had written him; but this was entirely an error – an error, into which he had most strangely involved himself, by the effervescent emotions of his heart, and his credulous vanity.

The character, the delicacy of Mary was still unimpeached; – She was still – alas! she was dying! Perhaps even now she had breathed her last!

Miss Moreton, on recovering from her fit, and finding that the cold, the insensate Montgomery had left her, could scarcely be persuaded to stay under his mothers roof for the remaining part of the night; but this Mrs. Montgomery insisted on, and, having laid her troublesome guest on her pillow, she besought her son to give her an explanation of the extraordinary scene which she had witnessed.

To his mother and his sisters, Montgomery would no longer have any reserve. He gave a short history of his first introduction to Mary Cuthbert, and of his succeeding visit to the Attic Villa. He painted Miss Moreton's character in the colours which he had viewed it in; and he took shame to himself, in the mixture of blindness and vanity which had bewildered him, so as to make him misconstrue her letter.

'Thus far, my dear Madam,' said Montgomery, 'I have explained myself, as it is necessary to your Frederic's peace of mind, that his mother should have no doubts of his conduct, but no farther shall I go. – *Never* shall Miss Moreton hear me confess the origin of my mistake – never shall the name of Mary Cuthbert be breathed by me in her hearing. – I cannot so profane my passion – a passion, of which the object of it must ever remain in ignorance. I took no steps to gain her affections; for, knowing my situation, it would have been base and cruel to have done so. The lovely girl is unacquainted with my partiality; but I know the selfish, the ungenerous disposition of Miss Moreton; and, if she beheld a rival in her ward, the situation of poor Mary would be worse than it is at present – the present, did I say? Alas! the *present* may be hers no longer!'

Montgomery paused to stifle his emotions. His mother and his sisters cast on him a fond, a commiserating glance.

'I have already written to the aunt of Miss Moreton, acquainting her of Miss Cuthbert's danger,' said Montgomery; 'and, if it please Heaven to let me hear of her safety, I shall exert all my fortitude to struggle against an hopeless passion, and will sedulously endeavour to lose every other feeling in that of son and brother!' and he respectfully kissed the hand of his mother, whose tears flowed silently down her cheeks, as her grateful heart was lifted up to Heaven, in the conscious exultation of having such a blessing still left to her in her son!

Montgomery purposely quitted the house at day-break, in order to elude another interview with Miss Moreton; and finding, by this behaviour, that he was resolved to continue inexorable, the disappointed heroine departed, sighing as she got into the chaise, and muttering to the civil good wishes of Arabella Montgomery, who attended her to the door – 'False, perjur'd Frederic!'[62]

Miss Moreton had now determined on going to London. There she might, in congenial society, try to forget Montgomery's perfidy. She took H— in her way, in order to make inquiries concerning her ward; but she had previously determined on not being troubled with her company, even were she fit to travel.

Spite of the taciturnity of Montgomery, her suspicions had been turned towards Mary; and she saw in her the insipid *Lucilia Edgermond* of Lord *Nelville's* present attachment.[63]

To be rivalled by such a mawkish, ignorant girl, in the affections of the only man for whom she had felt a passion, was torture; and had she had an interview with her unconscious ward, in the present state of her feelings, she would doubtless have exhibited pretty strong symptoms of anger.

Hearing that Mary was alive, and slowly mending, she contented herself with sending a laconic message to Captain Walsingham; informing him that he should hear from her again, and that she would then give orders for Miss Cuthbert's removal, when sufficiently recovered.

Miss Moreton proceeded to town. She took lodgings in — street, Covent-Garden. The Signora, the Monsieur, Germ, and Copy were in London; and she soon convened them round her, and they enjoyed with the Corinna, the pleasures of the metropolis, to which they were franked by her purse; and they had no sort of objection to partake of the *petit soupers* to which she afterwards invited them.

In the adulation of these sycophantic flatterers, *Corinna* derived some consolation for her rupture with Walwyn, and the pride-wounding behaviour of Montgomery.[64] The theatre was her favourite amusement. There, with her paper and her pencil, she criticised on actors and actresses; and there she attracted general notice by her extraordinary deportment, and the studious display of her manner.

The Signora introduced her to many persons of *genius*, in singing, dancing, and acting; and a *ci-devant chere ami* of that lady's, of good person and assured address, who had been hair-dresser, valet-de-chambre, strolling player, and stage-harlequin in rotation, now bid fair to wrest the palm of Miss Moreton's favour from all beside. His person was not so attractive, as was Montgomery's; but then Miss Moreton discovered that he was an enthusiastic disciple of *Sentiment*. He reminded her of the dear Chevalier, in his manners, in the softness of his accents, in the tender melancholy of his looks.

Matters were perfectly understood between the Signora and Lauzune (for so had she yclept this Proteus); and a liberal sum was to be paid into her hands on his succeeding with the heiress. The Monsieur played on his dear Cremona, and smiled at these arrangements; Copy was too absent to suspect them; and Germ was just now too deep in the mystery of *gas*, to *see* any farther than the parties would have him.

CHAPTER XXVI

'Where'er I turn, how new proofs pour upon me!
How happily this wondrous view supports
My former argument! How strongly strikes
Immortal life's full demonstration here!'[65]

YOUNG's Night Thoughts.

Reduced to a state of infantine weakness, the return of Mary Cuthbert's mental faculties was very sparingly followed by an accession of bodily strength; and, when she was perfectly sensible of her situation, and of the unkindness of Miss Moreton, in leaving her to the mercy of strangers, she seemed incapable of the least exertion for herself.

Her nurse, who had been won upon by the gentle patience of the invalid, with all the loquacity usually attendant on those of her occupation, and rejoiced at finding that she had once more an opportunity of making herself heard and understood, was loud in her praises of Dr. Saville's skill, and also of the kind and incessant attention of *the handsome officer* from the barracks.

Mary, to whom all that had passed was a mystery, expressed her gratitude to Dr. Saville, at their next interview. 'I am grateful to you, my good Sir,' said she, 'for the preservation of my life; grateful, as it is the will of the Almighty, that it should be prolonged; which is apparent by his having blessed the means which you have used for my recovery. Yet, in a prolongation of life, I see nothing to hope.'

'Oh! fie, fie, say not so, young lady,' said the Doctor; 'I must not hear that language. At your age, a very unnatural one, let me tell you – Come, come, I know more than you think for; you shall not always live with this confounded *quiz*, *odd-body* cousin of yours! and you have time before you, to make friends, who are more congenial to your turn of mind. To be sure, this Miss Moreton is the most uncommon heroine I ever met with in history or fable; and, I believe, nobody besides herself would have thought of putting you under the management of a gay red coat, and absolutely leaving him your whole and soul guardian. Ah! now you stare, and look prettily fearful; but the young fellow has conducted himself very well, and made over his right and title to you, with great heroism and wonderful self-denial, to an *old doctor* and an *older* nurse – and even now, he waits my permission, ere he pays you a congratulatory visit, though he comes here about twenty times in a day, and knows to half a second, how long you sit up.'

'I shall be glad to see Captain Walwyn, if you think it right, Sir, when you are here.'

'Walwyn, no, no; he is not the man; I have not such an opinion of his forbearance, believe me; Lesly Walsingham is the gentleman I am speaking of; and I am confident, that if good wishes could have helped you out of the disorder, he would have forestalled me.'

A faint suffusion crossed the pale cheek of Mary; the Doctor watched the minutest symptom; and, thinking the change indicated fatigue, he took his leave.

Lesly Walsingham was the next day introduced by Dr. Saville; and thinking that two visitors at once might be too much for the invalid, he took his leave, promising to call for his companion, when he thought it right for him to depart.

The air of tranquil serenity which was diffused over the delicate countenance of Mary, impressed Walsingham with respect and tenderness. During her illness he had had many opportunities of privately conversing with Dr. Saville; and if the good Doctor had been the restorer of Miss Cuthbert, he had performed a far greater cure on Walsingham, for he had dispelled the cloud of infidelity from his mind!

Dr. Saville's arguments carried great weight with them; for they came from man of science, and of great philosophical knowledge. He had attained the summit of human learning; yet he was candid and humble; for he was a Christian! 'I know,' said he, 'that my profession labours, (unjustly I trust,) under the stigma of infidelity; but, tell me, Walsingham, has any order of men a greater call for the comforts of the Gospel? When we witness the most heart-rending and distressful scenes; – when we, in vain, exert out utmost skill to preserve the wife to her afflicted husband; to save the blooming boy for his distracted mother; to detain the orphans friend on earth; *what* can console us under the failure of our endeavours, but the certainty of an hereafter; the glorious consolations of a Saviours mercy, and a Saviours love. We know in whom we have believed, and we trust all to him.'

Lesly Walsingham had thought more within the last three weeks, than he had during his preceding life. The transitory enjoyments of this world appeared as nothing, when the glories of another were unfolded to his vision; and he entered the sick room of Mary Cuthbert a new man. All his outrageous passions were chastened, tempered by the convictions of his heart; and he looked at her with the hallowed softness with which he would have approached an ethereal being!

Mary said but little, but that little was impressive. She spoke of her restoration to life as the mercy of Heaven; and piously clasped her hands as she said, 'I trust I shall not be unworthy of it!'

As she said these words; as her dove-like eyes were turned towards Heaven, and Walsingham was surveying her countenance, with an admiration as unbounded as it was free from every worldly idea, a light step was heard on the stair-case; the door opened, and Mary Cuthbert was strained to the bosom of Miss Davenport! while the surprised, the entranced Walsingham, knelt at her side, and clasping her hand in his, almost devoured it with kisses! 'Oh! Clara! Clara! Angel of Mercy!' cried he, 'Beatified messenger of heavenly love! Oh! Clara, hear your Lesly's recantation! behold him not almost, but the altogether Christian.'

Miss Davenport was busily engaged in encouraging and soothing the trembling and half-fainting Mary; but she remembered the beloved voice of Walsingham; the joyful sounds thrilled at her heart, and though she withdrew her hand, yet she did it not in anger.

Dr. Saville soon made the quartetto of this party. Explanations succeeded congratulations; and general satisfaction ensued.

Miss Davenport accounted for her unlooked-for appearance, by informing Mary Cuthbert, that she came deputed by Mrs. Deborah Moreton, to bring her back to Marlow.

'And is Miss Moreton returned to the Villa?' asked Mary.

'No, my love, she is not. It seems Mr. Montgomery became acquainted with your illness; and wrote an account of it to Mrs. Deborah Moreton.'

Mary felt a secret pleasure at hearing that she owed any thing to the kind interference of Montgomery.

Eager to accept the proffered invitation of Mrs. Moreton, the recovery of our invalid seemed to keep pace with her wishes. An explanation of the most happy kind ensued between Clara Davenport and Walsingham; and the judgment of Miss Davenport now gave a free sanction to the choice of her heart.

In less than a week, Mary Cuthbert was able to travel; and the two ladies left H—, attended by Lesly Walsingham, and followed by the hearty prayers of Dr. Saville.

Mary Cuthbert was much hurt at perceiving the alteration in the countenance and whole appearance of Mrs. Deborah Moreton. 'Ah! child,' said she, shaking her head, 'if the unheard of behaviour of my wild niece has almost precipitated you to the grave, it has likewise undermined my health; a gnawing canker has preyed at my heart for many months; and now, while I am in uncertainty about her, and do not know what wild freaks she may be about, and into what frightful schemes she may be plunging, I can never enjoy a moments peace of mind.

'Ah! my poor brother little knew what would become of his *free* education, as he called it, and his *unfettered notions.*'[66]

Mary Cuthbert tried, by every means in her power, to divert the mind of the old lady. She palliated the behaviour of Miss Moreton, though conscious that when represented in the mildest point of view, it must appear wholly unjustifiable.

'I had hoped,' would Mrs. Moreton say, 'that she would have tried to attract Mr. Montgomery. He is a sensible, steady young man, and I should like to have seen him her husband; but he saw what a strange fantastic creature she was, and would have nothing to say to her. I am sure you ought to be grateful to him to the end of your life, my dear; for, had it not been for his kind and considerate letter, you might have lain for ever at H—. *I* should never have heard of it.'

Mary *was* grateful to Montgomery; and she began to think that her gratitude was of a kind, which was calculated to give pain to her bosom. Insensibly she took the walks round the Villa, in which she had been accompanied by him; and she retraced every word which had there fallen from his lips.

The Attic Villa was undergoing repairs and alterations; but the servants were in ignorance of Miss Moreton's return, as well as of the place of her present abode.

Captain Walsingham had always been a favourite of Mrs. Moreton's. She had never known the cause which had produced a rupture between him and her favourite, Miss Davenport; but she was heartily glad, that any circumstance had produced their reconciliation; and when she looked at the bright prospect which was before them, she only wished that her niece had such an one.

But the prospects of the unfortunate Miss Moreton were closed for ever! Her untimely fate first reached her aunt, through the medium of the following letter from the Monsieur.

CHAPTER XXVII

'Great heights are hazardous to the weak head.'[67]

BLAIR'S GRAVE.
LETTER.
'MADAME MORE-*TON*.

'London, Wednesday, Twentieth

I HAVE de tres honneur to *inform* you, Madame, a *cat-as-tro-phee* has happen dat will aston-ish you ver, ver much *in-deed*. You, Madame, have, no doubt, heard of de ver dread-*ful con-fla-gra-ti-on* dat happen toder night at Covent-Garden-*Te-a-tre*. Ve vas all just come from de seeing of de play. Madame More-ton, she look ver vell, ver vell, indeed, in de green and de silver; de long vaists vas ver *be-coming* to pauvre Maamselle More-ton. Vell, ve return to de petit souper, at her apartment, La Belle Signora, Monsieur Lauzune, Monsieur *Jerme*, Monsieur *Coupee*, and votre tres humble servant. Vell, ve ver merry, ver merry, indeed, ven we heard great noise, great bus-*teel*, great ringing of de bells; and den dey said de grand *magnifique* building, de Co-vent-Gar-den *Te-a tre* was all on fire. Madame Moreton, she vent ver fast wid Monsieur *Coupee*, Monsieur *Jerme*, and Lauzune, to see de fire, grand *spec-ta-cle*, on de top of de house; but, helas! dey should not go, for dey did not know dat de house vas caught, till too late. Monsieur Lauzune he jump from *pa-ra-pet* walls, ver high, ver high, indeed; but he vas used to *de jumping*. Madame More-*ton* she follow him, but she no thought it so ver high leap; she vas killed, ver *instantaneously*, on de ver spot she fell down on. Oh! Mon Dieu! how dreadful acci-dent! Monsieur Jerme, Monsieur Coupee, dey both escape, by assistance of fire-men! but, helas! Madame More-ton could not vait. The Signora be ver much sorry, quite *au de despoir*; she not sing one note of de musique since. Charmante Madame Moreton met wid so ver tre-men-*dous* mis-*for*-tune tragique,

'Madame De-bor-*ah* More-*ton*,

'Javois de honneur to be, Madame, tres humble, tres Devoted Serviteur,

'JEAN JACQUES, LOUIS MYRTILLA.'

N.B. It may be observed, that Monsieur *accented* in writing, just as he pronounced in speaking.[68]

This accident, as related by the Monsieur, was too true, and was of too dreadful a kind to require any comment. Mary Cuthbert tried to console Mrs. Deborah Moreton; but she felt too much herself from the shock of this awful event, to be able to tranquillize her own emotions, or to compose her mind. After an affliction of such a nature, time must be required ere the mind can recover its tone; but Mrs. Deborah Moreton was able to exert herself before her young companion, and seemed to derive a new interest in life, whilst securing to Mary Cuthbert the fortune which had devolved to her by the death of her niece.[69]

'I have enough for myself,' said she; 'every farthing of the poor lost ones must go to you. Dear child, you will be regular, and steady; may it prove a greater blessing to you than it was to her!'

The sudden acquisition of fortune by such an appalling calamity, gave a superstitious impression to the mind of Mary Cuthbert. 'You give me these riches for a trial, Madam,' said she; 'as such they are sent me by Providence. Oh! may I, by a humble, by a right use of them, prove myself worthy of the distinguished favour!'

'That you *ever* will, I am sure,' said Mrs. Deborah Moreton; 'Oh! an hundred and a thousand times have I wished, that the poor lost one had been like *you*! but my dear child the assistance of *a clergyman* may be of some use to *keep* even *you* in the right way. – Don't blush now, Miss Cuthbert – Mr. Montgomery loves you; he is worthy of you; and – *but all in good time*, child, I hope to see you united.'

And in *good* time Mrs. Deborah Moreton is likely to see her wishes completed. Montgomery will become the happy pastor of his fathers flock; and Miss Cuthbert's fortune will enable them to gratify the benevolent feelings of their hearts. – The emoluments of the Elmsly living will, with the full consent of Mrs. Deborah Moreton and her favourite, be secured to Mrs. Montgomery and her daughters, who are to reside in a cottage near the parsonage.

Mary Cuthbert does not wish to inherit the Attic Villa. 'No, dearest Madam,' said she, while conversing with Mrs. Deborah Moreton on the subject, 'the Villa would bring us a thousand unpleasant recollections. – Comparisons would be made; we could not bear them; it would grieve us to hear them. – Peace to the ashes of the dead!' – 'Amen!' said Mrs. Deborah, lifting up her hands and eyes; 'the estate has not been many years in our family; I wish my poor brother had never bought it, from the very bottom of my heart; but no matter, I will sell it, Miss Cuthbert, and the money shall accumulate for your children!'

Thus we must draw our curtain, telling our readers that, in all human probability, Mr. and Mrs. Montgomery, and Mr. and Mrs. Walsingham will maintain an uninterrupted and friendly intercourse, and that Mrs. Deborah Moreton will be a witness of their happiness.

We fear that we shall be *accused* of the *murder* of Miss Moreton, our redoubt-able heroine; but, reader! in the intricacies of her *destiny*, we had *imposed* on ourselves no easy task. It was impossible to let a lady on stilts slide down *gen-tly* – and, (be merciful, O reader!) it was not *murder*, believe us, but accidental death.[70]

ENDNOTES

Volume I

1. *'What Caricature is in painting ... from it'*: This quotation is actually an extract from Henry Fielding's Preface to his 1742 novel *The History of Joseph Andrews, and his Friend Mr. Abraham Adams, Written in Imitation of the Manner of Cervantes, Author of Don Quixote*, 2 vols in 1 (London: Cooke's Edition, 1795), pp. iii–v. In it, Fielding introduces the difference between comic and burlesque in romance. He explains that burlesque writing is 'ever the exhibition of what is monstrous and unnatural, and where our delight, arises from the surprising absurdity, as in appropriating the manners of the highest to the lowest'. He then compares burlesque writing to caricature in painting, which aims to exhibit 'monsters not man, and all distortions and exaggerations'. By choosing this extracts as epigraph, the author seems to warn readers that the novel belongs to the burlesque kind of writing, aiming to ridicule characters.
2. *'When I see such games ... nothing up!'*: The extract is from William Cowper's *The Task*, Book III (in *The Poems of William Cowper, of the Inner Temple*, 2 vols (London: printed for J. Johnson, 1800), vol. 1, p. 100). First published in 1785, *The Task* became an extremely influential pre-romantic text towards the end of the eighteenth and the beginning of the nineteenth century. The passage refers to the vanity and deception of learning and to the happiness derived from domesticity and common sense. As in the case of the extract from Fielding, this quotation anticipates the expected reader's reaction, and the author's attitude, to the story of the Corinna of England.
3. *'Doom'd from each ... of the heart!'*: from John Langhorne's 'Hymn to Hope' (1761), *The Poetical Works of J. Langhorne, D.D with The Life of the Author* (London: Cooke's Edition, 1798), p. 158.
4. *with great success*: At the end of the eighteenth and the beginning of the nineteenth century Birmingham had become the first major industrial town in England, thanks to the exploitation of the near coalfields in Warwickshire and Staffordshire. It was also the birth place of the 'Lunar Society', founded in 1765 by the industrialist Matthew Boulton and other intellectuals, among which, Joseph Priestly. In 1802, Nelson and the Hamiltons visited Boulton's Soho Manufactory in Birmingham and in 1809, the year of composition of the novel, a statue was erected in honour of Nelson. It is possible that the author took inspiration from the emerging powerful industrial class for the character of Mr Moreton and for his quickly acquired fortune. It is also possible that the author found annoying the increasingly powerful influence that industrialists such as Matthew Boulton had on the cultural and intellectual circles of the town.

5.   *serious uncle*: Clarissa's circumstances are quite similar to Madame de Staël's eponymous character in her 1807 novel *Corinne, or Italy* (ed. and trans. Avriel H. Goldberger (New Brunswick and London: Rutgers University Press, 1987). Like Corinne, Clarissa has lost her mother in adolescence and is left to her rich father's care.

6.   *time-worn cloister*: The antithetical construction of the characters of the two cousins is clearly reminiscent of the relation between Corinne and her half-sister Lucile. While Lucile has been educated to become a timid, chaste, docile and domestic woman, Corinne has been accustomed to be at the centre of public attention, honoured and admired for her artistic talents. The difference between Clarissa and Mary is comically exaggerated in the novel, thus showing the author's intention not only to parody the original story of *Corinne, or Italy*, but also to question such antithetical constructions, which became extremely popular after the publication of Staël's novel. See: Eve Sourian, 'Germaine de Staël and the Position of Women in France, England and Germany', in Avriel H. Goldberger (ed.), *Woman as Mediatrix: Essays on Nineteenth-Century European Women Writers* (New York: Greenwood Press, 1987), pp. 31–8; Esther Wohlgemut, '"What do you do with her at home?" The Cosmopolitan and National Tale', *European Romantic Review*, 13:2 (June 2002), pp. 191–7; 'The Corinne Complex: Gender, Genius and National Identity', in Clarissa Campbell Orr (ed.), *Women in the Victorian Art World* (Manchester: Manchester University Press, 1995), pp. 89–106.

7.   'Even such ... ours': James Thomson, 'The Castle of Indolence', II.lxiii, in *The Poetical Works of James Thomson, With His Last Collections, Additions, and Improvements, With the Life of the Author* (London: Cooke's Edition, 1794), p. 285.

8.   *rewarder of talent*: The introduction of the character of Clarissa is to be read as a parody of the character of Corinne. Clarissa is described as a 'unique' character, 'different from the rest of her sex'; she is devoted to the 'impulse of taste' and she is 'a liberal rewarder of talent'. These features are also typical of Corinne. Reflecting on the uniqueness of Corinne's character, Oswald comments: 'but could anything compare with Corinne? Could the common run of laws apply to one whose genius and sensibility were the unifying bond of so many diverse qualities? Corinne was a miracle of nature' (Staël, *Corinne, or Italy*, p. 105).

9.   *conspicuously on the list*: The author here makes a consciously satirical use of the words 'talent and genius', which had become extremely popular amongst early nineteenth-century writers, especially women, after the publication of Germaine de Staël's *Delphine* (1802) and *Corinne*. From hence, the author italicizes references to 'over-used' terminology, which she often employs with satirical purposes. See, for example: Dino Felluga, *The Perversity of Poetry: Romantic Ideology and the Popular Male Poet of Genius* (New York: State University of New York Press, 2005), Gayle Levy, 'A Genius for the Modern Era: Madame de Staël's Corinne', *Nineteenth-Century French Studies*, 30:3–4 (Spring 2002), pp. 242–53, Ellen Moers, 'Madame de Staël and the Woman of Genius', *American Scholar*, 44 (1975), pp. 225–41.

10.   *"Wilt thou ... nightingale!"*: *Romeo and Juliet*, III.v. The original text is:
> Wilt thou be gone? It is not yet near day;
> It was the nightingale, and not the lark,
> That pierc'd the fearful *hollow* of thine *ears*.
> Nightly she sits on yon pomegranate tree.
> Believe me, love, it was the nightingale!

The author's satirical intent is not only directed to Corinne, but, more generally, to all people displaying talents and artistic abilities they do not actually possess.

11. of her every virtue: Educated to be a decorous, reserved and prudent woman, Mary Cuthbert represents a more conventional idea of womanhood than Clarissa. The italicized words, however, together with the exaggerated language that the author employs, seems to suggest that the author's approach to the character of Mary is also satirical. The author shows to be aware of the contemporary debate about the education of women and seems to ridicule any extreme position. For a selection of texts on the Romantic debate on female education see Pam Morris (ed.), *Conduct Literature for Women, Part IV 1770–1830* (London: Pickering and Chatto, 2006). Recent critical works on the subject include: Alan Richardson, *Literature, Education and Romanticism: Rreading as Sexual Practice 1780–1832* (Cambridge: Cambridge University Press, 1994); David Halpin, *Romanticism and Education: Love, Heroism and Imagination in Pedagogy* (London: Continuum International, 2007).

12. 'Here Freedom ... might inspire': James Thomson, 'The Castle of Indolence', I.xxxv, in *The Poetical Works of James Thomson*, p. 257.

13. *dawns within me*: This lines are reminiscent of Wordsworth's 'Be blest, by sight of thee from heaven / was sent Peace to my parting soul, / the fullness of content', part of 'Guilt and Sorrow, or Incidents upon Salisbury plain' (stanza LXX), composed in 1793–4 but published only in 1843. The poem was partially published as part of 'The Female Vagrant' in the 1798 edition of *Lyrical Ballads. The Poetical Works of William Wordsworth*, 6 vols. (London: Edward Moxon, 1843), vol. 5, p. 122.

14. *her father's table*: This is reminiscent of de Staël's *Corinne*. In the novel, as a young child, Corinne performs in front of guests and friends. In the attempt to please Lord Nelvil's father while in England, she 'displayed all [her] talents: [she] sang, [she] danced, [she] improvised for him; and with [her] wit held in check for so long was perhaps over lively when it burst its chains', with the effect of entirely alienating him and the possibility of marrying his son (Staël, *Corinne, or Italy*, p. 260).

15. *applause and admiration*: The references to 'romantic fervour and enthusiasm' and to '*energy*' is undoubtedly linked to Staël. The Romantic idea of enthusiasm found its origins in the French Enlightenment, particularly in Jean Jacques Rousseau's works, and successively, in the German philosophical thought of Kant and Schlegel. Staël was well acquainted with both Rousseau and the German philosophers. She first reflects on the emerging concept of 'enthusiasm' in her *Letters on the Works and Character of Jean Jacques Rousseau (Lettres sur les ouvrages et le character de Jean Jacques Rousseau)* published as early as 1788, with reference to *La Nouvelle Eloïse* and *Confessions*. She then continued to develop the romantic idea of 'enthusiasm' in her novels *Delphine*, and especially in *Corinne*, and in her philosophical treatise *On Germany*. In *Corinne*, Stael recurrently uses the word 'enthusiasm' to describe an attitude of devotion and total emotional and intellectual commitment to art and genius. In Book II, Chapter II, she defines 'enthusiasm' as 'that inexhaustible well of feelings and ideas' (*Corinne, or Italy*, p. 24); in Book IV, Chapter I, she refers to 'imagination, love, enthusiasm' as 'all that is divine in the human soul' (*Corinne, or Italy*, p. 51). In the novel 'enthusiasm' is often linked to the idea of 'energy of the soul', 'energy of the passions' and 'sensibility'. In *On Germany* (1810) she will dedicate a whole chapter to the definition of 'enthusiasm'. See also Jon Mee, *Romanticism, Enthusiasm and Regulation: Poetics and the Policing of Culture in the Romantic Period* (Oxford: Oxford University Press, 2005), Lawrence E. Klein and Anthony J. La Vope (eds), *Enthusiasm and Enlightenment in Europe, 1650–1850* (Los Angeles: University of California Press, 1998).

16. *music books*: The tambourine is a musical instrument typical of southern Italy. In *Corinne*, it is mentioned with regard to the 'tarantella' and other folkloristic dances which Corinne performs at Rome and Naples (Staël, *Corinne, or Italy*, p. 235).

17. *'Whether he ... trifler still'*: William Cowper, 'Charity', in *Poems*, 2 vols (London: J. Johnson, 1794–5), vol. 1, p. 198 (ll. 353–6).

18. *"Join the ... victory"*: Thomas Gray, 'The Fatal Sisters: an Ode', in *The Poetical Works of Thomas Gray With Some Accounts of his Life and Writings* (London: Longman, 1800), p. 58.

19. *"The spider's ... on bliss!"*: The original extract is: 'The spider's most attenuated thread / Is cord, is cable, to man's tender tie / On earthly bliss; it breaks at every breeze', from Edward Young, 'The Complaint. Night One: On Life, Death and Immortality', in *Night Thoughts; on Life, Death and Immortality* (London: Allen and West, 1800), p. 5. These lines, originally written in 1742, were becoming very common as epitaphs on gravestones towards the end of the eighteenth century. In 1795, William Blake was commissioned to illustrate the poem.

20. *her slaves*: The idea of '*genius*' is largely employed by Staël. In *Corinne*, 'genius' is mentioned in reference to Corinne's talents and to artistic genius in general. In Book II, Chapter I, for example, the word 'genius' is mentioned several times: 'Oswald quitted his lodgings to repair to the public square, where he heard everybody speaking of the genius and talents of Corinne' (Staël, *Corinne, or Italy*, p. 20); Corinne is welcomed at the Capitol in Rome with the words 'Long live Genius and Beauty', and Corinne is known as 'a woman illustrious only by the gift of genius' (Staël, *Corinne, or Italy*, p. 21). The word became extremely popular at the beginning of the nineteenth century. Here, the author is using it in an ironic vein, together with 'benevolence', 'philanthropy', and 'wit'. However, she also italicizes 'plain truths' and 'unenlightened', which suggests a similar ironic reference to Mrs. Moreton's more traditional and conservative ideas.

21. *'Stern rugged ... she bore!'*: The author has sarcastically altered the original extract: 'Stern rugged nurse! Thy rigid love / With patience many a year she bore', from Thomas Gray, 'Ode to Adversity', in *The Poetical Works of Thomas Gray*, p. 18.

22. *an old fool 'tis*: All French words used by the housemaid are misspelled here, stressing the artificiality of the language used by Clarissa and the difficulty of middle- and working-class people to understand and correctly employ them.

23. *almost celestial*: This is the first explicit reference to Germaine de Staël. Clarissa and the Chevalier are reading *Delphine*, one of Staël's most popular novels. Published simultaneously in Paris and in Geneva in December 1802, the novel was dedicated provocatively '*to Silent France*'. As Maria Fairweather observes, the novel was an immediate success and became the main topic of conversation in Paris. In the *Journal de Paris*, Roederer commented: 'Do you know why nobody was at the theatre the day before yesterday, or why today, which is Sunday, there will be few attending Mass? ... It is because the whole of Paris is behind closed doors reading Madame de Staël's new novel'. The eponymous heroine of the novel is actually a highly idealized form of Madame de Staël herself. Delphine, a beautiful young widow of independent means and independent views, has, like Staël, the gift of brilliant conversation, enthusiasm, a romantic and passionate nature, a belief in reason, a dislike of constraints and a love of liberty. She falls in love with a charismatic nobleman, Léonce de Mondoville, who is very careful of social conventions. Their love is threatened by Delphine's cousin, who persuades Léonce to marry her own daughter. The story is set during the French Revolution, particularly the years of Terror, and is full of political references to Napo-

leon and to contemporary Europe. See Maria Fairweather, *Madame de Staël* (London: Constable, 2005), pp. 283–5, and Germaine de Staël, *Delphine*, ed. Avriel H. Goldberger (Dekalb: Northern Illinois University Press, 1995).

24. *of her acquaintance*: Italics again suggest an ironic use of the words 'chaste' and 'virtuous'.

25. *applauded and caressed*: Britain and France had been at war for over a decade. France declared war against Britain in 1793 soon after the events of the French Revolution. The war continued up until the Piece of Amiens in 1802 and resumed in May 1803, carrying on until 1815 with the defeat of Napoleon. For more information about the British conservative response to the French Revolution, see Matthew Grenby, *The Anti-Jacobin Novel: British Conservatism and the French Revolution* (Cambridge: Cambridge University Press, 2001) and Philip Shaw (ed.), *Romantic Wars: Studies in Culture and Conflict 1793–1822* (Aldershot: Ashgate, 2000).

26   'Vain is the tree ... fruits': James Thomson, 'The Castle of Indolence', II.xii, in *The Poetical Works of James Thomson*, p. 272.

27. *her health*: This salon clearly reminds of Corinne's international salon in Rome, attended by Lord Nelvil and Count D' Eurfeuil in Book III, Chapter I. Corinne's circle of friends is mainly composed by French, British and Italian intellectuals and artists who spend the evening discussing the latest fashion in literature and art. As Lord Nelvil observes entering Corinne's sitting room, 'in each detail he noticed a harmonious blending of all that is most pleasing in three nations – France, England, and Italy: a taste for social discourse, a love of learning, and a feeling for the arts' (Staël, *Corinne, or Italy*, p. 36). The author's parodical reconstruction of Corinne's salon reproposes the same mixture of national cultures.

28   *over his wine*: The traditional practice of separating men and women after dinner is also, polemically mentioned in *Corinne*. In England, at her father's house, Corinne is surprised by her step-mother's signalling 'to the women that it was time to withdraw, and prepare tea, leaving the men alone at table for dessert'. Corinne reacts surprisingly: 'I did not know the first thing about this practice, so startling to Italians who can imagine no pleasure in social interchange without women [...]' (Staël, *Corinne, or Italy*, p. 253). Here, Clarissa seems to prefer the Italian way of conversation to her aunt's more traditional English division of the sexes.

29   *that potato*: This sentence is also a parody of a fundamental aspect of Staël's thought. In *On Literature* and *On Germany*, Staël discusses the limitation of the idea of national belonging and promotes integration and cooperation among different countries and different cultures, thus proposing herself as a cultural mediator between European states. In *On Germany*, in particular, she celebrates the possibility of choosing '*une patrie de la pensée*' (an intellectual homeland) over any imposed idea of national belonging (*Oeuvres Complètes*, 17 vols (Paris: Treuttel et Würtz, 1821), vol. 5).

30. *my existence*: Clarissa's opinions on marriage and relationships sarcastically echo Staël's own ideas. Corinne never contemplates marrying Lord Nelvil but she is ready to commit her whole life and to sacrifice her career to follow him in Britain, thus suggesting an implicit reflection on the limitations of marriage. In *On Germany*, Staël dedicates a chapter to 'Love within Marriage', where she discusses the pros and cons of the traditional idea of marriage and she particularly reflects on the inferior position of women in marriage. Staël's own life and numerous lovers suggest an anti-conformist approach to marriage (see *Major Writings of Germaine de Staël*, ed. Vivian Folkenflik (New York: Columbia University Press, 1987), p. 317).

31. *'Would you ... part?'*: The actual lines are: 'Would you that Sensibility resign? / And with those powers of Genius would you part?', from John Langhorne, 'To George Colman Esq. Prefixed to the Correspondence of Theodosius and Constantia', in *The Poetical Works of J. Langhorne*, p. 136.

32. *a reasonable being*: Clarissa's speech is shaped after Corinne's improvisation at the Capitol. In Book II, Chapter II, Prince Castel-Forte, one of most intimate friends and admirers of Corinne, introduces her improvisation by praising 'her sensibility', 'the talent of [her] genius and art' and referring to the 'impassioned sensibility inspiring Corinne's poetry'. He also called the audience's attention 'to the originality of Corinne's language, language so entirely born of her character and her way of feeling that no trace of affectation could ever alter a charm not only natural but involuntarily as well' (Staël, *Corinne, or Italy*, pp. 23–4). Corinne then starts her improvisation on the subject of *The Glory and Bliss of Italy*, which the audience had suggested. At the beginning of her speech she refers to Petrarch who had been the first to be crowned at the Capitol as poet laureate and she continues praising Italian literature and art. Clarissa's speech recreates the language, tone and subject of *The Glory and Bliss of Italy*, with the difference that the author makes her heroine's speech appear as artificial and as ridiculous as possible (Staël, *Corinne, or Italy*, pp. 26–9).

33. *from her society*: One of the most famous texts about bees circulating at the time was Rev. John Thorley's 'The History of Bees', *An Enquiry into the Nature, Order and Government of Bees* (London: J. Waugh, 1765). The text went through several editions up to 1803. The 'story of the Queen Bee' obviously refers to Clarissa's situation and to the numerous useless and untalented people who surround her.

34. *the tragic tale*: Monimia is the heroine of Thomas Otway's *The Orphan or the Unhappy Marriage* (1680), while Belvidera and Jesseir are the protagonists of Otway's *Venice Preserv'd* (1682). Calista is originally the protagonist of a seventeenth-century French tragedy, *Les Amours de Lysandre and Caliste* by Vital d' Audiguier first performed in 1612; the story was re-elaborated by John Fletcher and Philip Messinger in 1623 and published under the title *The Wandering Lovers* or, *The Lovers' Progress*. All these female heroines, including Cleopatra, have been the victims of unhappy love relationships.

35. *'Now while ... sleep'*: The original extract is: 'Now, while the drowsy world lies lost in sleep', from 'Winter: A Poem', in *The Poetical Works of James Thomson*, p. 118.

36. *in a roar*: The description of the character of Montgomery is reminiscent of Lord Nelvil in *Corinne*. In Book I, Chapter I, Nelvil is introduced as a reserved and melancholic hero: 'At twenty-five, he had wearied of life; his mind prejudged everything, and his wounded sensibility no longer had any taste for the illusions of the heart. [...] Yet his was a restless nature, sensitive and passionate, combining all the qualities that might sweep others along, and himself well, but unhappiness and remorse had left him hesitant to confront fate, whom he thought to mollify by demanding nothing of her' (Staël, *Corinne, or Italy*, pp. 3–4).

37. *grace or dignity*: Mary's role within the novel is increasingly associated with that of Lucile, Corinne's half-sister, in Staël's novel: that is to create a 'fold character' to Clarissa. While back in Britain, Lord Nelvil is struck by Lucile's chastity, docility and timidity, strikingly in contrast with Corinne's character. Lucile and Mary's upbringings are described in similar terms: 'Nelvil reflected on the life [Lucile] had led – so austere, so secluded – on her matchless beauty, deprived of all the world's pleasures as of its homage, and his soul was pervaded with the purest emotion. Lucile's mother, too, was worthy of the respect

she commanded. She was a person still harder on herself than on others' (Staël, *Corinne, or Italy*, p. 321).

38. '*Ah, little … misery*': 'Winter: A Poem', in *The Poetical Works of James Thomson*, p. 121
39. '*And as … at once*': 'Autumn: A Poem', in *The Poetical Works of James Thomson*, p. 84.
40. "*Along the … way*": from Thomas Gray's 'An Elegy Written in a Country Churchyard' in *The Poetical Works of Thomas Gray*, p. 94: 'Along the cool sequester'd vale of life / They kept the noiseless tenor of their way'.
41. "*Then though … ray*": Henrietta Maria Bowdler, *Fragments in Prose and Verse by a Young Lady Lately Deceased With Some Accounts of her Life and Character, by the Author of 'Sermons on the Doctrine and Duties of Christianity'* (Bath: n.p., 1808). This collection was so successful that it went trough several editions up until 1842.
42. *Chevalier D'Aubert*: This paragraph reveals an articulate and complex view of French emigrants in Britain. It seems that the author is taking here a more conservative view in support of the French nobility, but against the contamination of British habits with the more licentious French mores. See Gregory Claeys, *The French Revolution Debate in Britain: The Origin of Modern Politics* (Basingstoke: Palgrave, 1995).
43. *cheerful magnanimity*: Montgomery's attraction to the chaste and virtuous Mary Cuthbert mirrors the attraction that Lord Nelvil feels towards the timid Lucile in Staël's *Corinne*, with the only difference that Montgomery seems to be totally disgusted with the character of Clarissa, while Lord Nelvil is also deeply attracted to Corinne.
44. "*The banquet … sip!*": These lines do not seem to have any literary sources. They must be improvised by Walwyn to add to the poetic tone of the chapter.
45. '*They represent … virtues*': James Fordyce (1720–96), 'On Female Virtue', *Sermons to Young Women*, 2 vols (Dublin: Campbell and Shea, 1796), vol. 1, p. 70.
46. *does she not display*: This is another important and direct reference to Germaine de Staël's character and works. This obviously demonstrates that *The Corinna of England* was clearly composed as a provocatively conservative response to Staël's literary and philosophical production. In this and the following paragraphs Staël's first novel, *Delphine*, is discussed.
47. *intrinsic merit*: As soon as *Delphine* was published in 1802 it received controversial reviews. As an anti-Napoleonic novel, the press in Paris, regulated by Bonaparte, tore the novel apart. Fiévée, for example, one of Bonaparte's disciples, harshly criticized not only the novel's heroine, Delphine, but indirectly the author as well: 'Examine such women closely, you will see that they are violent in all their desires, demanding in all their relationships, and that it is even more difficult to be their friend that their lover. Listen carefully to these unhappy women; you will learn that they complain their melancholic sighing; their hearts are forever hurt by the ingratitude; they shout loudly for peace; peace which they can no longer find but in their graves. Look at them: they are big, fat, greasy and heavy' (cited in Maria Fairweather, *Madame de Staël*, pp. 285–6). Later on, Staël wrote an essay, *Some Reflections on the Moral Aims of Delphine*, in defence of her novel and against the charges of immorality, which was published only after her death. In defence of Delphine, she wrote; 'I believe it to be useful and strictly moral to demonstrate how people of superior intelligence can make more mistakes than others […] how a generous and sensitive can lead to many errors if it is not subject to strong moral principles […]' (cited in Maria Fairweather, *Madame de Staël*, p. 286).
48. *Deborah Moreton*: Matilda de Vernon is the daughter of Delphine's impoverished cousin, Madame Vernon, who will eventually marry Léonce.

49. *its peculiar care*: This sentence alludes to the seventeenth and eighteenth-century theory of the geographical, cultural and social differences between the north and the south of Europe. It was elaborated by the French author Montesquieu (1689–1755) and the Swiss author Bonstetten (1745–1832) respectively in *The Spirit of Law (L'Esprit des Lois* (1748)) and *Human Studies (Etudes de l'homme* (1821)). This difference was also re-elaborated by Staël in *On Literature* and *Germany* and fictionalized in *Corinne*. See: Silvia Bordoni, 'From Madame de Staël to Lord Byron: The Dialectics of European Romanticism', *Literary Compass*, 3 (2006), pp. 1–16.

50. *'The lovers ... retribution'*: John Nichols, *Biographical Anecdotes of William Hogarth* (London: Published by and for John Nichols, 1781), p. 84.

51. *Deborah Moreton's*: This episode suggests that Clarissa is not after all the frivolous, superficial and unaware character that the author has depicted so far. It seems to suggest, on the contrary, that Clarissa is consciously provocative and trying to challenge the moralistic and conservative view of a provincial town.

52. *"Music has ... oak!"*: William Congreve, *The Mourning Bride*, I.i (London: John Bell, 1791), p. 13.

53. *'It is difficult ... insignificant'*: James Fordyce, 'Sermon on Female Pity', *Sermons to Young Women*, p. 202.

54. *'"Do good ... its fame!"'*: Alexander Pope, 'Epistle to Dr. Arbuthnot, being the Prologue to the Satires', in *The Works of Alexander Pope*, 9 vols (London: Printed for B. Law and J. Johnson, 1797), vol. 4, p. 314.

55. *Provence rose*: The reference is most probably to Nicholas Rowe's *The Fair Penitent* (1703), which was one of the most frequently performed tragedies on the eighteenth-century stage. See Joseph Donohue (ed.), *The Cambridge History of British Theatre, 1660–1895* (Cambridge: Cambridge University Press, 2004), p. 96.

56. *attitudes and gestures*: This passage clearly alludes and parodies Corinne's discussion of Italian poetry during her improvisation at the Capitol and at her literary gathering in Rome. See Staël, *Corinne, or Italy*, Book II, Chapter I (pp. 27–9), and Book III, Chapter III (pp. 43–5).

57. *life and happiness*: Clarissa's mind is here starting to shape her relationship with Montgomery as an imitation of the relationship between Corinne and Lord Nelvil in Staël's novel, whereby the cold, reluctant and timid Nelvil is conquered and fascinated by the exuberant and artistic Corinne.

Volume II

1. *'Happy ... at the same time!'*: James Fordyce, 'Sermon on Female Virtue, Friendship and Conversation', in *Sermons to Young Women*, p. 76.

2. *her left had done*: Miss Devenport's judicious and magnanimous behaviour and the modesty and decency of her habitation are in striking contrast to Clarissa's.

3. *to her sex*: In the eighteenth and nineteenth centuries, needlework was considered part of the so called female accomplishments, together with music, watercolour painting, modern languages, comportment and manners, and was therefore an important aspect of a conventional education for women. See note 11 to Volume I.

4. *'A few ... to follow others'*: not identified.

5. *from the press:* This is obviously an ironic reference to Staël's *Corinne*, which was first published in France at the beginning of May 1807. This temporal reference would presumably set the story of the *Corinna of England* sometime after this date.

6. *the character of Corinna*: This comment suggests that the narrator has a controversial opinion of the novel. Although she considers the story of Corinne morally dubious and dangerously passionate, she is nevertheless able to appreciate Staël's historical and literary learning.

7. *her passion to Montgomery*: Clarissa's identification with Corinne and the perception of herself as the Corinna of England initiate a close parallelism between the story of Corinne and Clarissa's own story. In Clarissa's imagination, Montgomery will come to represent the gloomy and reserved Lord Nelvil, while Mary will progressively be identified with the chaste and timid Lucile, Corinne's half sister, who will eventually marry Lord Nelvil.

8. train *of lovers*: There is actually no evidence in *Corinne* that the heroine had encouraged the addresses of numerous admirers, and had apparently favoured the pretensions of a *train* of lovers. From the scene of the improvisation at the Capitol, we know that Corinne had a troop of admirers and she accepts everyone's praises, but also that she gives no one special preference and surely there is no reference to any lover. This is obviously a personal interpretation of the author who, by exaggerating the morally dubious behaviour of the heroine, is trying to present Corinne as a dangerously libertine character (Staël, *Corinne, or Italy*, p. 20).

9. *of her glory*: This is an ironic reference to Corinne's exclusivity and popularity. Prince Castelforte, one of her closest friends and admirers, considers her Italy's most famous woman and he often refers to her as the personification of Italy. The author is here replicating the connection between Corinne and the nation she represents, by stressing that Clarissa's talents and virtues had been borne on the *blast of Fame* through the extended dominions of Great Britain (Staël, *Corinne, or Italy*, pp. 24–5).

10. *he had ever heard of*: This is again a clear ironic reference to Corinne who is an *improvisatrice* with a renown ability to compose extemporaneous verses (see Book II, Chapter III of Staël, *Corinne, or Italy*). For an extensive analysis of the role of improvisation in Romantic literature see Angela Esterhammer, *Spontaneous Overflows and Revivifying Rays: Romanticism and the Discourse of Improvisation'* (Vancouver: Ronsdale Press, 2004), Angela Esterhammer, 'Improvisational Aesthetics: Byron, the Shelley Circle and Tommaso Sgricci', *Romanticism on the Net*, 43 (August 2006), http://www.erudit.org/revue/ron/2006/v/n43/013592ar.html and Angela Esterhammer, 'The Cosmopolitan Improvvisatore: Spontaneity and Performance in Romantic Poetics', *European Romantic Review*, 16 (2005), pp. 153–65.

11. *to become his wife*: This sentence seems to suggest a different ending to Corinne's story. In Staël's novel Lord Nelvil eventually prefers and marries the timid and chaste Lucile. To some extent, Clarissa's reverie of marrying Montgomery strengthens her identification with the character of Corinne, who had always wished to spend the rest of her life with Lord Nelvil, though marriage is never considered as a realistic option for Corinne.

12. *'Bare was ... her tresses'*: James Thomson, 'Britannia', in *The Poetical Works of James Thomson*, p. 145. The full quotation is: 'Bare was her throbbing bosom to the gale, / That, hoarse and hollow, from the bleak surge blew; / Loose flow'd her tresses'.

13. *here in Coventry*: According to Anglo-Saxon legends, Lady Godiva was a gentlewoman, patron of the arts, equestrienne, and tax protester. She lived *c.* 1040–80 AD. The legend says that Lady Godiva, in order to remove the heavy taxes that her husband Leofric had imposed on the citizens of Coventry, traversed completely naked on horseback through the entire village. A three-day festival dedicated to her was celebrated throughout the eighteenth and nineteenth centuries and is still celebrated

in July in Coventry. See Richard Barber, *Myths and Legends of the British Isles* (Wood-bridge: Boydell Press, 2004), p. 34.

14. *as her* Ladyship: It is not entirely clear, but the narrator is probably referring to the crowd gathered at Corinne's improvisation at the Capitol.

15. *she first broke silence*: This situation, in effect, is a parody of Corinne's appearance at the Capitol: 'At last four white horses drawing Corinne's chariot made their way into the midst of the throng. Corinne sat on the chariot built in the ancient style, and white-clad girls walked alongside. [...] Everyone came forward to see her from their windows which were decorated with potted plants and scarlet hangings' (*Corinne, or Italy*, p. 21).

16. *from all sides*: Clarissa's address to the crowd in terms of patriotic feelings is shaped after Corinne's improvisation. In Staël's novel, Corinne thus addresses the Italian crowd gath-ered to hear her: 'Italy, thou empire of the Sun; Italy to whom the world stands subject; Italy, cradle of learning, I salute thee.' The public reaction, however, is obviously differ-ent. While the Italian crowd welcome Corinne's speech with acclamation culminating in her coronation as poet laureate – '*Long live Corinne! Long live genius! Long live beauty!*' – Clarissa's speech is here received with laughters and huzzas as well as acclamations (Staël, *Corinne, or Italy*, pp. 26, 21).

17. *again spoke*: The quotation is from James Bland Burges, *The Exodiad: A Poem* (London: Lackington, Allen & Co., 1807), p. 170.

18. *now direct your labours*: In Staël's novel, Corinne, at her coronation at the Capitol, like Clarissa, presents herself in humble terms: 'Why is my humble forehead to receive the crown that Petrarch wore, that is left hanging from Tasso's funeral cypress tree?'. The author has clearly perceived the paradoxical attitude of Corinne and has exaggerated its comic aspects (Staël, *Corinne, or Italy*, p. 27).

19. *Adieu*: The first part of Clarissa's speech mimics Corinne's improvisation at the Capi-tol. By addressing the citizens of Coventry with a patriotic tone and by connecting her declamatory speech with the humanitarian gesture of Lady Godiva, Clarissa inserts her-self in a tradition of powerful and patriotic women who dared to question authoritative masculine power. Similarly, Corinne addresses the Italian people in a patriotic tone and presents her own improvisation as part of a long tradition of patriotic verses in Italian poetry, a tradition which was male dominated. See Staël, *Corinne, or Italy*, pp. 26–32.

20. *indecent expressions*: It is remarkable that Clarissa's unconventional speech is considered un-English by the crowd and associated with French liberal and revolutionary ideas.

21. *all that passed*: The appellation *The Corinna of Coventry* is a sarcastic reference to *Corinne*. Corinne's improvisation took place in Rome, the capital city of Italy, and one of the most famous towns in Europe for its history, art and literature. On the contrary, Coventry is a small and provincial English town, famous for its manufacturing industry rather than for artistic production.

22. '*E'en the lewd ... pleas'd me*': Thomas Otway, *Venice Preserved, or a Plot Discover'd. A Trag-edy* (London: Printed for Hindmarsh, 1682), p. 8.

23. *this account to himself*: 'The Spectacle de la Nature' sarcastically refers to the work of the French priest Noël Antoine Pluche (1688–1761). His *Spectacle de la Nature* (1732) was one of the most popular works of natural history and was widely translated and read all over Europe throughout the eighteenth century. *Spectacle de la Nature; or Nature Deline-ated. Translated from the French by J. Kelly* (London: James Hodges, 1743).

24. *of my existence*: In 1450, a rebellion broke out in protest against war taxation. It was led by a man called Jack Cade, who commanded an armed force recruited in Kent and Sus-sex. Cade marched on London, arriving on 3 July, but his rabble army was forced back at

London Bridge and dispersed before it had achieved anything of note. Cade was hunted down and killed on 12 July. It is unclear to which painting Copy is referring to. There are paintings of Jack Cade preaching at London Stone, Cannon Street but not in Smithfield. In *Henry VI, Part II*, IV.vi, Shakespeare explains that Cade decides to fight an army gathered together in Smithfield. Anne B. Rodrick, *The History of Great Britain* (Westfield: Greenwood Press, 2004), p. 58.

25. her *fame*: In *Corinne* Lord Nelvil witnesses with surprise and fascination Corinne's improvisation at the Capitol and it is on this occasion that he first feels attracted to her (Staël, *Corinne, or Italy*, p. 20).

26. *about the matter*: There is no evidence of any riots in Coventry around 1806 and 1807, so this presumably has no historical sources.

27. *that she imitates*: The reference here is to Helen of Troy who fell in love and flew with Paris, thus causing the war between Troy and Spart. This legendary story is narrated by Homer in his *Iliad*.

28. '*E'en so ... bowers*': James Thomson, *The Castle of Indolence* II.lxiii, in *The Poetical Works of James Thomson*, p. 285.

29. '*Above the ... schools!*': The original source of this quotation is unclear. Arthur Murphy in his comedy *The Way to Keep Him* (1760) attributes this poem to the poet Prior. The lines are slightly different: Above the fix'd and settled rules/ Of vice and virtue in the schools / The better Part should set before em, / A Grace, a manner, a decorum'. *The Way to Keep Him*, II. i (London: John Bell, 1792), p. 65.

30. '*If one ... in a day?*': William Shakespeare, *Cymbeline*, III. 2 (London: Randall, 1788), p. 30.

31. '*The timorous ... withdraws!*': 'The origin of the veil', in *The Poetical Works of J. Langhorne*, p. 78.

32. *it is in my power*: Clarissa's misuse of what the narrator describes as Staëlian language is sarcastic. In particular, her employment of a over sentimental language with regard to her journey through London mirrors Corinne's sentimental and intellectual description of her promenade through Rome with Nelvil (see Staël, *Corinne, or Italy*, Book IV, Chapters I, II).

33. *Lord Nelville*: The reference to Corinne's pedestrian tour of Rome with Lord Nelvil is here made explicit (see Staël, *Corinne, or Italy*, Book IV, Chapters I, II).

34. double life: The reference here is again to Book IV of *Corinne*, where Corinne takes Nelvil to visit several funerary monuments, first the tomb of Cecilia Metella and then the Columbaria tombs and to other tombs in Saint John Lateran, St Paul's, St Peter's and in the Vatican Museums (Staël, *Corinne, or Italy*, pp. 53–61).

35. *fair Dulcinea*: Walwyns's association between Dulcinea, the idealized woman whom Don Quixote is in love with, and Clarissa is not entirely clear.

36. dear hand: The author's sarcastic use of Staël's sentimental language is emphasized throughout the chapter by the use of italics.

37. *was doubtful*: This reference is to Book IV, Chapter VI of *Corinne*, where Lord Nelvil writes a note to Corinne announcing his ill health (Staël, *Corinne, or Italy*, p. 73).

38. *at the Villa*: The only female character with whom Corinne has a protective relationship is her half-sister Lucile. After Corinne left England for good, the two sisters meet again at the end of the novel, when Lucile is travelling through Italy with her husband Lord Nelvil and their daughter Juliette (Staël, *Corinne, or Italy*, Book XX, Chapters IV, V, pp. 410–49).

39. '*Let us ... fly!*': *The Fatal Sisters*, *The Poems of Gray* (London: T. Bensley, 1800), p. 55.

40. he *for glory* : This sentence is probably the sarcastic alteration of 'Love and Glory', a musical piece quite popular at the beginning of the nineteenth century, composed by Thomas Dibdin and von Ahn Carse: 'she died for love, and he for glory' (*Musical Times*, 47:766 (December 1906), pp. 823–6.

41. *the whole world*: Paradoxically, Clarissa criticizes Mary for being the victim of sentimental reading which alters her perception of reality. It is clear, however, that the author wants to show that it is Clarissa's fervid imagination that is the result of an exaggerated reading of sentimental literature, particularly of Staël's novels.

42. *'Come ... assuage'*: James Thomson, 'A Nuptial Song', in *The Poetical Works of James Thomson*, p. 314.

43. *"On some ... requires"*: Thomas Gray, 'Elegy Written in a Country Churchyard', in *The Poems of Gray*, p. 82. The original lines are slightly different: 'On some fond breast the parting soul relies / Some pious drops the closing eye requires'.

44. *to assist me*: Both Mary and Clarissa's moral attitudes are strongly exaggerated. Mary is excessively devoted to the defence of her female propriety, while Clarissa's sense of decorum is almost inexistent.

45. *Miss Moreton*: see note 34 to Volume I.

46. *proof of affection*: To some extent, Clarissa's change of attitude towards marriage mirrors Corinne's own devotion to Lord Nelvil. Accustomed, like Clarissa, to a free and financially independent state, Corinne is clearly ready to devote her whole life to Nelvil, and she even contemplates marrying him: 'If I could spend my life at your side without our marrying, I would prefer not to be joined to you in marriage, although it would mean losing a great happiness as well as an honour that in my eyes is the highest of all' (Staël, *Corinne, or Italy* p. 271).

47. *rather than his*: The narrator's tone is here evidently sarcastic, since Clarissa's liberal manners have not made at all clear to whom her affections are directed.

48. *'Heaven ... banish'd maid!'*: Alexander Pope, *Eloisa to Abelard*, *The Poetical Works of Alexander Pope*, 3 vols. (London: C. Cooke, 1800), vol. 1, p. 92. The original lines are as follow: 'Heav'n first taught letters for some wretch'd aid, / some banish'd lover or some captive maid'.

49. *he went down stairs*: The reference here is most probably to Shakespeare's *Macbeth*, V.iii: 'And that which should accompany old age,/ As honour, love, obedience, troops of friends, / I must not look to have; but in their stead, / Curses, not loud, but deep, mouth honoured, breath,/ which the poor heart would fain deny and dare not' (London: Lowndes, 1794), p. 58.

50. *'Heard you ... woe!'*: John Langhorne, *Hymns*, in *The Poetical Works of J. Langhorne*, p. 163.

51. *"learn to fly"*: These lines are from Oliver Goldsmith's *The Deserted Village*, in *The Poems of Oliver Goldsmith* (London: T. Bentley, 1800), p. 41.

52. *of conscience*: The reference here is probably to Lady Macbeth's speech in Shakespeare's *Macbeth*, I.v (p. 16):

> The rauen himselfe is hoarse,
> That croaks the fatall entrance of *Duncan*
> Under my Battlements. Come you Spirits,
> That tend on mortall thoughts, unsex me here,
> And fill me from the Crowne to the Toe, top-full
> Of direst Cruelty: make thick my blood,
> Stop up the access, and passage to Remorse,

That no compunctious visitings of Nature
Shake my fell purpose, nor keep peace between
The effect, and it. Come to my Womans Brests,
And take my Milk for Gall, you murd'ring Ministers,
Where-ever, in your sightlesse substances,
You wait on Nature's Mischiefe. Come thick Night,
And pall thee in the dunnest smoake of Hell,
That my keene Knife see not the Wound it makes,
Nor Heaven peepe through the Blanket of the darke,
To cry, hold, hold.

53. *than the observance*: The reference is to Shakespeare's *Hamlet*, I.iv: Ay, marry, ist:/ But to my mind, though I am native here/ And to the manner born, it is a custom/ More honourd in the breach than the observance. (Manchester: R & W. Dean, 1800), p. 19

54. *Dr. Saville's*: Walsingham seems to have views on marriage similar to those of Clarissa, and therefore of Corinne. Although defined by the author as a 'modern philosopher', Walsingham is overall a positive character, thus revealing a more optimistic view of the contemporary sentimental and liberal strain.

55. *'Heaven first ... captive* maid': Alexander Pope, *Eloisa to Abelard*; see note 48 to Volume I.

56. *I may expect it*: In Staël's novel, Corinne and Oswald also exchange several letters expressing their reciprocal feelings (Staël, *Corinne, or Italy*, Book IV, Chapter I, p.50; Book VI, Chapter III, pp. 98–9; Book XX, Chapter III, pp. 405–10).

57. *'O ... Mores!'*: This Latin sentence was pronounced by the Roman Consul Cicero while condemning Catilina's conspiracy against the Republic. See Cicero Marcus Tullius, *Selected Political Speeches* (Harmondsworth: Penguin Books, 1969), p. 69.

58. *'Fallacious ... train!'*: *Elegies*, in *The Poetical Works of J. Langhorne*, p. 143.

59. *an ordinary level*: This sentence reminds of Corinne's sense of exclusivity. In the novel, Oswald describes her as follow: '[..] but could anything compare with Corinne? Could the common run of laws apply to one whose genius and sensibility were the unifying bond of so many diverse qualities? Corinne was a miracle of nature'. The fact that Corinne's character is often misunderstood while in Britain is also emphasized by Mr Edgermond's words: 'A woman like that is not made to live in England. Only English-women are right for England. [...] *what would you do with her at home?*' (Staël, *Corinne, or Italy*, pp. 105, 133).

60. *strong hysterics*: Clarissa perceives her situation to be similar to Corinne's. Like Staël's heroine, she feels she has been abandoned by her lover in favour of the more timid, decent and proper Mary Cuthbert.

61 *'Ah! ... lover's pain'*: Hymn to Hope, *The Poetical Works of John Langhorne*, 2 vols. (London: T. Becket and A. De Hondt, 1766), vol. 1, p. 12.

62. *perjur'd Frederic*: The reference here could be to Shakespeare's *The Two Gentlemen of Verona* (London: R. Butters, 1790), p. 48. Thus Silvia addresses Protheus in Act V, Scene I:

Had I been seized by a hungry lion,
I would have been a breakfast to the best,
Rather than have false Proteus rescue me.
O! heaven be judge how I love Valentine,
Whose lifes as tender to me as my soul.
And full as much—for more there cannot be—

> I do detest false perjurd Proteus.
>
> Therefore be gone, solicit me no more.

63. *present attachment*: The reference to Corinne's half sister, Lucile, whom Lord Nelvil will eventually marry, preferring her to Corinne, is here made explicit.

64. *favourite amusement*: This is, sarcastically, a very different behaviour from that of Corinne's, who, after Nelvil's departure for Britain, lived in solitude and isolation, first in Venice and then in Florence (Staël, *Corinne, or Italy*, Book XVII, Chapter I, pp. 332–4; Book XVIII, Chapters I, II, III, IV, pp. 358–68).

65. *'Where'er ... demonstration here!'*: Edward Young, *The Infidel Reclaimed, Night Thoughts* (London: T. Wills, 1800), p. 143.

66. unfettered notions: Mrs. Moreton seems to blame her brother's liberal education for the eccentricity of Clarissa. This issue enters a much wider debate on female education which was current at the beginning of the nineteenth century and to which the publication of Staël's *Corinne, or Italy* had highly contributed. See note 11 to Volume I.

67. *'Great ... weak head'*: Robert Blair, *The Grave, a Poem* (Stirling: C. Randall, 1800), p. 14.

68. *in speaking*: The artificial language that the Chevalier creates in this letter by mixing French and English serves the purpose of satirizing the tragic accident that caused the death of Clarissa.

69. *of her niece*: The episode of Clarissa's death, although tragic, satirizes the end of *Corinne, or Italy*: both heroines are destined to die, thus stressing the sentimental nature of their lives. Corinne, however, dies a tragic death after discovering Nelvil's marriage with Lucile (Staël, *Corinne, or Italy*, Book XX, Chapter V, pp. 418–19).

70. *accidental death*: The end of the novel clearly parodies the end of *Corinne*: Mary, who represents the moral, timid and ordinary heroine, triumphs by marrying the hero, Montgomery, while the unordinary heroine, Clarissa, is wiped out from the story.

SILENT CORRECTIONS

6   demeanour] demeanor
11 fervour] fervor
12 sofa] sopha
14 tambourine] tamborine
14 sofa] sopha
15 veranda] viranda
17 hers] her's
18 scissors] scissars
18 fiddler] fidler
18 veranda] viranda
19 hers] her's
19 theirs] their's
19 hers] her's
20 inaptly] unaptly
20 choose] chuse
21 curtsey] curtesy
23 scrape-grace] scape-grace
23 racketing] racketting
24 tease] teaze
24 spoken] spoke
24 hurt] hurted
24 garnet] sernet
24 tied] tyed
25 curtsey] curtesy
27 showing] shewing
28 hers] her's
28 potato] potatoe
29 ours] our's
29 choose] chuse
31 impassioned] empassioned
32 entirely] interely
32 curtsey] curtesy
33 ?] y'clep
33 sophisticated] sophistical
39 shrubbery] shurbbery
40 grieves] griefs

41   befall] befal
44   showed] shewed
45   curtsey] curtesy
46   portrayed] pourtrayed
49   sofa] sopha
49   portraying] pourtraying
50   asperient] aperinet
51   Leonce] Leonee
52   Leonce] Leonee
53   fiddler] fidler
56   curtsey] curtesy
56   curtsey] curtesy
57   courtesan] courtezan
57   spinet] spinnet
57   spinet] spinnet
59   cipher] cypher
62   unparalleled] unparalelled
62   sofa] sopha
62   curtsied] curtesied
63   curtsied] curtesyed
72   expenses] expences
72   reconcilable] reconcileable
73   irreconcilable] irreconcileable
74   seamstress] sempstress
76   torn] lorn
79   portrayed] pourtrayed
79   impassioned] empassioned
79   ecstatic] extatic
79   acme] acmé
80   choose] chuse
80   Persian] persian
82   burdens] burthens
82   chisel] chissel
83   curtsied] curtesyed
85   ecstatic] extatic
86   show] shew
89   frenzical] phrenzical
96   indefinable] undefinable
96   sentinels] centinels
96   sentinel] centinel
96   show] shew
97   ecstatic] extatic
98   surprise] surprize
99   surprise] surprize
99   surprise] surprize
99   surprise] surprize
100 choose] chuse
100 show] shew

101 crowded] crouded
106 embosom] unbosom
111 shown] shewn
112 enclose] inclose
112 expenses] expences
113 surprise] surprize
113 surprise] surprize
116 ecstasy] extacy
118 dependence] dependance
120 portrayed] pourtrayed
123 grieves] griefs
126 surprise] surprize
126 expense] expence
126 show] shew
126 unparalleled] unparalelled
133 ethereal] etherial

www.ingramcontent.com/pod-product-compliance
Ingram Content Group UK Ltd.
Pitfield, Milton Keynes, MK11 3LW, UK
UKHW020350010325
455677UK00021B/384